The Art of the Meet Cute

NC BARTON

THE ART OF THE MEET CUTE

A SMALL TOWN FOUND FAMILY ROMANCE

FORTUNE FALLS

NC BARTON

For Alaina, my sister, my very first critique partner, my first ever pre-order, my partner in crime (writing) my fiercest and most loyal fan. I love you.

CHAPTER 1

TWENTY-ONE DAYS UNTIL THE RETREAT

As I weave through the crowd, holding a glass of wine, the sheen of the glass reflects the bare minimum of my features back to me—blunt black bangs, strong eyebrows, dark lashes, and red lipstick. It looks like a painting. Is that a good idea for a series? Wine portraits? I could call it *Simulacrum Sips. Red Wine Reflections.*

No.

It's a terrible idea. Plus, I don't have time…ever.

A bead of sweat runs down the nape of my neck, tracing the outline of my spine, finding the edge of my backless dress. Despite it being the first week of October, it's hot as balls, and this over-crowded wine-and-cheese fueled room is not helping matters.

One thing I haven't gotten used to in my four years in LA is the lack of seasons. Some people will argue the point, but those people have never lived in a place where fall rolls in like spreading out your favorite knit blanket. Where the leaves get so orange in the right light the trees look like they're on fire.

A gentleman with slicked-back white hair and a wide smile grabs my arm, handing me an empty glass and pulling me out of my spiral.

"Refill, dear. What was your name again?"

Inhale one, two, three. Exhale one, two, three. I'm not a server at this opening. It's not my job to fetch wine for the guests. I recognize this man as one of our repeat customers, though. He doesn't buy art often, but when he does, it's very expensive.

"Zara." Looking up from his empty glass, I flash my largest smile and hope it doesn't give away any of my annoyance. This was supposed to wrap up half an hour ago. I should know better than to make plans after an opening.

I make my way to the bar, dodging the wild hand gestures of the artist of the hour. His close-cut dark hair is sticking up at odd, yet very intentional, angles, and I overhear some of his spiel. "It's an exploration of small town America as future ghost towns. My aim is to capture the richness and culture that we're all going to lose to internet shopping."

Resisting the urge to roll my eyes, I keep moving. I know for a fact the artist was born and raised in Brooklyn and moved to LA right out of art school. What does he know about small town America? In fact, he was Marlene's assistant a few years ago. And now look at him. Solo show at a prestigious gallery. Just what I want. He is talented, but he got this show because of that job. Now my job.

Not that he doesn't deserve the show. The paintings are gorgeous. Main Street with the ocean behind it and large pine tree covered mountains on either side. Worn brick buildings portrayed in such detail I can practically feel the rough texture under my fingertips. It looks like home.

Handing the wineglass to the bartender, I wait for her to open another bottle. My head is pounding. I've spent too long in my high, tight ponytail. I'm dying to let it down, but that would look unprofessional.

My phone buzzes in the pocket of my dress, but pulling it out to check would also be unprofessional, and if Marlene hates anything…well, she hates a lot of things, but being unprofessional has to be top of the list. She's said it time and time again, and I've seen many gallery attendants let go for texting on the job, even in an empty gallery. I need this job. I just got this promotion to Marlene's assistant last week when her other assistant... quit? Was fired? No one's sure what happened. I can't fuck this up. The phone will have to wait.

Marlene catches my eye across the room and gives me a wink. She's cleaning up on this show. The red dots are on more paintings than not.

When I hand the wine back to the gentleman, his fingers linger on mine a beat too long.

"Thanks, doll," he says with a smirk. "Are you sure you're old enough to serve this?"

I'm twenty-nine, and while I may look a bit younger, this man, who must be nearly sixty, is clearly flirting with me.

"I'm old enough." And you're too old, I think but don't say.

"Has anyone ever told you you're a dead ringer for Audrey Hepburn?"

I smile. I have heard this before. It's the fair skin, dark hair, striking eyebrows, and brown eyes. I play it up with my baby bangs and high ponytail. Hey, if it worked for Audrey. I haven't heard it in quite such a lascivious manner before, though. "A couple times. Enjoy your wine."

As I make my retreat, Marlene motions with her head, beckoning me over, her sleek copper bob not moving with the gesture. I quickly make my way to her side. Her heels are high—her neckline low. The black pencil skirt she's wearing comes down to mid-calf, and her silk flowy halter top dips to nearly her navel. If I tried a neckline that low, it'd be *Debbie Does the Art World*, but on rail-thin Marlene, the effect is elegant, as per usual with her. She says through a smile, "Let's start shooing them out. Close the bar."

A hot, humid hour later, Marlene is walking the artist out the door as the remaining servers finish cleaning up.

"It was a smash!" Marlene slaps him on the back. "I'll meet you at Jackalope after we finish up here."

She clicks the door shut with a heavy sigh. "Whew."

I smile. "You can say that again."

Marlene claps her hands together. "It was a massive success. We did it, Ashford!"

Marlene insists on calling me by my last name like she's the coach of some sports game.

I raise my fist in the air. "Woo hoo!"

She gives me a side-eye—too much enthusiasm maybe?—before stopping at one of the paintings with a red dot indicating it's sold. The picture is another brick building, the rough texture lit by a lamp-post emitting buttery yellow light in an otherwise blue-tinted paint-ing. The neon bar sign pops off the canvas in shades of hot pink.

Marlene traces the air near the sign, her red nails clashing with the fuchsia. "People love this small town aesthetic."

"Hmm."

Marlene shifts her gaze to me. "You don't?"

"No, I do. It's..." I let out a long breath, blowing my bangs. "I'm from a small town, so it's...familiar, I guess. Beautifully painted, though."

Marlene tilts her head to the side in a bird-like gesture, or maybe more like one of those velociraptors from *Jurassic Park*. "Are you?"

I nod and busy myself gathering glasses, but she doesn't take her ice-blue eyes off me.

"Where are you from?"

"It's a little town on the Oregon Coast."

She keeps staring, so I go on.

"Fortune Falls."

"Fortune Falls?"

"Yep." I'm used to the reaction. It's an unusual name, it sounds almost magical. When I first moved there, it was, then as I got older, it felt more like a gilded cage. Impossibly small, everyone knows everyone else's business, and when you're seventeen, that's the last thing you want.

The corner of Marlene's lips quivers into a smile. "You know we have the artist retreat coming up."

Marlene is renowned for her retreats. There's always a hand-picked selection of famous and talented artists in attendance, as well as the artist-in-residence who presents and holds workshops for the other artists. Last year's artist-in-residence was none other than Kehinde Wiley, and two years ago, it was Cindy Sherman. I've been trying to find out who this year's artist is, but Marlene keeps the A-in-R a secret until the first day of the retreat, surprisingly, even to her assistant.

"Right, we have the place all booked outside Malibu." I confirmed with them last week.

Marlene slices a hand through the air. "No. I'm over Malibu." She points to the painting, her long red nail like the laser of her level she uses to double-check all the paintings. "I want to go somewhere like here."

An idea springs to mind, but I bite my lip. I shouldn't say it. It's a terrible idea. But looking at Marlene's face as she gazes at the painting, my need to impress her wins out. "I might know a place…"

"Really?" She turns to me. "With enough space? We need accommodations for five artists, the A-in-R, and you and me. Room for them to work as well."

"I'm not sure…" My brain maps out the town and lands on the cabins. "I think so."

"You don't sound sure. I need lots of pictures of the accommodations. You'll need to go scout it."

My stomach drops. "My car broke down."

I can practically hear Marlene blink.

"It doesn't matter how you get there. Charge the expenses to the gallery—within reason, of course, don't hire a private jet." She snaps her fingers. "Train—you should take the train. I was just talking to an artist that swears by them. That way if Fall of Fortune—"

I stop myself from correcting her. It might actually be a more accurate name.

"—doesn't work, you can gaze out the window and find a charming small town that will. We have to get moving on this pronto."

I get out my phone, ignoring the voicemail, and scroll to the Amtrak website. Shit. No route goes directly there. My Google search finds another train. Sunrise Express goes all the way from LA to Fortune Falls in a "speedy" 38 hours.

"There's a train leaving first thing in the morning."

Marlene gives my shoulder a little pat. "Good, good. Don't forget to send pics." She grabs her leather slouch bag, a lot like mine but about ten times the price since hers is designer and I found mine at the St. Vincent De Paul. "Set the alarm once everyone is gone."

After the last of the servers are gone, I let out a long exhale and sit in the uncomfortable but stylish wire mesh chair. I'm about to pull out my phone to check the voicemail when there's a small knock on the glass.

Grace is standing at the door, looking put together in a dark denim skirt and black tank. Put together and very pissed off, her pale pink lips cemented in a fine line. I hurry to the door.

"Grace, I'm so sorry."

"You should be."

I step aside and let her in. "Things got crazy here, and I just couldn't get away." I walk over to the bar and hold up one of the open bottles. "Drink?"

She shrugs. I pour each of us a glass, and we sit together on the cold concrete floor.

I take off my boots, my feet aching from the long hours spent in them. Unwinding the elastic, I finally take down my hair. My head tingles, and I breathe a sigh of relief.

"So, this is where you spend all your time."

I half smile and look around. She's not wrong. I spend more time here than I do anywhere else.

"This is it."

Grace nods, her thick blonde hair bobbing. "It's nice."

We sit in silence for a bit. Grace and I have been roommates for almost a year now, but we still haven't moved into that comfortable silence place. But I'm too exhausted for small talk—that's not entirely true. Even when I'm not exhausted, it's not my strong suit.

Grace breaks the quiet. "Zara, I'm not sure how to say this—"

My stomach tightens. I had a feeling this was coming, but I really didn't want it to, so I didn't give it too much thought.

"Sam and I want to live together, and since it's my name on the lease..." She takes a hearty sip of her wine.

I use the pause to jump in. "This is perfect." The smile I slap on my face is so fake it actually hurts. "I was thinking of finding my own place anyway."

The lie hangs in the air between us. But If I have to leave anyway, I don't want her to feel like she had to kick me out. I'll leave on my own terms.

"I can be out in a couple weeks," I say and try to smile.

The fact that the artist retreat is right after I move out isn't great, but I can find a place. I have before. I always land on my feet. Maybe I'll just put my stuff in storage and figure it out after the retreat. Why do something today when you can put it off until tomorrow?

The smile on my face is genuine when I say, "This is a big step for you two. Congratulations."

Grace lets out a laugh. "Yeah, we've been talking about it for a couple months. I think that he's the one."

The one. I sip my wine so I won't roll my eyes. I believe in the one for tonight, but it's been a long, long time since I believed in a fairytale happily ever after. As I set my wineglass down, my thoughts tumble out. "The 'one' is a concept manufactured by Hallmark and Hollywood. People are just people, messy, imperfect, bumping around into each other like jellyfish in the sea."

Jellyfish? What am I even saying? Today has been too long.

Grace laughs again, this one a little less boisterous. "Whoa. Tell me how you really feel."

"Sorry, that was—"

"I prefer seahorses, they mate for life." Grace twirls a strand of hair.

"Do they?"

"They do." Grace reaches for the wine, pouring more in her glass and then mine. "Maybe you just haven't met the right person. You know Sam has a friend…"

"Nope." I soften my tone and try again. "No, thank you. I'm too busy to date right now, anyway." Gotta find a place to live, scout a retreat, along with all my usual gallery duties, and maybe, just maybe, if I find a speck of time in there, I can paint a new series.

CHAPTER 2
TWENTY DAYS UNTIL THE RETREAT

The morning light is bouncing around the train car, reflecting my face back to me as I stare out the window, reminding me of my wine portrait idea. This idea might have something to it —not just wine, but different reflections, on different days, in different locations, the only constant being me.

The leather seat is smooth under my palm as I reach for my phone where I tucked it next to me. I ruminate on it as the California landscape whizzes by. When I boarded the train an hour ago, my seatmates were a family of three: mama, daddy, and tiny screaming baby, so I immediately staked out a table in the bar.

I don't know what I was thinking not buying an actual room for this trip. Not true. I know exactly what I was thinking: *Marlene will be so impressed with how frugal and efficient I am. Gold star Zara.*

As the landscape shifts to rows of dark green and golden vines, the reflection shifts. The image gets stronger with the darker landscape outside. At this point, I don't even care if it's a good idea—I need to paint this. I need to capture this ephemeral moment of me staring back at me, on my way home. Something I wasn't expecting to do ever.

Pulling out my cell, I go to snap a picture, but my phone is now prominent in the window. That's not the look I'm going for.

This isn't about selfies. I lean forward and try to prop my phone on the armrest. Now it just shows my back, not the window. Shit.

Thinking on my feet, I wrench my arm back behind me and for the first time in my life wish I had one of those selfie sticks. From this angle, I can't push the button, so I turn on the timer and reposition. Tilting my face just so, I count in my head.

Ten, nine, eight, seven, six, five, four, three—

Crash.

My arm jerks back, spinning me in my seat. As I tumble into the aisle and onto the floor, my phone flies out of my hand. Except it's not the floor. Underneath me is solid, warm muscles under soft cotton. I angle my face up to take in a stubbled jaw, steely blue eyes, and chestnut hair a little shaggy around the ears.

"Are you okay?"

"I…"

In one swift move, the man underneath me helps me to my feet like I weigh nothing more than a feather. Standing face to face, I see just how tall he is. He must have a foot on me, not that I'm particularly tall, but still. In two long strides, he retrieves my phone and hands it back to me.

"Thanks."

"The train lurched," he says, rubbing a hand on the back of his neck, his triceps popping.

I smooth down the tight skirt of my sweater dress.

"Did you get the shot at least?"

The thought of this very tall, extremely handsome man watching me take an elaborate selfie sets my neck on fire. It's probably beet red. I open the picture app on my phone to the last photo, which must've been taken while the phone was midair. Both our faces are frozen in a blur of horror. A giggle escapes me as I show it to him.

He laughs too. It's such a deep timbre of a chortle that it makes me laugh more. Soon, I'm clutching my stomach and he's wiping a tear from his eye. A woman with a toddler is walking our way, so I quickly duck into my seat, and he takes the seat across from me.

"I'm thinking that wasn't what you were going for?"

I shake my head. "No. I was trying to take a picture of the reflection in the window."

He shifts his head over to my side of the table, leaning in so close his scent fills the air—leather, spice, and something else I can't quite put my finger on, but it's fresh. Like a morning mist.

"That's a pretty picture," he says, holding eye contact with me on his way back to his seat. Oh lord, where did this man come from?

I shrug off my jean jacket and roll the sleeves of my dress up my forearms, the train car feeling suddenly warm.

"Do you want my help to take it?"

I shake my head, staring back at the window. The reflection has changed, once again. It's not what I'm yearning to paint. "That's okay. I'm Zara by the way."

He smiles, it's a little crooked, slightly larger on one side than the other. "It's nice to meet you, Zara Bytheway."

I grin at the dad joke.

"I'm Oli, Oliver really, but everyone calls me Oli."

"It's nice to meet you, Oliver Really."

He laughs. "I was going to grab a coffee, would you like one?"

The corners of my mouth turn up with wild abandon. "Yes, please."

He smiles, and our eyes linger. The moment stretches on and on like one long uninterrupted brush stroke.

Oli breaks away first, laughing a little to himself. "Great. I'll be right back."

I let out a long exhale. Truth be told, I'm not usually one for chatting up strange men. Usually when guys approach me, I brush them off. I don't have time. What's the point? But there's something about Oli. When our eyes meet, it feels like the air is filled with static electricity.

Oli saunters off toward the café counter, and I enjoy the view from the back with his long legs moving effortlessly. His jeans are snug, but not too tight, low on his hips and splattered with paint specks. Is he a painter like me? Or maybe he's in construction? I turn back around and peer into the reflection this time, checking my makeup. Pulling out my red lipstick, I quickly swipe on a fresh coat.

I'm putting the lipstick back in my bag as Oli sets a paper cup in front of me. The earthy aroma steaming out of the hole in the lid makes my mouth water. He sets his down then pulls sugars and creams out of his pocket before he sits.

"I wasn't sure how you take it."

I pick up a couple packets. "Two sugars, no cream."

He repeats it, as if practicing for a test later. I bite the side of my lip to stop myself from saying, "Ahhh."

"So, Oli…"

"Yes, Zara?"

I'm not sure what to say, honestly. I detest the usual getting to know you small talk questions, but surely some must be necessary. "What do you do?"

Oli frowns as he dumps two creams and one sugar in his coffee. "Zara Bytheway, what do any of us do?"

"Well, Mr. Really, I work in a gallery, and you…"

Oli's eyes go wide. "Do you? Crazy. I'm an artist, sort of."

"How can you sort of be an artist?"

He shrugs. "It's all a matter of perspective."

"Have you made anything I may have seen?"

His eyes don't meet mine when he says, "Probably not. I'm not very good. What's your favorite color?"

The subject change is abrupt, but maybe he's in a slump too. It's painful to talk about your art when it feels like it's going nowhere—if anyone can understand that, it's me. So, I don't push. "Black."

His smile is full to the brim with mischief. "I can see that." He gestures to my form-fitting black turtleneck sweater dress.

"What about you?"

"Usually green. But today it's black."

Heat pinches my cheeks. He is so cute.

I sit back in my chair, sipping my coffee, the slightly sweet, rich liquid surprisingly good for something bought on a train. We stare out the window, the ground dry and covered in sagebrush, a sharp contrast to the cloudless turquoise sky. It's beautiful. If I were a landscape painter, I would want to capture this.

But I'm not. I love nature, but I'm much more inspired by people. I slide my gaze over to Oli. He's staring out the window, his strong hands wrapped around his cup, his eyes more blue than gray as the landscape switches to jagged red hills.

Oli turns his attention back to me. "Would you rather fly or breathe underwater?"

Without hesitation, I answer, "Breathe underwater."

"That was fast." He tilts his head to the side. "Have you thought about this before?"

"No, but lots of people drown every day. Way more than are falling from great heights."

A wrinkle appears on his brow. "So, you'd rather breathe underwater because you'll be less likely to die?"

"Obviously. Let me guess, you want to fly."

"Hell yeah, I want to fly. Think of all the places you could reach."

The laugh that escapes me is so loud it startles the couple across the aisle from us. I mouth *sorry* to the woman and lower my voice. "What could you possibly need to reach that you can't already. You've gotta be what, like six-three?"

"Six-five."

"There you go—if you can't reach it, nobody can or probably should."

His eyes flash. "Nothing good ever came from doing what you 'should.'"

Reaching into his side bag, he pulls out a flask, as if his manifesto statement on rebellion reminded him it was in there. He pours a little in his cup and gestures to mine.

I nod. "Just a nip."

"A nip it is."

He tucks the flask away and holds out his coffee for a cheers. We touch our paper cups together and both drink as the landscape rolling by shifts once again, the deep blue ocean coming into view. I move my leg, and our knees lightly brush under the table—his jeans rough on my bare skin. It's more delicious than the coffee.

He nudges me with his leg. "Your turn."

"My turn for what?" I ask wrapping my hands around my cup, the paper sleeve rough under my palm.

"To ask a question."

"Ahhh." So it's a game. I'm great at games. "What's your favorite book?"

He smiles. "*Einstein's Dreams*. It's all these short stories about different ways time could work. Fucked me up after I read it. What about you?"

"*Another Roadside Attraction* by Tom Robbins—have you read it?"

Oli shakes his head. "After a raging adolescent crush on Uma Thurman, I read *Even Cowgirls Get the Blues*. Same guy, right?"

"Yep. Have a thing for blondes, huh?"

His smile is devilish. "I preferred her black hair in *Pulp Fiction*, actually."

Heat creeps up the back of my neck while simultaneously shooting to my thighs. Holy shit—he actually said that.

"Why is it your favorite?" he asks, pulling me out of my thoughts.

I run my hand over the smooth Formica table, grounding myself. "He describes this painting of a hot dog in such amazing, epic detail. It goes on for pages and pages. I'm convinced no painting has ever existed or will ever exist that's more exquisite than that hot dog painting."

"The one that was never actually painted?"

"Yep." I sip my coffee.

His blue eyes light up as they bore into mine. The charge between us is so palpable you can practically see an electric current, like one of those static machines.

"I love that. It's the next book I'm reading." He pulls out his phone, breaking our eye contact. "Done. Just bought the e-book."

I smile. "It's your turn."

A large man jostles Oli on his way by. "Want to check out the Vista car?"

I don't know what that is, I didn't research this train more than buying the ticket, but right now, I would follow Oli almost anywhere. "Yes, I do."

CHAPTER 3

As I sling my leather tote on my shoulder, Oli grabs my hand. His palm is rough and calloused. His large hand dwarfs mine, but it feels good—both safe and dangerous at the same time.

He leads me through the narrow aisle, the yellow diamond patterned carpet muffling the sound of our feet, down two cars and then up a narrow set of stairs. The car is about the same size as the bar car, but the roof and the sides are all made entirely of windows. Sunlight streams in, the blue sky now dotted with enormous white puffy clouds. Oli quickly snags the two open seats in the back of the car. The leather is slick under my dress as I sit down, delighted by the cushiness of the seat.

"Wow, this is incredible," I say, running my hands along the armrests and gazing out at the rolling waves.

"It is one of my favorite places in the world."

I take him in. His blue-gray eyes are focused out the window at the ocean beyond, a soft smile on his face. "What are some of your other favorite places?"

He turns his eyes on me, and I nearly suck in a breath. He's startlingly handsome. "Glacier, Lost Lake outside of Mount Hood, Rockaway Beach. LA is nice, sometimes. I like cities, but only for a day or two. I like how easy it is to blend in. Nobody notices you. It's comforting, but also lonely at the same time."

I nod, cradling my coffee in my hands. "That's exactly how I feel living in LA. Sometimes it feels like it's where I'm meant to be. I love my job. I love the gallery. I love the art scene, most days. But like today, no one knows I'm even gone except my roommate. Part of me misses that about living in a small town. It was annoying, being seventeen and having everyone know my business, but at the same time comforting. When someone asked how you were you could answer any way you wanted; either way, they usually already knew."

He smiles, but there is some sadness to it. "You're from a small town, too?"

I sigh. I didn't mean to say all that. It just tumbled out. "I am. I'm actually going home for the first time in over ten years."

Oli whistles. "Wow. That's big."

I shrug, trying to fluff off the weight of his words. But there's no denying it, it's big. Monumental, even.

"Have you seen your family in that time?" His eyes are warm as he asks, no judgment, just curiosity across his strong features.

"Yeah. My mom moved before I did. I stayed and finished high school. Scholarship to the Chicago Art Institute, then off to LA. Anyway, if I visit Mom, it's wherever she's living. She moves around a lot. Used to anyway."

There's a beat of silence, where Oli is looking at me, maybe waiting to see if I'll go on. I smooth my hair, more for something to do with my hands than any hair feeling out of place.

I quickly change the subject, not wanting to dwell on my mom. "What about you? Do you visit home often?"

"No." He takes a large sip of his coffee. "My home is a little tense."

"Tense?" I raise an eyebrow at him.

He laughs. "To put it lightly. My dad doesn't like what I do for a living. So, it makes things awkward."

"Not a fan of the arts?"

He laughs, but it's unlike the ones I've heard before. There's no joy to it. "You could say that again."

"What's he do?"

"He's a sheriff."

"Ahh."

He leans in closer, so close to my face I smell his leather and mist scent. My breath is jagged. His eyes move over my face, slow and purposeful. Is he going to kiss me?

My mouth parts a fraction. His hand comes up to my cheek and plucks a speck off the tip of my cheekbone. He holds it up to me between his pointer finger and thumb, a small black eyelash. "Make a wish."

Closing my eyes, the wish that comes to mind is more flashes than words. Oli's hands on the small of my back, pulling me close to him, pressing our bodies against the cool glass of the train car, his lips on mine, on my neck, on my...

I open my eyes and blow the lash out of his hands.

"What did you wish?" he asks, his voice low and gravely, like he could read my mind.

I shake my head. "If I tell you, it won't come true."

He smirks, and we hold eye contact for a long moment.

A couple walks by us on their way out of the car, yelling loudly. "I know all about her. I saw the messages. Don't try to lie to me."

Oli frowns, turning back to the window. "Ain't love grand?"

I imagine Oli with a woman, not me, maybe someone blonde with a cute bob, walking hand in hand down the beach. Something about the picture doesn't ring quite true. He gives off such a lone-wolf vibe.

Before thinking about whether or not I should, I ask, "Have you ever been in love?"

He purses his lips to the side, eyes squinting, brows furrowed as if he's searching his brain for the answer. "I thought I was."

I smile. "You thought so?"

"I loved her. I did. But I don't think she ever really loved me.

We were together a little over a year. And there was always something about her that didn't feel quite right. But I shoved that little voice aside, because the rest of it...whew, it felt right. Seeing her, hearing her laugh—I did the most ridiculous shit to make her laugh. Touching her. It was all-consuming. Like swimming underwater. But then she left me for a buddy of mine. Ex-buddy. He was a better artist, famous, tons of connections. That shit mattered to her. More than I realized."

His eyes are pure gray, glimmering a bit.

"That's awful." And I mean it. How could you choose someone else with this man in your life?

He reaches out and touches my knee again, lightly, almost casually. Almost, if it weren't for that charge. Does he feel it too?

"The awful thing is that it wasn't. Don't get me wrong, I was devastated, but part of me always knew she'd find someone better, and she did. Once I pulled myself up off the floor, I went and had a cheeseburger. It was like it was all meant to be."

I sigh, my thigh tingling under his touch. I put my hand on top of his, his skin warm underneath my palm.

"What about you? Have you been in love?"

I trace his fingers as he moves his hand to a spot a little higher on my thigh. "Yes. Once. His name was Ben, is Ben. He's not dead, as far as I know."

"Ah Benjamin. What happened with him?"

I smile at Oli's condescending tone as he says Ben's full name. "Ben and I dated all through junior high and high school. When I moved to town, it was love at first sight. Or he always said that."

"It wasn't for you?"

I shrug. "When I saw him, I thought he was cute. There were no violins or thunderclaps, but he was adorable with his brown hair, short in the back and long on the sides, and a dimple. He asked me to get French fries, and we were Ben and Zara for the next five years."

Oli whistles. "Wow. That's a long time."

"Yeah, it didn't feel like it, but it was also teenage years. We had school and curfews. There were family vacations. A lot of it was spent apart, saying we wished we were together."

"Saying it?"

Oli doesn't let things slip.

A long, slow breath passes between my lips. "I know I loved him. I know it. And it didn't fade as much as change. As the years went by, I saw him more and more as a good friend. The passion I once had wasn't there anymore. Plus, we wanted different things. I wanted to get the fuck out of town, and he wanted to stay, run his dad's business."

"So, you broke up with him?"

"Something like that." My pulse beats faster, guilt sinking in the pit of my stomach. How did we end up talking about Ben?

"What's your favorite movie?"

Not my most elegant segue, but Oli lets it slide.

We talk for hours, flitting from one topic to the next as the landscape shifts outside like slides flipping through a projector.

The train pulls into a station, stopping with loud pops and creaks. The announcer comes over the speaker. "San Luis Obispo stop, one hour."

Oli holds out his hand to me. "Should we go find some food?"

I smile, slipping my hand into his.

We leave the train, him leading the way but still holding my hand. Sparklers ignite in my chest. It's silly to feel this excited about a man I just met, but the sweet gesture of his hand in mine makes me feel like I'm a teenager and the boy I liked just asked me to dance.

We descend the stairs and find the exit. An ocean breeze blows lightly on my cheeks, and I inhale the fresh air deeply. The train station, a white stone building with a red tile roof, stands before us. I gesture to it. "They probably have a café in there."

He smirks, a twinkle in his eyes, blue in this light. "We can do better."

We walk down the sidewalk lined with trees, the tops bejeweled bright yellow and orange against the glowing amber of the sun's descent. The blowing wind sends dry leaves skittering down the road, like glitter. Oli seems to know right where he's going.

I ask, "Have you been here before?"

"Once or twice."

We wind down the road. My breath catches in my throat as we pass a small stencil on the brick walls of a building. I'm so shocked, I drop Oli's hand and hurry to the side of the building, running my fingertips over the rough brick.

It's a solid black silhouette of a young girl with a puffy dress, something you'd see in a storybook from the 1950s. She's holding out her hand to a flock of colorful birds flying away. As the birds get farther, their shape changes, first to black and white skeletons, then to bones, then to white fragments.

Oli joins me, seeming to be more interested in my face than the painting.

"Do you know what this is?" I ask.

"Graffiti?" Oli turns his gaze to the painting. "A statement on life and death. The fleeting nature of youth?"

I laugh, but he could be right. "Well, maybe. But I meant more, do you know who it's by?"

"Nope."

"And you call yourself an artist," I tease, smiling.

He smirks, his dimple popping. "Never said a good one. We better keep heading to the café if we want to get back on the train in time."

He walks away. I pull my phone out and take pictures of the art. Once I have enough shots, I catch up to Oli.

"It's an OG."

Oli frowns? "An OJ? Like the juice?"

I let out a sigh. "No. An OG. He's an internationally famous graffiti artist. Have you heard of Banksy?"

He opens the door for me. Soft music, the tinkle of silverware, and light chatter of the other guests surround me, as well as the heavenly scent of French fries. Oli slides into an open booth, and

I sit across from him, running my hands over the worn wood table.

"OG is like Banksy but slightly less famous."

"Slightly less, huh?' Oli opens the enormous menu, his face hidden behind it.

My nerves are still buzzing. I smile, looking back over the photos I took. "I've never seen one in real life."

A woman with a massive smile and itty-bitty waist comes over to take our order. Oli orders a club sandwich. Since I haven't even picked up my menu yet, I get the same. After she leaves, I go back to looking at the photos.

Oli puts away his menu. "What's so special about this graffiti?"

I shake my head. "It's not just graffiti, at least not how most people would think about it. It's art for everyone. You don't have to pay a hefty museum admission, or get side-eyed by some uppity gallery attendant. Anyone and everyone can see it. It's art weaved into the fabric of our everyday lives. Brightening it, or making us pause. It's the extraordinary in the ordinary."

Oli tilts his head to the side, his blue-gray eyes thoughtful. "That's beautiful."

I smile and fiddle with the sugar packets, feeling suddenly self-conscious about getting carried away.

Oli reaches out touching my hand. "Do you have a favorite piece?"

I intertwine my fingers with his, my skin heating with the contact. "The one we just saw is for sure my favorite now."

He laughs.

"I have some others, though." I scroll to an OGs fan page on Instagram, showing Oli a few I love. We lose ourselves talking about what some of them could mean. The server brings us our food, and we keep talking all through the meal.

When I put my phone away, I notice the time. "Shit. What time was it when we left?"

Oli furrows his brow. "Around four thirty, I think."
I show him my phone, the time glowing—five thirty-two.

CHAPTER 4

Oli pays our check at the counter then grabs my hand. We run, hand in hand, down the sidewalk, my booties smacking against the concrete. I hitch my skirt up to run a little faster. Despite the dire situation, Oli watches as I do, giving me a mischievous smile and an eyebrow raise.

I laugh. "Not now. Run faster!"

He turns his gaze back toward the sidewalk. As we get closer to the station, the train is making all sorts of clicking and bursts of air sounds. It sounds like it's getting ready to leave, but mercifully, it hasn't left yet.

We run to the train, show the attendant the tickets on our phones, and climb aboard. I lean back against the side of the train car to steady my racing heart. Oli's hand is above me on the wall, he's nearly doubled over catching his breath. He laughs, and it's so joyful, so full of life, I laugh too. With his other hand, he runs it lightly on my hip as we laugh, still breathless.

The laughter fades, but his hand remains cupping my hip. I look up into his strong face, his jaw so square. I trace it lightly with my finger, the stubble rough under my touch. His eyes bore into mine as he leans his head down.

Footsteps and a very deliberate throat-clearing has Oli

jumping away from me. A man in a blue uniform with a bushy mustache and eyebrows to match says, "Keep the path clear please."

He moves past us, his mustache turned up at the corners like it's hiding a smirk.

Oli is rubbing a hand on the back of his neck. I play with the belt loop of his jeans, wanting him to press back into me, but we can't. I can't risk getting kicked off this train. I have to find a location for the retreat. Pretty sure if I don't, I can kiss my job goodbye.

Kiss. My eyes find Oli's lips. It might be worth it.

"Do you want to play a game?"

A smile spreads across my face. "Yes."

He laughs. "You're agreeing without even knowing the game?"

"I trust you." I'm stunned silent by this. How can I trust him already? I hardly know him. There's something about him, though. When I talk, he listens with his whole body. Leaning in. And even when I was talking about Ben, there's no judgment. "What's the game?"

"Hide and seek."

I laugh. "Okay." I place my palms over my eyes, my hands cool on my flushed cheeks. "One, two, three…"

There is a rustle of fabric as Oli moves past me. I continue the counting in my head, giving him three extra beats.

Removing my hands from my eyes, I glance around the car. His footsteps went to the right, so I move that way to a business-class car with rows of seats. I peek behind a few of the chairs, but he's not here. My heart skips a beat. What if I can't find him? What if I never see him again? We should've exchanged numbers. This was so stupid. What was I thinking, agreeing to hide and seek on a train?

I take a large inhale. I can do this. Moving lightly through the train car, I go to the next one. It's another business-class car. If I were Oli, which way would I go? The next car must be a sleeper car. Closed door after closed door lines the narrow hallway. The next car is the same. I move through the tight hallway, inspecting the doors. I should probably go back the other way to the lounge car. Then something catches my eye. The door at the very end of the hall is slightly ajar, a strap from a messenger bag caught in it.

Would Oli hide in someone's room?

I creep closer, peeking through the crack in the door. Dark jeans, worn shirt, steel-blue eyes. The door opens, and Oli grabs my hand, pulling me into the room, moving the bag and closing the door completely this time. The room is gorgeous. There's a strong art deco theme, with intricate inlaid wood designs covering the walls, giving the entire space a rosy, golden glow. There's a small beige couch with mustard-yellow velvet pillows and a surprisingly large white bed, the headboard covered in the same pillows. In front of a massive window is a table with a built-in seat on either side, a bottle of red wine sits in the middle with two glasses and a bag of chips.

"Holy shit. This is crazy."

Oli plops down on the bed, propping up on his side. "It's modeled after the Orient Express."

"It's crazy. But come on, we have to go. If they find us in here, they'll kick us out. How'd you even know this one would be empty? Can you imagine being able to afford something like this someday?"

Oli stands, his smile completely gone. He nods almost in a daze. "Yeah, that would be crazy."

He grabs the bottle of wine and puts it behind his back, placing his fingers on his lips. "They'll never miss it."

My insides fizzle and spark. We tiptoe like spies out of the sleeper car. Oli grabs a table in the dining car, and while the attendant is getting something from the back, I grab two clear plastic cups.

I sit across from Oli at the small table for two. Out the window, the ocean waves roll in and out in a hypnotic rhythm. Oli opens the screw top, pouring us each a glass, the red liquid catching the light and sparkling like a jewel. He hands me one. I sip my wine, letting the earthy notes sit on my tongue pleasantly.

The sun is setting in earnest now, the light a soft pink. It shines through the window, caressing Oli's cheek like a tender lover. I want to paint it, it's so beautiful.

Oli notices me staring at him. "What?"

I shake my head. "The light is beautiful right now."

He moves his eyes around the room, landing squarely on me. A large slow smile spreads across his face, just like honey. "It certainly is."

Oli sighs as he stares out the window. "I think this is the nicest train ride I've ever been on."

I laugh. "This is the first train I've ever been on."

"Really?"

"Yeah. I fly or drive. I would've driven this time if my car hadn't died."

He places a hand on my knee under the table, his eyes more blue than gray in the waning sunlight streaming through the window. "I'm so glad your car died."

I put my hand over his. "Me too."

I'm about to ask if he rides trains a lot when he sets his wine down on the little table. He scoots over in his seat, patting the spot next to him. "The view is better from here."

I look out the window. It looks very similar, but I want to be close to him. I move to his side. He puts a hand on my leg, and we snuggle close, sipping our wine in a comfortable silence as the world passes by.

Stars start to appear in the sky one by one, reflecting off the water. He points outside to the jagged rocks of the dark bay. "I think this is Lover's Bay."

"No, that's a line."

His smile is champagne fizzing my insides and going straight to my head. "Do I need a line?"

I shake my head and whisper, "No."

Setting his glass down, Oli takes my face in both hands. Our lips meet. It's so soft. A butterfly landing on a flower, a whisper of a touch at first. Then the pressure increases. White hot desire runs through my veins. I want to consume this man. I snake my hands around his neck, pulling him closer to me. He moves his hand to my hip then moves up, grazing my ribs, skimming my breast and finding his way to the back of my neck, sending goosebumps down my arms. His lips are delicious, sweet and earthy like the wine. My skin is on fire. Time stops, the train fades away. There are no noises but our breaths mingling.

When the kiss ends, Oli's eyes flash as he drinks me in. "You are so beautiful," he says softly.

"So are you."

I lean my head on his shoulder, and we turn back to the window. The soft rocking of the train eventually makes it too hard to keep my eyes open.

CHAPTER 5

NINETEEN DAYS UNTIL THE RETREAT

Cold blue morning light spills into the dining car as I stretch my limbs, not remembering how little room I have. My shin hits the metal bar underneath the table. Oli is leaning against the window, his eyes closed, his breaths even. I get up and find a bathroom, staring into the mirror for a long time. My eyes look bright, my cheeks rosy. Despite spending all night sleeping upright on the train, I'm not looking too shabby. I splash some cold water on my face and remove my dress, trying to take a bit of a sink shower. After I'm dressed again and feeling a bit more presentable, I head back.

When I get to our table, it's empty. I glance over at the snack counter, but no one is there either. Oli wouldn't leave without saying goodbye, would he?

I take a seat, picking up my jacket from the bench and digging out my phone. The battery is at 12%. I should've got my charger out of my bag last night, but I was busy, very busy. My mind flashes to Oli's hands on my face, his lips on mine—

The door to the dining car opens.

Oli walks though, balancing two coffees, one on top of the other, and pulling a yellow suitcase behind him. There's an oddly familiar metal rattle as he pulls his suitcase, but I can't quite place it.

He hands me a paper cup. "There's a smaller dining car down that way. This one doesn't open until nine. Two sugars, no cream."

My chest feels warm, and I'm sure the smile on my face is pure puppy love. He remembers how I take my coffee. He's dressed in the same jeans, paint splattered in the same spots, but a fresh shirt. This one is light blue with a skeleton on it. "Thank you."

I sip my coffee and wish I had also thought of going to my suitcase for fresh clothes.

Oli sets his coffee on the table and moves his suitcase next to him on the seat. He sits next to it with a large sigh. "My stop is next."

My tender heart plummets to my stomach. "Oh."

He hands me his phone. "Can I have your number?"

My breath catches in my throat. As much as the thought of not seeing him again fills me with a deep sorrow, the thought of trying to see each other, or date, makes panic crackle in my chest. I don't even know where he lives.

Oli notices my hesitation and shakes his head, the tips of his ears turning pink. "If you don't...I mean..."

His face is so sweet. I type my number in along with my first name and hand him back the phone. He smiles and taps on the screen.

"I just texted you, so now you have my number too." He moves to my side of the table, playing with a strand of my hair. "I have a busy couple of months, but I'd like to see you again. On a train or otherwise."

I smile as he buries himself in my neck.

The train slows, making popping and screeching sounds. The announcer comes over the loudspeaker. "Next stop Dunes City."

Oli groans, letting the full weight of his body droop on me for a moment.

It's delicious.

I wrap my arms around his neck. He lifts his head, his breath hot on my cheek. I lean forward, and we kiss. His lips are so soft, his touch so tender. I no longer have to breathe. I am stardust.

Then we part, and my breath returns in a whoosh, like when it comes back after falling off the monkey bars.

"I'll text you," he says, his steely eyes shimmering with sincerity.

I don't know what to say. This was all so unexpected. I don't want to say goodbye, so I bring my hand to my mouth and blow a kiss instead. He catches it and makes his way down the aisle. I watch from the window as he rolls away his bright-yellow suitcase covered in stickers.

Once he's out of view, I lay my head back, staring at the inlaid wood ceiling but seeing only flashes of Oli. I close my eyes to see them better.

THE LIGHT when I wake again is even colder than before. Gray clouds blanket the sky, and raindrops hit the window at a steady pace. My stomach feels hollow. Where are we? Searching the view for clues on how far we've gone, I'm distracted once again by my reflection in the window. My stark features and pale skin echo back to me so strongly it's like looking in a mirror. Do I look different after last night? After meeting Oli. Can one night change a person?

Picking up my phone to take a reference photo, I find that it's dead. Shit. Why didn't I grab the charger? After I take one last look at the reflection, trying to commit the more important details to memory—the way my hair is sticking up at odd angles, most likely from Oli's large hands—I get up. I make my way to the snack counter through the steady rocking of the train. Once there, I order fresh coffee and a plain bagel. As the attendant is pouring the heavenly liquid, the rich aroma filling my nose, I ask, "How far is it to Fortune Falls?"

The man checks his computer screen. "About two hours."

The clock behind him on the wall says it's already past noon. I slept longer than I thought. The lounge car is full of people eating lunch, laughing, and chatting. I take my food back to my original seat. The family that I was seated next to is nowhere to be seen. I set my stuff down then grab my suitcase. I dig through my bag, stopping now and then for a bite of bagel. There is no phone charger. I can picture it clearly, plugged in next to my nightstand at home. I was in such a hurry, I didn't remember to pack it.

Well, that will make pulling into Fortune Falls a little more challenging than I originally anticipated. Shit.

The rain falls steadily out the window, splashing in puddles, soaking into pine trees. It gets heavier as we finally slow, the pops of air and squeal of brakes sending fresh tendrils of anxiety straight to my toes. Grabbing my suitcase, I wheel it through the hall. A train attendant in a crisp blue uniform helps me get it down the stairs, even though it's not particularly heavy. I thank him and wheel it across the brick platform, suddenly at a loss of what to do with myself.

The air smells so familiar, the salty sweet tang of the ocean— too far to see, but the scent permeates every inch of this town. The earthy scent of wet leaves reminds me of so many walks to school, when the rain pelted down but Ben and I never seemed to mind. Our intertwined hands dripped with the icy drops.

I button my jean jacket, not much more protection from the rain, but it's something, and wheel my suitcase around to the front of the station, standing under the awning and trying to figure out what to do.

The room I booked at the Inn is only a few blocks from here, I think. I glance around the streets. It's after two on a Saturday afternoon. Where can I go to get my bearings and find the address?

Then it comes to me. The Vern. I've only ever been inside once, with a fresh fake ID when I was sixteen. It was promptly confiscated, and I was sent packing. But it's dry, warm, open, and this is the most important thing, I know how to get there from here. I walk the four short blocks to Main Street and wheel my suitcase through the rain to the end of the street where the smashed-up tavern sign hangs over a brick building, only the last letters, VERN, lit up. The bright red wooden door is closed, but the pink neon sign in the window flashes OPEN.

As I open the door, loud cheers greet me. I nearly turn right around, until I realize they're all directed at the screen in the back showing a football game. There is an open spot at the bar, in the corner, so I wheel my suitcase across the hardwood floor, tucking it between the barstool and the wall. I take off my completely soaked jacket and lay it on top of my luggage.

The man behind the bar with slicked-back black hair and warm brown eyes hands me a very full glass of red wine. I shake my head, even though that glass of wine looks amazing right about now. "I didn't order this."

The corners of the man's brown eyes crinkle as he smiles, wide and genuine. He points behind me. "It's from that man right over there."

I turn, my wet hair sprinkling tiny droplets around me as I do. Standing there, leaning against the pool table in a green flannel shirt, dark jeans, and worn-to-the-bones Redwing boots is Ben. My Ben.

The bartender wipes his hands on his jeans. "He wanted me to tell you welcome home."

CHAPTER 6

B en raises his tall can of Pabst in my direction. A silent cheers. I want to smile, or return the gesture with my gifted glass of wine, but I'm frozen. I knew running into him was a possibility. An inevitability, really. I just didn't think it would happen so soon.

Gulping my wine, I'm about to head over to Ben when a crowd of laughing women moves between us. One stops right in my face.

"Holy hell. Zara? Zara Ashford?"

Shaking myself out of my gaze, I focus on the woman in front of me. Deep auburn hair hanging down to her back, bright-blue eyes, and a smattering of freckles on her pert nose. "Meg?"

Meg pulls me in for a massive hug, her hair brushing my cheek. It still smells like the rose shampoo she found in seventh grade and declared the best five-dollar shampoo on the market. At a sleepover years ago, she told me that when she's a famous actress, she'll still use this shampoo and her Maybelline mascara to keep her grounded. Looks like the whole famous actress thing didn't pan out.

"What are you doing here?"

One of the other girls calls out, "Come on, Meg. It's shot o'clock!"

I laugh.

"I'll be there in a second." Meg waves her away.

She's just as tall and thin as she was the last time I saw her at our high school graduation. She's wearing a pair of hip-hugging jeans, a tight white sweater, and a shiny pink sash that says *Bride-to-Be* in sparkly silver letters.

Meg motions to the group of girls also in sashes that say things like *Hot Mess* and *Sexy and Single*. She smiles, and for a flash it feels like we're back sitting in her kitchen with the smell of warm cookies in the oven. "It's my bachelorette party."

I run my fingers along the sash, the satin smooth under my fingers. "I see that. Congratulations. Who are you marrying?"

Meg's cheeks flush pink, and my breath snags in my throat. What if it's Ben?

"Tommy Carter."

A giggle bubbles, and before I know it, we're doubled over laughing. "What about being so grateful not having to see his smug face anymore?"

All through high school, they hated each other. They both ran for class president, Tommy won. They both were up for valedictorian, Meg won. When we were about to graduate, Meg said one thing she was looking forward to was not having to see him every day.

She shrugs. "Turns out I love that smug face. Come join us. I want to hear what's been going on with you."

I grab my suitcase to bring over to the table and glance back to where Ben was standing before. He's gone. Probably for the best. I'm not ready to talk to him. Yet.

Holding up my phone to the bartender, I ask, "Do you have a charger by any chance?"

He grabs it. "I can plug it in back here."

"Thanks."

With butterflies in my stomach, I make my way over to the

circular booth in the corner. I stash my luggage on the side of the red vinyl seat and slide in next to Meg. She throws an arm around my shoulder. "Girls, this is Zara. She was my best friend in high school."

Meg points to a petite blonde woman with a pale-pink tank top on despite the chilly weather and the sash that says *Sexy and Single.* "This is Carly."

Carly waves her nails that are the exact same shade as her top.

Next, she points to the woman with long brown hair that falls in soft curls around her shoulders. Her sash says *Hot Mess.* "This is Amanda."

Finally, she points to a woman in a green sweater with a sash that says *Diva.* "And Bridget is my maid of honor."

Bridget. I haven't thought about her in so long. She looks just like she did in high school. Same long honey-blonde hair, same purse to her lips.

Bridget hands out the shots. Her face pinches when she gets to me. "I didn't know you'd be joining us. I can go get you—"

I hold up my wine. "I'm good."

Her face breaks into a dazzling smile as she holds up her shot. "To the bride, bitches."

They whoop and holler and throw back the shots.

Carly leans in, her green eyes fixed on me. "Where have you been?"

Sitting back in my chair, I try to put some distance between us. "Excuse me?"

"Well," she says, twirling her wineglass on the table. "If you and Meg were best friends since you've been in training bras, then why haven't we ever met you?"

"Uh…"

Bridget chimes in, picking up her wine, her long black nails clinking on the glass. "Zara bailed right after high school. No one has heard from her since. Where have you been hiding?"

"Down girl," Meg says playfully, but there's an edge to it. "Zara just got here."

"Right. Sorry. It's my curious nature." She sits back, bringing the pink wine to her lips.

"Bridget is a lawyer."

"Ahh." I have no idea what to say to that. Great. Good job. Why? "That's awesome."

"What do you do?" Carly asks, her tone much warmer than her lawyer friend.

"I work at an art gallery in LA."

"Fancy. I always knew you'd do something with your art." Meg smiles. "Zara makes the most amazing paintings. You know the one of the snake plant hanging in my kitchen? She painted that."

My cheeks flush as my heart fills. "You still have that?"

"Of course, I do. I love that painting."

The fact that even after I left without a word to anyone, she kept my painting, and after ten years of being gone, welcomed me into her bachelorette celebration, it's beyond what I deserve. Tears prick the back of my eyes, and I quickly change the subject before I get too emotional. "What do you do for work, Meg?"

"I work at the library."

We pass the afternoon catching up and celebrating the bride-to-be. After a couple hours, I ask Meg, "Hey, remember camp in seventh grade?"

"Yes, how could I forget. We danced around the fire in the middle of the night on the full moon and swore our allegiance."

I laugh, the memory coming back now. "Sisters of the fire."

"Yes, bitch. Sisters of the fire. That same year, I kissed that boy...what was his name?"

"Nathan? I nearly forgot about that."

The girls dissolve into chatter about first kisses.

I place a hand on Meg's arm. "Do you know if Mr. Willard still owns the cabins?"

Meg bites her lip, her eyes shimmering. "He passed. Probably four years ago now."

My stomach turns over uncomfortably. Mr. Willard was old,

but he was always old, white hair as far back as I can remember. But dead? I knew when I left, life would move on—I didn't think about when it wouldn't. "What happened?"

"Heart attack. He left the place to..." Meg takes a long drink of her wine, emptying her glass. She doesn't need to go on, I know what she's going to say.

I finish the sentence for her, "Ben."

<hr />

AFTER A COUPLE more glasses of wine, Bridget announces it's time to move on to her house for face masks, pizza, and *Sweet Home Alabama*.

"You should come!" Meg says, clasping my hands. The scowl on Bridget's face tells me I really shouldn't.

"I should check in before it gets too late."

Meg throws her arms around me, wrapping me in a bear hug. "Don't be a stranger. My number's the same."

I hug her back, the feeling both familiar and foreign. "I'll text you."

She says, "Do it now so I'll have your number."

I check my pocket for my phone then remember it's still behind the bar charging. "I will as soon as it's charged. I promise."

The bachelorette party bustles out the door to some whoops and whistles from the football fans. I make my way to the bar, wheeling my suitcase behind me.

"Can I pay my tab and get my phone?"

The bartender unplugs my phone and hands it to me. "Tab's paid."

"Ahh, they didn't have to do that."

The bartender points to the door the last of the party is leaving out of. "They didn't. Ben did."

My breath hitches. "Is he still here?" I turn, scanning the bar.

"Nope. Left a little bit ago. Made sure your drinks went on his tab, though."

"Do you know how I could get a hold of him?" The bartender's brown eyes narrow. "I'd like to thank him."

A gentleman in a worn Carhart jacket pushes his glass toward the bar. "Another one, Kyle."

Kyle goes to refill it, saying over his shoulder, "I think Meg has his number."

Maybe I could text Meg.

He hands the older gentlemen his beer then raises his finger. "I hear he goes to the Stonehouse Café every Sunday."

Of course, Sunday morning breakfast just like he had with Mr. Willard every week.

Kyle asks, "You know where it is?"

"I know the place. Thanks." I try to turn on my phone, but the screen remains black. "Hey, do you know where the Fortune Falls Inn is?"

Kyle points. "About two blocks that way, just past the book store, towards the water."

"Thanks."

Stepping outside the warm bar, I'm met with an icy wind and light drizzle. The sky has darkened to a menacing shade of gray. It doesn't look like it'll stay a light rain for very long. I walk the two blocks down Main Street, my boots kicking water up on my legs with each step, past a cute little bookstore with a circular sign that reads *Story Club Books* hanging in front, blowing in the wind. At the very end of the street is a large house covered in cedar shingles. There's a wraparound porch and a massive spire. I remember this house. When I was a kid, I thought it was some sort of castle because of its architecture. I never realized it was an inn.

The lobby is all dark wood and cozy red upholstery. The large stone fireplace is lit, emitting a wonderful warmth. I wipe my feet on the doormat that says *Welcome Inn*. A woman in a floral dress, with earbuds in, is dusting the lampshade near the fire.

She notices me. "Ah, you must be Ms. Ashford."

"That's me."

The woman whistles. "You nearly missed the check-in window." She pulls out her earbuds, tucking them in her pocket. "You're lucky my cozy mystery just got good. I'm Mrs. Pepper." She moves her attention away from the lampshade for the first time in the conversation, and her eyes go wide as quarters. "Good lord. You got caught in it. Let's get you to your room so you can get in dry clothes." She hurries behind the desk, grabbing a key, an actual key, with a red tassel keychain. "Come on, then."

"You can just point me in the right direction."

She waves her hand and starts walking. "It's a bit of a maze. Come on, dear."

I follow her up the terracotta-colored tiled stairs. On the second floor is another fireplace and a small sitting area with bookshelves covering the walls. We walk right past it down the long hallway to the last room. Mrs. Pepper puts the key in the lock and opens the door. The room is gorgeous. A four-poster bed covered in a seafoam-green comforter sits to the right as I walk in. There's a leather chair next to the fireplace, with a chunky knit blanket draped over it, and the fireplace is already lit. There's a window seat with pillows that match the comforter. The view looks out onto the ocean, waves crashing with increasing force.

"Bathroom is right through there." Mrs. Pepper points at the closed door. "Anything else you need, dear? Did you eat?"

"I'm fine." Thanks to the bachelorette party snacks. "This is perfect, thank you." And it is really, if I was here under other circumstances.

Mrs. Pepper leaves, and I shrug off my jacket and peel off my wet clothes. I go to the bathroom and run a bath in the clawfoot tub. There's a window in here as well that looks out at the ocean.

I try to turn on my phone again. This time, the screen comes to life, the little white apple lighting up. Setting it next to the tub, I sink into the warm water, washing off all the chill from the rain that's still going strong out the window.

When I pick up my phone, the first notification is a text. I open it, and an altogether different kind of warmth spreads across my chest.

Oli: I wish we were still on the train right now or you were here.

There's a blurry picture clearly taken out the window of a train of a tree with bright orange leaves.

Lining up my phone, I prop my leg up out of the water and snap a pic. The ocean view, the bath, and my legs are the only things visible. Sexy, but not too sexy.

I send it to Oli.

Me: It's a big tub. Definitely room for two.

I set my phone to the side. I really do wish Oli were here. He could make this feel like a vacation, take my mind off the task at hand. How am I going to ask Ben for a favor after what I did?

CHAPTER 7
EIGHTEEN DAYS UNTIL THE RETREAT

First thing in the morning, I head out for Stonehouse Café. Apparently, there are only three Lyfts in Fortune Falls and all of them are busy. But Mrs. Peppers points me in the direction of the bike that is free for guests to use.

Glad I chose jeans when getting dressed and that, so far, the morning is dry, I hop on the bright-red bike with a wicker basket in the front and start to ride. The wind rushes through my hair, whipping my ponytail behind me. The first mile is swift; it's the next two that make my muscles burn and leave me sweating and panting as the road goes up and up and up. It's been too long since I've been to a spin class. The effort is honestly a welcome distraction from the task at hand.

The final half mile is too steep, so I hop off the bike and walk it the rest of the way, the clouds rolling by in deepening shades of gray. A few fat rain drops fall as I lean my bike against a nearby tree in the gravel lot of the Stonehouse Café. The river stone covered house is nestled in the large pine trees, overlooking the ocean. The café hasn't changed a bit. Memories flow in like the waves below, one after another. Ben and I getting French fries on a rainy Saturday afternoon after a hike. Grabbing milkshakes after a hard day at school. Eating burgers, me in my black prom dress, him in his tux.

I take a deep breath, my stomach turning in knots. I'm not sure if I'm more nervous that I'll find Ben or I won't. My fingers touch the brass handle, the cool metal grounding me. As I open the door, a blast of warm air greets me along with the aroma of freshly made cinnamon rolls and rich coffee. "Take Me Home, Country Roads" plays over the speakers, but the chatter of all the guests and clanks of silverware on porcelain nearly drown it out.

I scan the faces at the tables but don't see Ben.

A woman in a red sweater saunters to the wood podium. "Breakfast, hun?"

My stomach rumbles at the mention of it, and possibly the cinnamon rolls. "Sure."

She points to an empty stool at the long wooden bar. "You're in luck. One spot's open at the counter."

She bustles off. I seat myself between two gentlemen, one in a crisp white shirt, sleeves rolled up reading the paper, the other in a puffy red vest focused on his eggs. Neither of them is Ben. Maneuvering carefully to not bump my neighbors, I hang my jean jacket on the hook underneath the bar. A man with a massive white mustache and a pitcher slides up behind the counter. "Coffee?"

"Yes, please. And a cinnamon roll."

The man's mustache curves up as he pours my coffee then moves on to fill the next cup.

"Still have a sweet tooth?"

The deep, familiar voice reverberates in my chest.

It's at once familiar and strange. Deeper than I remember. I look down to the end of the counter. Ben is smirking at me. His dark-brown hair sticks out here and there underneath his navy-blue beanie, bringing out his dark-blue eyes shimmering with mischief.

The man next to me eating eggs points to his own seat. "Want to switch me?" he asks through a mouthful of eggs.

Ben grabs his coffee. "Sure. Thanks, Norm."

My nerve endings crackle. This is happening. I can do this. I can hold a polite, pleasant conversation with the man I lost my virginity to, ran out on our engagement, and haven't spoken to in ten years.

Ben sits on the stool next to me, angling his body toward me instead of the counter. "Zara Ashford."

"Ben Willard."

We look at each other. I'm at a loss of what to say next. What is there to say? How am I going to ask him if we can rent his property? I can't. I won't. I'll tell Marlene we need to find another town.

The man with the mustache sets down my cinnamon roll.

Ben chuckles, turning back to his mug. "I don't know how you can eat that in the morning and not get sick."

I pick up my fork, sawing into the delightfully oozy roll. My mouth is watering. "Iron stomach."

"Still?"

I smile as I take a massive bite, the sugary sweetness and the spice of the cinnamon are absolute heaven in a pastry.

"Not a lot has changed, then?" Ben turns his gaze back to his coffee for a beat. We both know that's not true.

He clears his throat. "What brings you back to town?"

Setting my fork down, I take a sip of coffee. Could it be just this easy? "Well, I work for a gallery and we host an annual artist's retreat. We're looking for a location to hold the next one."

"And you suggested Fortune Falls?" he asks with a slight eyebrow raise.

I didn't exactly mean to. This homecoming was absolutely not what I had in mind. But I did. And here we are. "Yep."

Ben bobs his head. "They have lots of rooms at the Inn. And there's that place a little further south, the spa in Beachside."

Moving my next bite around on my plate, I don't meet his gaze as I say, "We were actually looking for something a little more rustic."

I glance up, and his lips have set into a hard line, the sharp edge of his jaw clenched. "Anywhere in particular?"

"Camp Ironwood."

Ben blows out a heavy breath.

"Do you still rent out the cabins?"

There's a hint of a frown as he says, "We do. Well, I do. It's just me running it now."

"I heard about your dad. I'm so sorry, Ben. I had no idea."

"You haven't been back in a decade, so how would you know?"

His words, while completely true, are a slap in the face.

"Thank you, though. For your sympathies."

There is a heavy silence that Ben breaks. "When would this retreat be?"

"It's coming up really fast. Would the camp be available from October twenty-third to November twenty-sixth?"

He gulps his coffee, finishing his cup. "If you leave me your email, I can look into it."

I scramble through my purse for a pen. I find one, but of course, I can't find any paper. Ben hands me a napkin. For the briefest moment, our fingers touch. It's an odd sensation. Suddenly, I'm back in front of that waterfall and he's slipping a ring on my finger. He pulls his hand away, bringing me back to the present.

I write my email and number on the napkin and slide it across the counter, careful to not make skin-to-skin contact again.

"I'll get back to you soon." His eyes drill into me, while I try to read his thoughts. I felt like I could, once upon a time. But those days are long gone. I have no idea what he's thinking.

"It's nice to see you, Zara. You look good."

And with that, Ben heads out the door, his boots making a light thud with each step across the wood floor. I push my cinnamon roll away. My appetite is gone, and in its place is a sickly nausea. Maybe not such an iron stomach after all.

A DAY GOES BY. Then two. I pass the time walking on the beach. I buy a book from the bookstore across the street from the Inn, but am too distracted to lose myself in the story. Every three minutes, I'm staring at my screen, waiting to hear from Ben. An email or text, but there's nothing. Just a few texts from Oli. Pictures and wishing I was there or he was here.

I ride the train back to LA on the third day, all the while looking for Oli, but what would be the odds of taking the same train again.

Snapping a picture of the landscape whizzing by, I send it to Oli along with a text.

Me: Any chance you're also on the southbound Sunlight Express?

Gazing out the window, I search for another town, somewhere else we could hold the retreat that might be as quaint or charming. I can't return to the gallery empty-handed, but with no word from Ben, it looks like that's exactly what I'll be doing. I can't even text him, because I didn't get his number, and when I left town a decade ago, I very deliberately deleted it. I needed a fresh start. I knew I'd use his number and go back—and I just couldn't, not after all that happened.

My reflection stares back at me, my dark hair in loose waves around my face. Once again, I try to get a picture so I can maybe paint it one day, if I ever have time to paint again. I crane my arm back to line up the shot, setting the timer. And Oli's face comes to mind when he ran into me, when we first met.

Checking the shot, I have a text notification from an unknown number.

Unknown: Those dates will work. I emailed the paperwork and the invoice.

A wave of relief washes over me, followed swiftly by a larger wave of pure terror. We're going to hold an artists' retreat on

Ben's property. This is great, exactly what Marlene wanted, and it's absolutely terrible.

I save Ben's contact info then quickly read through the email with all the paperwork. Staff will be onsite. Meals can be provided in the dining room for an elevated "sleep-away camp" experience. The manager will be onsite to help with anything we might need. Manager—it doesn't say who. Should I ask? I start to text back.

Me: Great. Who is the onsite manager?

But I delete it. What does it matter if it's Ben? It's a big property from what I remember. And we held a conversation today just fine. Neither of us burst into flames. I type another text.

Me: This all looks great. I'll get everything signed and get the invoice paid ASAP.

I hit send then write another one, hoping it contains the gratitude I really do feel.

Me: Thank you.

The text back is instant, and I'm expecting something heartfelt back, something like *you're welcome* or maybe even *anything for you*. But it's from Oli.

Oli: I wish I was, but I'm working. I'm working pretty much the rest of October and most of November, but I was wondering if you would be interested in meeting me on the Sunlight Express sometime in the winter? Maybe for Thanksgiving?

My cheeks flush at the prospect of seeing Oli again. I check my calendar. The retreat runs from Friday, October twenty-fourth to the Wednesday before Thanksgiving. If Marlene is cool driving herself back, I should be free. This plan will actually work. In fact, it's perfect.

Me: Yes!

CHAPTER 8
ONE DAY UNTIL THE RETREAT

The next two weeks, I work more than I ever have in my life. Emails and actual paper invites are sent out to the five approved artists attending the retreat this year. Marlene handles all the correspondence with the artist-in-residence. The identity of whom she's still keeping top secret.

When I'm not working, I'm packing. I move all my stuff into storage until I have time to find a place. I have a few friends I can stay with when I get back, until I find another place to live.

Thursday morning, we're up well before the sun. I load all the supplies—canvases, paints, clay, and more alcohol than most respectable bars—into Marlene's Mercedes SUV. We hit the road, me driving and Marlene breathing deeply with a silk mask firmly over her eyes in the passenger seat. It's a sixteen-hour drive, according to GPS, but at the speed I'm going, we'll be there in thirteen, fourteen tops. The retreat starts tomorrow afternoon. We set everything up tonight, then I pick up the A-in-R at seven o'clock. Everything has to be done by then. My nerves fizzle uncomfortably, and I press down on the gas a little harder.

Marlene wakes up hours later, shifting in her seat and lifting her mask. "Where are we?"

"We just passed Sacramento."

Marlene reaches in the back for her purse and pulls out the file. I've seen that file more over the past week than I have my own bed. "Let's go over it again."

She holds up a picture of a man with dark hair and even darker eyes. "Miguel Garcia, ceramist originally from Brazil but living in Brooklyn now. No dietary restrictions."

Marlene says in a sultry voice, "And extremely attractive."

I don't say anything, one because I'm not the kind of girl that gossips about guys like that, and two because it feels like a test.

"What? You don't think he's attractive?"

"He's fine, I guess. It's just not what I'm focused on at the moment."

"If he asked you out, what would you say?"

This is definitely a test. "I'd politely decline."

"Good, good. This retreat..." Marlene pauses, stepping her fingers. "It feels special. It *is* special. Relationships form quickly—which is exactly what we want. But we must remain professional. One of my assistants, this was a few years back, started dating an artist from the retreat. It was all sunshine and kittens for the first couple months and then right as a group show was coming up that this artist had several pieces in, things went sour between them. He didn't want to show at the gallery anymore. Ever. To this day, I can't get him to be a part of a show."

I nod. "Understood."

"I knew you'd get it." Marlene gives a half smile. "Next."

She holds up the next photo of a pale, very blonde woman with bright-blue framed glasses that bring out the blue in her eyes.

"Alice Anderson. Photographer originally from Chicago, but lives in..."

Shit, I know this. It's somewhere different. Not New York and not California. Where was it again?

"Austin?"

"Correct," Marlene says this time with no lightness to her face. "Next."

We go through the rest of the artists one by one. After a few stops for bathroom breaks and food, we make the turn off for the cabins, just a little outside Fortune Falls. The trees are dense, and as we drive up the dirt road, they get thicker, so thick it feels like night is closing in.

Marlene must notice the shift, too, because she says, "More trees than I expected."

I hold in a laugh. We've gone over the pictures of the site and maps. She knows it's nestled in the middle of the forest next to a lake. How did she not expect so many trees?

We keep driving, and the trees shift from mostly pine to ones with stunning golden-yellow leaves, some with fiery orange tips. The lake comes into view, reflecting the blue sky and the yellow and greens of the trees. I park the SUV in the gravel lot next to the main lodge. As I get out of the car, the blood rushes to my feet. Marlene makes a beeline inside, and I head to the edge of the lake. It's been years since I've been here. Not since prom night, when Ben took me to cabin three. He had so many candles lit, and my first thought was, were they lit the whole time we were at prom? He could've burned down his family's property.

I bend to grab a rock, catching sight of my reflection in the water's edge, and I think about those paintings again. I put the smooth rock in my sweater pocket, exchanging it for my phone. I snap a quick picture. There's a text from Oli, a picture on a train, autumn leaves out his window.

"So you're into nature photography now, huh?"

I turn to find Ben in his blue plaid jacket, dark jeans, and worn boots. "Not exactly. The place looks nice."

Ben shrugs. "I made some renovations after dad died."

Marlene joins us.

"I'll give you both the tour." Ben leads us to a golf cart. We drive around the dirt paths, wide enough for the cart but too narrow for a vehicle. The cabins are all nestled next to the lake, each one on its own little piece of land with trees lining the back and the sides, so it feels secluded. There are ten cabins, but we're only going to use seven. At the end of the long path is a larger cabin. Ben gestures as he turns the cart to the left away from it. "That's where I am, if you ever need anything. Course, most days you can find me in my office in the main lodge and you both have my cell."

We keep driving, this time away from the lake and into the trees. Ben parks the cart and points to an even narrower trail. "Down that way is the amphitheater. Do you want to keep going or go look at it now?"

Marlene is tapping on her phone. "No time. We have to set up the cabins. The artists will be arriving soon."

Ben turns the cart back on and keeps driving, making the loop back to the main lodge. Once we're back, I get to work unloading the SUV, putting supplies in the rickety wagons provided by the site.

I stop to head inside and grab some much needed coffee, and when I get back outside, my packed wagon is completely empty.

Then I see Ben sitting in the driver's seat of the cart, the back loaded with all the things for the cabins.

I don't need his help. I don't want his help. Being more indebted to him than I already am seems like a truly terrible idea. But as per usual, he gave his help without me asking, and without seeing what I actually wanted.

We just got here, though. This is not the hill I'm going to die on. I take a hearty sip of coffee then say, "Thank you."

Ben smiles.

I grab the file from the back, slipping the NDA out, my stomach twisting in uncomfortable knots. I don't want to ask Ben to sign this. But the mystery artist-in-residence is insisting everyone, absolutely everyone, sign one. I sit in the passenger seat and hand him the paper and a pen.

His eyes scan the document, his mouth setting into a tight line. "What's this?"

"One of the artists coming this year is, apparently, quite famous, and they want to make sure they are protected from the press. It just means you can't talk about what's going on here at the Vern."

Ben's eyes meet mine. "Why would I want to?

I shrug. "I had to sign one, too."

Ben scrawls on the paper, handing it back to me.

I hand him a couple more and swallow hard. "Could you have your staff sign these, too?"

He grabs them without looking at me, stuffing them under the seat. "Sure."

I work for hours. Every cabin has a personal basket tailored to each artist. Bedding is provided, but I change the pillowcases to silk and add a hand-knit throw blanket onto each bed. Each bathroom gets its own scented candle. A rain jacket is hung in each closet, all bright yellow, but each size tailored to the artist. Snacks based on personal preferences are stocked in the small cupboard. Every cabin has a toaster oven, coffee maker, and a hot plate, even though all our meals will be provided at the main lodge.

I'm just slipping a rose-colored pillowcase on the only king-sized bed we have when the door bursts open, and I drop the pillow on the floor.

A woman with dark-brown hair pulled back in a tight bun walks inside in heels so high, I wonder if she knew about the dirt trails before dressing this morning. "This is quaint."

A man in a three-piece suit with stark-white hair follows behind her, holding a leather bag.

"Hmm," he says, eyebrows raised. Not really agreeing, but not disagreeing either. I recognize them both from the file, honestly, I would've recognized them without it. Genevieve and Andre Laurent, the internationally famous art couple known for massive installations that take over entire sections of cities.

I quickly pick up the pillow, and Genevieve wrinkles her nose. "You have another pillowcase, I assume." She rubs the pointed toe of her shiny black shoe along the, admittedly, dusty hardwood floor.

"Yes, of course." And I do. Mine. But it's fine. I'm more

worried that now they see me as the help instead of as a peer. Not that we're peers. And technically, I am the help, but I'm not a maid. I quickly grab another pillowcase from the cart and zip it on. Taking a deep breath of fresh air, I push my shoulders back before walking in and trying again.

"I'm Zara," I say as I thrust out a hand to Genevieve. She eyes it for a beat then shakes it. "Marlene's assistant."

She gives me a tight smile.

"I loved the piece you did at the Louvre last year. The brush strokes in the paintings felt frenetic."

They project paintings onto buildings, sometimes they are original paintings, sometimes it's the *Mona Lisa*. One of my favorites was when they projected *The Starry Night* onto the Empire State building.

Andre gives a curt nod. He's usually the one that makes the paintings, if they are original. "Thank you."

"I'm also a painter."

Andre tilts his head in a way that feels like *of course you are*. "What kind of work do you make?"

Fuck. Why did I even say anything? What do I paint? I haven't completed a series since my BFA show nearly five years ago. Not to say I haven't started, painted one or two then abandoned it. But what about this new idea, the reflections?

"I paint quiet moments of introspection in our increasingly exhibitionist society."

Andre purses his lips. "Sounds intriguing."

It does. All that's missing is the actual work. I leave Genevieve and Andre to get settled and continue setting up the rest of the cabins. The sun dips low in the sky. I'm still putting the finishing touches on—making sure everything is perfect for the arrival of the rest of the artists.

My stomach growls so loud I swear birds scatter. Once the last cabin is set up, I take my flashlight and wrap my sweater tighter around my torso. The air has cooled considerably since we got here. I head down the dirt trail to the main lodge. The only thing left to do tonight is pick up the artist-in-residence from the train station at seven.

The blast of warm air that greets me is a welcome reprieve from the chilly night. Marlene is in a leather wingback chair by the fire, her glass of red wine shimmering in the firelight. Andre and Genevieve are in two matching chairs on the other side of the fire, both with wine in hand. Genevieve has changed out of the stilettos into a chunky heeled boot. Still heels, but a little more appropriate for the terrain. Jealousy spikes. I'd love to grab a glass, sit next to the fire, and talk art, but there's still work to do.

"There you are," Marlene says with an enthusiasm that tells me that's probably not her first glass. "Ben was just about to look for you."

Ben comes out of the swinging door to the kitchen, his white T-shirt snug on his muscular frame. He's definitely not the wiry kid from when we were seventeen. "We were getting worried." He crosses the room to a table with a bottle of wine and several glasses. "Drink?"

I shake my head. "I have to drive to town in…" I check my watch. Shit. It's 6:32 p.m.—if I leave right now, I might not be too late. "I have to go."

"Ah yes. Our artist-in-residence should be arriving in Fortune Falls soon." Marlene claps.

Genevieve says, "I can't wait to see who it is that warrants all the extra paperwork."

"It'll be worth it. Trust me," Marlene says then turns her attention back on me. "He has a bright-yellow suitcase. He said you won't be able to miss it."

Bright-yellow suitcase? The image snags in my brain, but there's no time to think about it too hard.

Rushing, I speed through the dark dirt roads, my foot at the ready to slam on the breaks if a deer pops out of the trees. A quick twenty minutes later, I'm pulling up to the train station, feeling just as frazzled as I probably look. I do a quick check in the visor mirror. Yep, I'm a total mess. The mascara I swiped on before we left at four this morning is all mostly under my eyes, my top knot is more messy than it is cute. But I'm already late, so there's no time to fix it. Quickly I wipe under my eyes then exit the car, searching for the mystery artist.

The suitcase catches my attention first, battered butter yellow, covered in stickers and splattered with paint. The same suitcase that was pulled down the aisle on the Sunshine Express.

The hand holding it is covered in paint, too, as are his jeans, the exact same ones from a couple weeks ago. He's holding his phone in his other hand, looking down. His head snaps up, like he can sense me staring at him. Our eyes lock.

It's Oli.

CHAPTER 9

I'm torn. Part of me wants to run into his arms and nestle into his neck. The other part of me wants to head right back to the car. This can't be happening. The artist-in-residence is Oli? No. Nope.

I could head back to the cabins. Say he never showed. Of course, that wouldn't work, he'd probably just call Marlene and she'd think I'm incompetent. She'd fire me. Although she'll probably fire me anyway once she finds out I kissed the artist-in-residence. Shit. She can't find out.

We'll keep our hands to ourselves.

The picture of professional colleagues.

Oli's handsome face visibly lightens when he sees me. His lips crack into a wide smile, and my hard resolve melts into a pile of goo. This is going to be harder than I thought. Oli weaves his way through the small crowd of people making their way off the train.

He releases his grip on his suitcase, and it falls to the ground, hitting the cement with a clang. He swoops me up and spins me around. A giggle escapes me that is so pure and joyous I hardly recognize it as my own voice.

He sets me down and brings his lips to mine. I melt into him. What's the harm in one kiss before we start the hands-off policy?

His lips are soft but hungry. His hands are gentle on the small of my back. When we part, I'm breathless.

"What are you doing here?" he asks with a smile, his hand still lingering on the side of my hip.

I don't want to tell him; I don't want this moment to end. Unfortunately, it must. I take a step back, and his hand falls to his side. "I'm here to pick you up. I'm Marlene's assistant."

His mouth drops open slightly. "You're Ashford?"

He goes back to pick up his suitcase before I can answer.

I lead him to the SUV. Once we're all buckled and on the road, I say, "So, you're a *famous* artist."

He tilts his head. "Sort of."

"Must be a pretty big deal if we all had to sign NDAs?"

Out of the corner of my eye, I see him shift uncomfortably. "I've been burned a few times. Even by people I considered close. My medium of choice needs to be secret."

The rattle of metal in his suitcase on the train. It all clicks now. "Oh shit. You're a graffiti artist."

He runs a hand over his face. "I am. My work is done as my alter ego, like Batman."

I laugh. "Batman?"

"Yep." He smirks. "Just like Batman."

"What's your secret identity then, Bruce Wayne?"

There's a pause, long enough that I take my eyes off the road to steal a glance at him, the strong planes of his face lit by the moon streaming in through the windshield. Then all the pieces fall into place. When I found that OG piece and Oli didn't know who he was? There's not an artist working today in any medium that doesn't know who OG is.

"Holy shit. You're OG."

He smiles and puts both hands up in an emoji like gesture.

Oli is OG. I can't wrap my head around the fact that one, I know who OG is—something I never thought possible—and two, I kissed OG. We're...well... I don't even know what we are. Friends? Lovers? No, friends. But why wouldn't he tell me?

"I can't believe it. You let me go on and on about the cultural significance of your work."

Oli chuckles. "It was very flattering."

My cheeks flame, and I'm suddenly grateful for the dark car.

"I can't say anything until the big reveal. I signed stuff, too. But you get to stay, right, for the whole retreat?"

"Yeah."

"Then you'll see," he says as he puts an affectionate hand on my thigh.

I take a deep breath. The longer I let this go, the more painful it will be. "About the retreat."

I'm not sure how to say this. I don't want to say this.

Oli moves his hand, turning in his seat to face me a little more, but I can't look over. The road has shifted, the streetlights are gone, and the dense trees block out the moonlight. All my attention needs to be on the road.

"What about the retreat?"

"Marlene is particular about professional conduct from her employees."

"That's a mouthful. What does that mean?"

Despite the strong headlights from the SUV, the night is impossibly dark. The road seems even windier than when I left.

"Zara, what are you saying?"

I glance at him but can't make out his expression.

Movement catches my eye from the trees. I slam on the brakes and Oli braces himself with a hand on the dash as a deer darts out onto the road and freezes in the headlights. It's a young buck, its antlers a pristine white, its coat shining in the lights.

My heart is hammering in my chest. The deer moves on, hopping back into the trees, rustling the bushes as it goes. I throw the car in park, my leg holding the brake shaking.

"That was close."

I don't say anything, feeling just as frozen as that deer.

Oli puts a tentative hand on my shoulder, runs it down my

arm, and settles it on my thigh, sending tingles up my leg. "Zara, are you okay?"

"I'm fine." Exhaling a long slow breath, I turn to face him in my seat. "We can't see each other."

"Yeah, it's dark as shit." He turns on the dome light, and his features come into view in the nearly blinding light. His eyes light up, looking so blue it's too much. He's too handsome, and the light is too bright. It was better in the dark. I turn the light back off.

"That's not what I mean. I mean Marlene will fire me if she knows we..." I was going to say have a relationship, but I stop myself. We've kissed. I don't want to be presumptuous that it meant anything to Oli. Maybe he kisses girls on trains all the time. "We...I have to be professional."

I move his hand off my thigh, even though it physically pains me to do it, and place it back in his lap.

"Ahh." His voice sounds small.

We sit in the dark car, silent for a moment. Putting the car back in drive, I turn my attention to the road.

"What if I talked to her?" Oli asks.

"Pretty sure that would get me fired, too."

"I see."

The car is so quiet it sets my nerves on edge. I turn up the stereo. Under the crackle and fuzz of static, Faith Hill's "This Kiss" plays, as if the universe is mocking my resolve not to kiss the man next me.

Oli shifts in his seat, and I can feel his gaze on my face. "I understand. But just to be clear, if it weren't for your job, you would want to see me?"

The corners of my lips turn up. He's so cute. "I really would."

He sighs. "Good. I'm glad it isn't one sided, because truth be told, I'd like to see a lot of you. All of you. Naked, if you didn't catch my drift."

I laugh. "I get it."

"And you *need* this job?"

I sigh. Because I do. I've worked so hard to get here. Long hours, scraping by on two jobs. This promotion is a big step in the right direction. "I do."

"Okay."

There is a beat of silence. It's not awkward, but it feels sullen.

Oli adjusts the knob, stopping some of the static, turns up the radio, and starts singing along, breaking the dour mood. He sings not just the chorus, but every single word.

"A Faith Hill fan, huh?"

"I have three older sisters. Do you know how many times I've seen *Practical Magic*?"

He sings louder, and I join in.

The song changes, and Oli turns to me. "I think you're a Sally."

"What does that mean?"

"Like from the movie. My sisters have a theory. Everyone at the core of them is either a Sally or a Gilly."

I take a moment to process this. Sally was the one set against falling in love. She was focused on what she needed to do. But she could also be cold. Yep. Sounds like me to a tee. But I wonder what exactly Oli means. "Is being a Sally a good thing?"

Oli shrugs. "Neither are good or bad. Just that you seem sensible. And you'd look great in cut-offs and rubber boots."

I laugh. "Since Gilly was in love with a psychopath, I'm going to take that as a compliment. Although, I'd much rather have Gilly's clothes. Those slips!"

Oli laughs.

By the time I pull up to the trail leading to Oli's cabin and park the car, I'm confident we can be friends and I can keep my job. "We have to walk the rest of the way."

He nods.

I grab the small flashlight out of the back, turn it on, and lead us with the circle of yellow light down the dirt path to Oli's cabin. His is the largest of all of them, and the furthest from the lodge.

We get to his cabin, a large A-frame structure with a little porch that I strung large Edison bulb string lights from. They illuminate the fire pit out front and several Adirondack chairs circle around it.

"This is amazing," Oli says, stopping to take it in.

I bite my lip to stop from grinning like an idiot, pleased and a little proud he likes it. "Wait until you see inside."

Walking up the porch steps, I open the door, gesturing for Oli to go first. He steps by me, and I get a strong whiff of his scent, leather, spice and mist.

I watch him as he wanders the room. There's a queen-size bed with a red-and-white quilted bedspread. The pillows are encased in the red silk covers I placed on them, as well as the sheets beneath. There's a wood stove in the corner, lit for his arrival. A desk sits by the window facing the lake beyond, the moon shining on the water. A rickety wooden door to the other side leads out to the back deck. Oli disappears into the bathroom, modest but workable, with a standup shower and stone floors.

He comes back out. "This is great."

"Some of the other artists have already arrived, but I think Marlene wanted to keep the big reveal of...well, you until tomorrow."

I reach into my pocket and hand him a map of the property. Our fingers graze, and his eyes lock on mine, my lips suddenly feeling fuller, my throat dry.

"There's snacks here." I turn to the small kitchenette. "Tea, coffee, and a couple of bottles of wine."

He moves past me to check it out and holds up one of the bottles. "Stay for a glass?"

That's professional, right? Having a friendly drink with the artist of the hour. I search my soul: if this artist wasn't Oli, would I still agree? I would. It's only polite. "Sure."

He pours two glasses, and we take them onto the back porch, the sounds of distant frogs echoing through the night. We sit on the wood planks, our feet on the stairs below. Beyond, there's a narrow path, hardly visible through the brush, that leads down to the lake.

Oli takes a long sip of his wine, his neck arching back, his Adam's apple bobbing. I want to sink my teeth into him, but instead I take a small drink of my wine, the earthy, rich taste not doing anything to quench my desire.

Shifting slightly, Oli sets his wine down and moves a little closer to me on the porch. Or was that me moving closer to him? Either way, we are sitting so close now when one of us moves our thighs brush.

Oli clears his throat. "I completely respect your situation. I do."

I move my hand to the porch, my finger grazing his thigh lightly. "Thank you for understanding."

His hand moves next to mine, our pinkies touching lightly. My entire body floods with a wave of warmth. Flashes of our night on the train together fill my mind. I want to climb on top of him and feel his lips on mine again. Lift off my shirt and feel the cool night air on my goose-fleshed skin. The desire is so strong I rise.

"I have to go. There's still some things I need to get done for tomorrow."

His eyes are fixed on mine, like he could read my thoughts, like he was thinking the same thing. "I admire your dedication."

I practically run through his cabin and out the front door.

CHAPTER 10

C louds have moved in, blocking out the moon. My phone flashlight hardly illuminates the path. I was in such a hurry I left my flashlight on the porch. But I barrel down the path anyway, putting as much space between me and Oli as possible.

Why does the artist-in-residence have to be Oli? Six months after the retreat, there is a group show at Gallery Six including all the artists in attendance. And the artist-in-residence usually continues working with the gallery. The show we had in June was an A-in-R from one of these retreats five years ago.

Maybe it's for the best. I don't need the distraction. I can focus on my job, and if I have any spare time at all, I can paint. That's what I need to do. The whole point of working so hard at the gallery is to get my foot in the door, to have my own show some-day. I don't have time to chase dick, and it's not like we would've turned into anything more. If my time with Ben showed me anything it's that fairytale happy endings only happen in the movies.

I'm so focused on my internal rant that I'm startled when I look up to see a woman walking down the path. She's bathed in a circle of light from her lantern, her long white-blonde hair and pale skin glowing like some kind of apparition.

As she gets closer, I recognize her from her picture. It's Alice Anderson. She was supposed to arrive tomorrow afternoon, but she's early. She's stopped in the middle of the path looking at one of the maps of the property that Marlene or Ben must've given her, unless she printed it out on her own from the emails I've sent.

"Hello there."

She jumps. Of course, I scared her, I'm dressed all in black with no real light to speak of. I hold up my hands. "I'm Zara Ashford, from the gallery."

"Ah, yes. I'm Alice, and I'm completely lost." She holds the paper out to me with a small smile. "Help."

I laugh. "I know the way."

I lead her to her cabin, which is actually in the opposite direction she was going.

"I swear, I'm usually better at his stuff. But I've been traveling for…I'm not even sure. Two days. Three. What day is it?"

"Thursday."

"Shit. Three then."

Alice has a breathy voice that makes everything she says sound like a secret. I find myself leaning in closer to catch every word.

"Where were you?"

"Iceland. Sort of. I was on a little island, off Iceland. I was photographing an all-women's commune with the Northern lights as the backdrop."

"That's so cool."

She lets out a long breath and flicks her hair behind her shoulder. "It is. Sometimes I forget that. The women were amazing, but I was there for three months. Three months is a long time with no men. I'm not sure how they do it, spending their lives that way."

"Maybe they get used to it."

"I sure didn't. Don't get me wrong, it was amazing. They have powerful friendships. I'm in awe of them. I've always been so focused on my career, my friendships are few and far between."

Her words strike a chord with me. I left my best friend when I cut ties with this town. Honestly, I'm not sure she's as close as I thought all those years, anyway. Not after what I heard. In college, I kept my head down, too busy with school and work to cultivate many friendships. It's been the same since I moved to LA. My roommate is my closest friend, and I hardly know her.

Alice is bubbling with chatter like an uncorked bottle of champagne. "I missed men. Not even just fucking. But their smell." She sighs. "Ignore me—I'm jet lagged and rambling. I just hope there will be attractive men at this retreat."

My mind immediately goes to Oli, and my muscles go taught at the thought of him and beautiful Alice chatting it up.

"There are some." Thankfully, we arrive at her small, green cabin, which in the dark night looks gray, so I don't feel like I need to elaborate anymore. I turn on the string lights illuminating the small porch. Alice has one of the smaller cabins. We figured she wouldn't need a studio space in her lodging since she's a photographer. And there's a desk inside where she can lay out her gear.

I motion to the cabin. "This is it. Want me to show you around?"

"I just want to crawl in bed. Thank you for showing me the way and listening to my unhinged ramblings." She lumbers her duffle-like backpack up the stairs and disappears inside the cabin.

Back at the main lodge, the fire in the hearth is embers and no one is there. I check the time on my watch. It's nearly eleven and way past my bedtime, seeing as I've been up and going since four this morning.

I drag myself to my cabin, wash my face, put on my nightgown, and crawl under the covers, my mind still spinning in circles. Oli is a few cabins away. I wonder if he's thinking about me right now.

THERE'S NOT enough coffee in the world to put a pep in my step this morning. As soon as the sun peeked up over the lake, I was up, dressing quickly in black jeans, a black pullover sweater, and my black leather Chelsea boots while my coffee brews. I pour the heavenly liquid in a travel mug and head to the dining hall to make sure everything is ready for breakfast. A shrill bird, that is far chipper than any animal has the right to be this early, sings loudly in the distance. The air feels crisp on my face, waking me up a bit more, making me less grumpy and more excited for today.

Heading past the lobby, the fire lit in the hearth, I head straight for the dining room. When I was a kid, it was a dark room with a vaulted ceiling filled with long Formica tables. Entering the space, I see Ben has transformed this as well. The ceiling is still high with massive, exposed wood beams. The cafeteria tables are gone, replaced with square bistro tables covered in cream tablecloths. On a long table in the corner of the room, there are plates, cutlery, and cups. The walls have been redone to include more windows—in fact, windows cover most of the space. The room is no longer dark, but filled with light, despite the overhead circular steel and glass chandeliers being off.

The sun is coming up over the lake, the clouds glowing gold, the pine trees in black silhouette. Streaks of hazy pink and baby blue dominate the sky, mirrored in the lake below. I step closer to the window, catching sight of my own reflection overlaid on all these colors, and my fingers once again itch to paint.

"Gorgeous, isn't it?" Ben says, holding a tray of bacon and setting it on a long table by the wall.

"It really is." I'm confused why Ben is here. When his dad owned the place, he had a full staff and an onsite manager. Ben told me once that Mr. Willard came for parties, and to schmooze when important people were here, but he didn't live here. He lived at the Big House—their name, not mine. It's a massive mansion that's been in Ben's family for generations. Ben comes from old money. So I'm confused by him working here, living here. Does he always, or is he here because of me?

"Everything is all set for breakfast. Not sure when everyone was going to get up, so I told the staff to keep it open until around ten."

"That works." I take a sip of my coffee, my mouth salivating over the scent of bacon. "Ben, do you live here now?"

He doesn't meet my eye when he mumbles, "Yes," then heads back through the swinging door into the kitchen. A few minutes later, he returns with a platter of scrambled eggs, so sunny and yellow they look almost like a work of art on their own.

"Since when?"

Ben looks up, his eyes catching mine, and I suddenly regret my line of questioning. He holds steady eye contact as he answers, "Since you left. I needed some space on my own. Turns out, I like living out here. And running the lodge gives me a sense of purpose." He shrugs. "I'm good at it."

"What about your writing?" When we were in high school, Ben always said he wanted to be a writer. His plan was to go to Brown and write the next great American novel, like Jonathan Safran Foer.

Ben looks past me out the window and sighs then meets my gaze once again. "It's a long story. I'd be happy to tell you all about it sometime while you're here. Maybe—"

"This is gorgeous!" Marlene trills as she saunters into the dining hall, her heeled boots pounding on the wood floor. "Look at that sky."

The sunrise has shifted to include more blues than gold, the trees coming into focus, revealing some with vibrant red leaves.

Ben doesn't take his eyes off me when he says, "It's gorgeous."

He disappears back into the kitchen.

Genevieve and Andre join us next, both quiet this morning. Andre makes himself a plate of food while Genevieve sticks to coffee. Marlene puts a hand on my arm, whispering in my ear, "Ashford, take the a-in-r a plate of food."

"Of course." I rise and make Oli a plate, my chest a swirl of emotions. Excited to see him this morning. Nervous I have to see him and not touch him.

I cover the plate of food with a cloth napkin and head down the trail, the crisp air rushing in my face, blowing the end of my ponytail back.

As I climb the stairs to Oli's door, my apprehension grows. Taking a deep breath, I shift the plate to one hand and knock lightly. Footsteps approach as my stomach flips.

The wood door swings open, and I'm face to face with a bare chest, a smattering of dark chest hair dusting his defined pecs, thinning as it travels across his stomach to a line that goes down, down, down into a tight pair of black boxer briefs. My eyes snap up, finding Oli's steel gray ones, alight with amusement.

"Do you always answer the door like this?" is all I can think to ask.

He smiles, running a hand over his stubbled jaw, the sound practically ringing in my ears. I want to run my teeth along that jaw.

"I just woke up," he says, his voice husky with sleep. "Plus, I saw it was you through the window. Didn't think you'd mind," he says with a wink.

A wink that makes my knees wobble. I sigh. He's not going to make this easy. "I brought you food."

He takes the plate. "Care to join me?"

He opens the door to his room, the blankets rumpled on his bed. My mind flashes unhelpfully to me walking him in, pushing him on that bed, and climbing on top of him.

"No," I say with a little too much conviction. A little softer, I add, "I have to pick up Louise Walker."

"Holy shit! I didn't know she was coming."

"Have you two met?"

He shakes his head. "Just a fan."

"I'll see you at 4 p.m. in the main lodge. That's when you get to meet the rest of the artists." Most of the artists, anyway. Miguel was supposed to be here last night, but as far as I know, he hasn't arrived yet.

Oli yawns, bringing his hand to his mouth, each muscle of his stomach tightening with the motion, and warmth rushes through my center and straight between my legs. Time to go.

"See you then," I quickly throw over my shoulder as I make a beeline for the trail.

CHAPTER 11
THIRTY-THREE DAYS LEFT OF THE RETREAT

I drive the now familiar road into town, past Fortune Falls, heading for the small airport in New Haven where I'm picking up Louise Walker. It's a couple hours away. The ride there is a nice break; no one to impress, nothing to do but drive and listen to music, the fall sun beaming this morning, the blue sky dotted with puffy white clouds. I drive through a patch of trees, all their leaves golden, wind sending some fluttering down as if on cue. It's stunning.

Once I start to get closer, my nerves fizz. What am I going to talk to Louise Walker, *the Louise Walker*, about on the way back? Two hours in the car with a famous painter, one I've looked up to and admired since I was a girl. In school, I took a class about her: *Feminism, Postmodernism and the Magic of Louise Walker*. The whole class, one entire quarter, focused on her, and we didn't even get to all of it—that's how much work she's done.

Pulling up to the small airport, I get out, my heart in my throat. I'm usually not this star struck. In the summer, Chris Hemsworth came to the gallery and I was the picture of a professional. But this is altogether a different story.

The sun warms my face as I wait outside the sliding glass doors, in the area with other Uber drivers. Louise is notorious for not liking her picture taken, but I have an older book of her work. In the back is a small black-and-white picture of her at an opening hugging David Bowie. She had dark hair and sharp features. That was years ago. Hopefully, I'll be able to spot her from it though.

I scan the crowd for a similar face. A tall woman, with a long, elegant neck and even longer white hair, strides out the doors, and I stand straighter. Her leather jacket is flapping behind her like she makes her own wind.

"Louise?" I say, but she keeps walking to a waiting family of two toe-headed girls jumping up and down. "Grandma!"

The woman bends to pick the smallest one up, and an ache settles in my chest. I try to rub it away with a balled fist.

"Zara?"

I turn, dropping my hand, to find a woman in a long, colorful quilted coat with oversize purple buttons and short purple hair to match.

"Mrs. Walker?"

"Ms." She smiles, a gold tooth shining in the side of her mouth, with a tiny diamond in it. I'm stunned. Anything I may have expected, this—she—isn't it.

"Shall we?" Louise says with a chipper smile.

I shake myself. "Yes, of course." I grab the handle of her wheeling suitcase, leading the way to the SUV.

Louise whistles. "That's some car." She looks up at me with mischief in her blue eyes. "Can I drive?"

I laugh, more out of shock than anything. "Uh…"

She waves a hand at me, her nails short, but still with traces of paint on them. I resist the urge to grab her hand and look closer. She hasn't shown in nearly a decade, I assumed she wasn't working either.

"I'm kidding. Mostly."

We pull on the road, and Louise changes the radio station, finding a Chappell Roan song and turning it up. She rolls down the window, sticking her hand out and rolling on the waves of the wind, like a teenager on her way to summer camp.

"What do you make, Zara?"

"Sorry, what?"

"Art. You're Marlene's assistant. You must make art. No one would have that job otherwise."

She has a solid point. "I'm a painter."

Louise pulls her hand in and claps. "Like me!"

The fact that she's comparing what we do, that it's even in the same realm, floors and delights me.

She smiles, so wide it's like beaming light. "We're going to have a lot of fun."

As we drive through Fortune Falls, Louise perks up even more, sitting forward and practically bouncing in her seat.

When we come to Main Street, she points to the busted Vern sign. "We need to stop."

"Lunch is waiting at the lodge."

She makes a fart noise. "Is tequila?"

"Actually, yes, there is."

Louise puts both her hands together in a prayer-like gesture, her eyes going wide. We don't have anything pressing until drinks this afternoon. I need to figure out why Miguel didn't show up last night, but I can probably do that on my phone. "Okay."

As I pull over and park on the side of the street, Louise whoops.

The bar is dark compared to the bright day outside. "There's a back patio, should we sit out there?"

"Here is perfect." Louise pulls up a stool at the bar.

The same bartender is working, handing a card back to a woman with a bag of food and shiny blonde hair. She turns, and I see it's Bridget. Fuck. Doesn't anybody work in this town?

"Zara." Bridget's gaze takes in me and then Louise, her lips settling into a smug smile. "Is this your grandma? You *do* have family of your own. The way you latched on to Ben's in high school, we all thought you didn't."

Before I can correct her, Bridget is holding out her hand to

Louise to shake. Louise looks at it but makes no move to take it. Instead, she says, "Just because I'm an old lady doesn't mean I'm someone's grandmother or mother, for that matter. It's a hurtful and stupid assumption."

Bridget backs up as if Louise slapped her. "Sorry."

Louise waves her away, turning her attention to the bartender and ordering a tequila sunrise.

Bridget seems still stunned. "I better get this food back to the office."

I take a seat next to Louise, who is happily munching on a bowl of peanuts. "What's with her?" she asks me, crooking her thumb at Bridget as she heads out the door.

"She hates me."

"Because you don't have a grandma?"

I shake my head and laugh. "It's a long story."

The bartender hands Louise a highball glass filled with a rosy, pink liquid. She throws him a wink and takes a long drink. He asks if I want anything, but I shake my head as I start sending an email to Miguel.

When Louise sets her drink down, she says, "I have time."

I sigh, not wanting to talk about it, but her piercing blue eyes don't let up. "I moved here my first year of middle school with my mom. She got a job at the aquarium. We found a basement apartment for rent in our budget. Anyway, I met Ben and we started dating."

Louise nods. "That one has the case of the green-eyed monster, then?"

"Something like that, I think. Bridget insists they were only ever good friends. She actually was my friend, too. Not super close, but we all hung out, went to movies, football games. Typical high school stuff."

Louise slurps her drink. "So, what's with all the family stuff?"

"My mom started dating a guy in the military. He had to move to California at the end of my junior year, and my mom wanted to go with him. Wanted us to move, again. Ben's parents offered to let me live at their house and finish my senior year at Fortune Falls High. My mom agreed, and I moved in."

Louise whistles. "Wow. Living with the family at sixteen."

"Nearly seventeen, but yeah."

"So, she hates you for living with her crush."

I'm silent. I don't want to get into the rest. The rumors. Why I left. So I just say, "I think so." I hold up my phone. "Will you excuse me?"

A cold wind greets me as I step outside onto the back porch. Dark clouds have blown in, and the smell in the air has changed. It still has that salt tang that permeates the whole town (even up in the wooded hills by the lake, you can still make out that faint smell of the ocean). But now there's also the sweet smell that comes before the rain.

The number I have for Miguel goes straight to voicemail. With a heavy breath, I dial Marlene and brace myself to give her the news that Miguel is MIA.

"Ashford, where are you? Is Louise's flight delayed?"

"No, she just…" what? Needed a stiff drink in the local dive bar? "She needed to stretch her legs. We're headed to camp soon. I'm calling because I haven't been able to get a hold of Miguel."

"He called me last night. He's having issues with his installation at MOMA. Hopefully, he'll join us next week."

"Oh." So I've been worrying and bothering him for nothing.

"Be back by four! We don't want to spoil the big reveal."

The big reveal. Oli is in fact OG, probably the most famous graffiti artist working today. I still can't believe it.

LOUISE ASKS me to take her straight to her cabin so she can lie down before meeting the rest of what she refers to as "the gang."

There are only a few hours until cocktails with the artist-in-residence at the lodge. After tossing and turning all night, I should lie down, try to nap, or maybe try to sketch out one of my ideas for a painting. Getting out my sketchbook and my pencils, I settle on the porch, scrolling through my photos, trying to find the one of the reflection on the train. My eyes land on the blurry one of Oli's shocked face from when we met.

The corners of my lips curl up, and my chest warms as I remember the rest of that day.

A text appears, as if his skin was burning at my mental touch.

Oli: What are you doing?

I bite my lip, debating how to respond. Then I text him the blurry photo.

Me: Reminiscing

The sky opens up, and rain pounds the wooden roof covering the porch. Three dots appear, then disappear, then reappear.

A photo appears of me, my cheek dimly lit by the golden glow of the wall lamp on the train, my jean jacket wrapped around my front like a blanket, my face turned toward the window, my reflection staring back at me.

I had no idea he took this. It's perfect, and not just because I look smoking hot in the tawny light. The reflection in the window is exactly what I've been trying to capture. The rain picks up, as does the wind, and tiny specks of water drop onto my sketchbook, s I move inside. Kicking off my shoes, I settle on the bed, nestling in the soft blankets as rain pounds the roof.

A text appears next.

Oli: This is the picture I use when I "reminisce" ;)

A laugh escapes me.

Me: Not what I was talking about.

A minute goes by, then two, and I hope I haven't ended the conversation. Then my phone lights up.

Oli: What are you doing right now?

I lean back on the bed, glancing at my abandoned sketchbook, and wonder if I should be honest or sexy. But if I'm sexy, then what? Are we going to sext and pretend it never happened? We have to be here together for a month. We can't start out like this if I want to keep my job. I opt for honesty.

Me: I was trying to sketch
Oli: Can I see?

I open my book again to the blank, now slightly damp, page.

Me: No.

My phone buzzes in my hand. Oli is trying to FaceTime me. I sit up a bit and flick on the bedside lamp then press accept. Oli's scruffy face fills the screen, the rain loud through the phone and on the roof. He's in a soft gray shirt and navy-blue cardigan.

"Why can't I see?"

I let out a long sigh. "Fine." I hold up the blank page to my phone. "This is it."

He furrows his brow. "Very minimalist."

I laugh, throwing the book on the bed.

"Did I interrupt? Should I let you go?" Oli asks.

"No. This is how it's been every time I sit down to sketch for a while now. It's not you."

"What kind of art do you make? I mean, you sketch your ideas, but are you a sculptor? A performance artist?" He asks the last one with a smirk.

"I paint. Just a lonely painter. No audience for me."

"Lonely?"

My cheeks warm. It's true. I meant it as in I don't perform my art. I make it alone, and when it's hanging for an audience, I'm not there to see it except at the opening. But as Oli says it back to me, I realize it's true on every level. *I am lonely.* I've been so focused on working my way up, getting my foot in the door, and trying to create a body of work worth showing. I haven't let anyone in since I left Fortune Falls.

"Painting all by myself, sometimes it is really isolating."

Oli brings the phone closer. "It's such a different process than mine."

"How so?" I've always been interested in how other people make art, but the solitary part never felt like a variable. Unless you're a duo like Genevieve and Andre.

"When I make the stencils, that's all by myself, and when I

sketch ideas, so it's similar there. When I put a piece up, though, I have a crew. We work together."

"My process is very solitary," I confess. "In fact, I don't think I've made a painting with someone else in the room since art school."

"Maybe that will be different this month. It's fun to make art with people, even if you're working on your own stuff. It's a special connection. A rare spark."

His eyes flicker with mischief, and I wonder if we're still talking about art.

CHAPTER 12

Throwing on my yellow slicker, I head for the lodge a bit early to get everything set up for the big reveal presentation, the rain still pelting down.

The lodge is quiet, just the crackle of the fire in the hearth. There's a large screen pulled down near the couches that wasn't there before and a projector stand set up. Ben walks out of the swinging doors in a cream cable-knit sweater and a chocolate brown beanie, putting batteries into a remote in his hand. He looks up, and his brow furrows. It's a facial expression I've seen so often, but not for so long, that it momentarily freezes me.

"Zara, you're soaked."

I look down and see that I am, in fact, dripping water all over the hardwood floors. "I'm sorry."

Ben waves me away. "We can clean that, no problem. Hang up your coat and warm up by the fire."

The order prickles my skin. I do hang up my coat, but instead of going to the fire, I head to the projector. The laptop plugged into it is a sleek black MacBook Air, one I don't recognize. I press the spacebar to try to make it come alive as Oli walks confidently from down the hall in the same navy-blue sweater that he was wearing while we FaceTimed. We talked for nearly an hour about nothing really, but it felt...I'm not even sure, but not like nothing.

"Hey, there." Oli waves a reproachful finger at me. "No peeking."

I hold my hands up and back away. "You have a Powerpoint?"

Oli's lip quirks up at the side, making his dimple pop. "Of course, I do. I'm a professional." He throws me a wink, and my chest warms. Then instantly freezes as I catch the look Ben gives me.

I take a deep, breath shaking it off. "Everything's all set, then?"

There's a bar in the corner, and the bartender is polishing glasses. A buffet table next to it is filled with appetizers: everything from bacon-wrapped dates to mini mushroom quiches.

Ben says, "We're all set."

I wonder again why he's here. If I weren't a part of this retreat, would he still be overseeing everything so closely? Is this what he does now?

The main door to the lodge opens, bringing in a gust of wind and a damp but very chipper Marlene. She strolls in, hanging up her silver rain jacket, her thigh-high leather boots smacking against the hardwood floors as she heads straight past me for Oli. "Are you ready?"

"I think so," Oli says, but something about the slight quiver in his voice doesn't sell it. It dawns on me that Oli might be nervous at how these other prestigious artists may receive him. It makes me want to run to his side and whisper reassurances in his ear.

Marlene grabs Oli by both arms, making intense eye contact. "Everyone has signed the NDAs. You have nothing to worry about."

He gives one resolute nod. "Then I'm all set."

Marlene gives his arms one last squeeze before letting go. "Wonderful. Now grab a drink and hide in the back until you hear your cue."

Oli walks past Marlene, brushing my hand lightly as he walks past.

Andre and Genevieve arrive first and both order martinis, settling in on the loveseat. Alice comes in next, her hair absolutely drenched, her camera hanging around her neck wrapped in plastic. She orders a red wine and takes it to the wingback chair closest to the screen. She catches my eye and gives me a warm smile.

Louise is the last to arrive, wearing her quilted coat, now soaked. She shivers as she hangs it on the coat rack, slipping a little on the now wet floor.

I hurry over. "Here come sit. I'll get you a blanket."

"That would be nice, dear, thank you. And a tequila sunrise if they have it."

A staff member appears with a mop, and I stop them, asking where I can find a blanket. They say they'll get one. I ask the bartender for a tequila sunrise. As he hands me the swirling pink drink, the other staff member hands me a faux-fur blanket. After thanking them both, I take them to Louise and ask the group, "Would anyone else like a blanket or need anything?"

"No, we're fine," Genevieve says, placing a hand on Andre's knee.

"What about you, Alice?"

She shrugs. "Nah, I definitely got caught in it, but I'm okay."

Marlene claps her hands, striding down the hall. "Ah, we're all here. Except Miguel, but he's hoping to be here in a few days."

She taps a few things on the laptop, bringing the projector to life. The image of an old train yard, a dilapidated, rusty cable car sitting at an angle, with a massive piece of graffiti on the side appears. In the corner is a tiny silhouette of the same girl with the fifties-style dress that Oli and I saw on the side of the building. It's the girl he uses in a lot of his pieces, but it's one I haven't seen before.

My cheeks warm at the memory of me going on and on about graffiti at the little café. I can't believe he pretended it wasn't him, that it wasn't his piece I was gushing about.

Marlene clears her throat, a controller in one hand and a glass of red wine in the other. "Thank you all so much for being here. We are going to have a productive and life-changing time, I can feel it."

She holds up her glass, and the others do the same.

"Chin, chin," Louise says before taking a hearty sip.

"As all of you know," Marlene says, walking from behind the laptop to sit in the open spot on the couch, "I pride myself on inviting the best of the best. I'm thrilled you could all make it. And to make it worth your time, we must learn from someone truly exceptional in their field. Without further ado." Marlene presses a button on the controller in her hand and music comes over the speakers in the walls, so elegantly hidden I didn't notice them before.

Oli comes out of the back. The tips of his ears are a little pink. He gives a half wave and sits in the open wingback chair. Marlene tosses him the remote.

"I'm thrilled to introduce you to Oliver Grant, but you all know him better as OG."

A collective gasp ripples around the room like a wave. I have to admit, it feels nice to have been in on the secret, even if he never outright confirmed it. The room sits in stunned silence for what feels like an eternity. In actuality, it's more like two minutes.

The first to break it is Alice. "Like, as in *the* OG?"

Oli nods, squeezing the remote in his hand, his forearm flexing with the motion. "Guilty as charged. Literally. That's me. Thank you all, by the way, for signing the NDA. I know it's unusual, but the secret identity thing is pretty important to the whole operation."

"Why?" Genevieve asks, bouncing her crossed leg.

"At first, it was so I didn't get arrested. I never graffitied anyone's active business then." Oli clicks the remote, and the projector switches to one of his early pieces. "I didn't want to deface anyone's property that might not have the means to fix it. I stuck to abandoned buildings. Or billboards. Most of my work now is in pre-approved spots."

Oli walks us through the slide show of his work, but I find it hard to concentrate. I still can't believe he's OG. But now, looking back, maybe it was obvious. The paint flecks on his hands, the rattle of the suitcase. But who expects to run into an uber-famous graffiti artist on a train?

On the last slide, Oli turns back to the group. "This is my first time revealing to a group of strangers, basically, who I am and what I do." He laughs a little. "It's terrifying."

A titter of laughter thrums through the group as Oli sits back in his chair with a sigh. "I have my own thoughts for how our time together might go, but I was wondering what you all are thinking. What are you hoping to accomplish this month or get out of this retreat?"

Again, the room falls into silence. I wish I had gotten a drink, but to get up now seems rude.

Louise leans forward. "Oli, I admire your ability to be vulnerable with us. So, I'm going to be brave, too. If I'm being honest, this month I was hoping to paint something that was *good* enough to show. I paint. I paint all the time. But it's been years since I felt that spark of creativity. Whatever I paint now has to be spectacular. It must live up to my past works." Her shoulders slump a bit. "I'm not sure I can do it. And I don't need the money. So, I paint and then I throw it away, or paint over it. Nothing sticks. I'd like to make something that sticks."

Oli is nodding attentively. I'm struck by her honesty. She didn't have to share that with us, but by doing so, the whole room feels more intimate.

Oli says, "You might benefit from a secret identity."

She laughs, moving the blanket and grabbing her glass from the coffee table. "You know, that's not a bad idea."

Alice is sitting cross-legged in her chair looking at Oli with an unreadable expression on her face. Oli must feel her staring, because he turns to her next. "What about you? What would you like to work on with your time here?"

Her eyes flit around the room, taking each of us in. "I got some great shots of a family of deer on my walk this afternoon, and I need to edit the portraits I took in Iceland."

Oli's lips purse to the side, but he remains silent.

Alice sighs. "I have the opposite problem as Louise. I work all the time. ALL THE TIME." She takes a large gulp of her wine. "I have so many ideas, and there's never enough time to accomplish them all."

Oli leans in attentively. "I get that."

Alice turns her attention to Genevieve and Andre. "What about you two?"

Andre's eyes move to Genevieve as he waits for her to answer. "We have some projects in the works and thought it might be a good way to unplug and think about new ideas."

"You don't want to tell them about the retrospective?" Andre mumbles behind his glass.

Genevieve shoots daggers at her husband.

Oli's eyebrows go up, but he doesn't press.

Genevieve sighs. "We have a retrospective of our work at the Getty next year."

"Wow, that's great. Congratulations," Oli says.

Marlene puts a hand on Genevieve's knee. "It's such an honor."

Andre laughs. "See. It's a good thing."

Genevieve gets up, knocking Marlene's hand off. "It is an honor, I get that, but it also feels like being sent out to pasture. We're not dead yet. We still have so much to do, so much to say. It's not time to look back yet." She heads to the bar and hands her glass to the bartender.

Oli gets up and grabs a drink, too. I ask Louise if she wants another, and she hands me her glass.

I stand in line behind Oli and overhear him say to Genevieve, "Thank you for sharing."

Genevieve grabs her drink and turns to him with shrewd eyes and a hint of a smile on her lips. "Maybe we could collaborate on something new while we're here? An original Genevieve, Andre, and OG might shake up the art world."

Oli tilts his head to the side. "I was hoping we could all collaborate."

"The entire group?"

"Yeah."

"Hmmm." Genevieve's nose wrinkles as she scans the room. "I'm not sure how that will work. Our art is all so different."

"That's what will make it great," Oli says with a smile so joyous, I can feel it in my toes.

Genevieve takes a sip of her drink as Oli orders a whiskey.

"Or a total failure," she quips.

"If it is, what better place to fail? We're out here in the woods where no one can see it." Oli turns to me, whiskey in his hand and a sparkle in his eyes. "What do you think, Zara?"

I'm stunned by him turning his attention on me, including me in this. "I...uh..." I glance around at the eclectic group of artists gathered in the room. Each one of them brave enough to share something this evening. "It might be beautiful."

CHAPTER 13

The rest of the night passes pleasantly, the conversation turning more lighthearted and less soul bearing as we head into dinner in the dining room. The meal is scrumptious, the wine is flowing, and by the time the meal ends, a smile is fixed on my lips.

At the end of the meal, each artist heads back one by one until it's just me, Marlene, and Oli left sitting in front of the fire.

"The first night was a success, I'd say." Marlene downs the rest of her glass then sets it on the table next to her.

Oli smiles. "It's a great group."

"I'm turning in. I'll see you bright and early for your first lesson tomorrow. Goodnight."

She kisses Oli on the cheek. Then comes over to me, whispering in my ear, "Make sure he doesn't stay up too late. We have to get cracking."

I nod.

As soon as she heads out the main door, Oli leans forward, putting his hand on my knee. "I wanted to tell you who I was. I really did. I just have to be careful and—"

"Oli, it's okay. I understand."

He leans back with a sigh. "I was worried you'd be—"

"We should probably go to bed soon." I cut him off again.

Would I have loved for him to confide in me? Yes. But he certainly doesn't owe me anything because of one kiss on a train.

Oli's eyebrows raise, and heat rises to my cheeks. "I mean to our respective beds. I was told not to let you stay up too late."

Oli smiles. "Okay." Setting his drink down, he stands, holding out his hand to me. "Shall we?"

I put my hand in his, his skin rough but warm. The clouds have cleared, just a smattering here and there. The stars fill the sky like a Jackson Pollock.

Squeezing his hand in mine, I say, "Do you always hold hands with your colleagues?"

He laughs, running his thumb over my knuckles, reminding me of when he ran his hand through my hair as our lips met on the train. A shiver runs down my spine. "It's a new practice. If anyone sees us, we can tell them I'm afraid of the dark." His smile is wide. "Want to go for a little walk?"

"It's already quite a walk to your cabin."

"True."

We head down the dark path, watching out for puddles left from the downpour.

"You never said what you want to accomplish with your time here," Oli says.

"Well, it's my job to be here, so…"

"You don't have any goals beyond that for your work this month?"

I swallow hard. I'm not sure how much I want to share. His career, his art, is in a different realm of existence than mine. But he was so honest with everyone, and it's inspiring.

"I want to paint a series of reflections. I'd love to make some good connections with the other artists. My main goal with my art is to have a solo show of my work, hopefully in the next year or so…but I need to actually paint the series first."

"What's been holding you back?"

"Time. Energy. Funds. Well, I have the paint and some canvases."

Oli runs his thumb over mine. "Time and energy are big obstacles. Hopefully, you can find both here."

We're at Oli's cabin, but he doesn't drop my hand. He turns to me, his eyes gray in the dim light of the moon. "Would you like to come in?"

My heart leaps out of my chest and practically runs for his door. But I can't follow it. I have to stay professional. And with the way Oli is looking at me right now, the feel of his hand in mine, there's no way I could stay businesslike once the door shut and we were truly alone. "I can't."

Oli squeezes my hand. "It's cool. I get it. I just want to show you this one thing and then I'll kick you right out. I need my sleep if I'm leading a group of highly accomplished artists in a lesson tomorrow."

The last of my steely reserve falters at his boyish grin. My foot makes a move toward the door, but my stomach lurches.

I can't.

If I go in that cabin, I'm going to kiss him, and I can't kiss him. I squeeze his hand before I drop it, putting both of mine in my pockets so I won't reach for him. "Maybe you can show me tomorrow. I have to go."

He reaches for my face, tucks a stray strand of hair behind my ear, his fingers brushing my cheek along the way. "Until tomorrow, then."

I turn to go, walking to my cabin as fast as I can in the slick mud without falling.

BREAKFAST IS buffet style in the lodge, set out at seven in the morning. I'm there at five till. I tossed and turned all night, kicking myself for not going into Oli's cabin. What did he want to show me? I could've gone to see. As long as it wasn't his hard dick, I'm sure we could've kept it clean.

I pour myself a massive cup of coffee and take it out to the front porch stairs, wrapping my sweater tighter around my body. The dark night has faded into pearly grays and pale pinks, all reflected on the still water of the lake.

Louise walks up the steps, a bit slower this morning. "Mind if I join you?"

"Not at all."

After a few minutes, Louise returns with her own cup of coffee and a muffin. She sits gingerly on the top stair.

"Is your cabin comfortable?" I ask, trying my best not to show I've noticed her tender movements this morning.

Sucking her teeth, she shrugs. "It's not my Tempur-Pedic mattress, but it was fine. This is something."

She gestures out at the sunrise that has deepened. The pink intensifies, and the gray shifts to a deep blue. We sit in silence, sipping our coffee, watching the light show. Alice walks down the dock, her camera hung around her neck. She lies down on her belly, raising her camera to her face, looking every bit of the professional photographer that she is.

Louise blows out a raspberry. "That child has too much energy."

I motion to the sky. "She's probably just inspired."

"Yeah. Yeah. Ignore me. I'm grumpy this morning."

Oli walks down the path with Genevieve and Andre, and I wonder where Marlene is. We all make our way inside. Alice joins us after a bit, her cheeks rosy and her eyes bright.

I smile. Alice's energy is infectious—to me anyway. It seems to piss Louise off. Even though it shouldn't, I find that extremely amusing. "Get some good shots?"

She comes over and shows me her camera. The sky was gorgeous, but the way she's framed it, with the rough wood of the dock in the foreground, it looks once-in-a-lifetime exceptional. "You are *very* talented."

Alice's cheeks turn as pink as the sky on her little camera screen. "No one could fuck up a sunrise like that."

Ben comes out of the kitchen holding a tray of muffins. And I'm struck again by his presence.

Oli approaches him, and they start talking in hushed tones, my stomach flip flopping at the sight of them together. I can't hear what they're saying, but the snippet I do catch is, "all set."

As everyone is finishing up, Marlene strolls into the dining hall in a shaggy fur coat and a cashmere beanie. "Good morning, everyone. Are we ready to make some art?"

There are murmurs among the group, none of them very enthusiastic, except for Alice, who says, "Hell, yeah."

Oli clears his throat. "The best graffiti works with its environment. It doesn't exist in a bubble. A big part of my process is getting to know the area where I'm going to put a piece. When I was growing up, it was easy. It was home. I knew every nook and cranny of Park City. Which, considering its size, wasn't hard to do. But even when I'm commissioned to do a piece, I try to spend some time exploring. That's what we're going to do this morning."

Genevieve's mouth falls open. She points the toe of her heeled boot. "I'm not dressed for a hike."

Oli smiles. "We're not hiking today. My buddy here"—Oli motions to Ben, whose neck has gone beet red—"has arranged everything for us. Grab your coats and let's go!"

My *buddy*?

Oli's already out the door, headed to the water's edge, where four double kayaks are waiting for us. Once he's standing right in front of them, he motions to the boats like Vanna White. "Kayaks."

Ben walks us through the safety precautions and helps everyone with their life jackets. He points everyone to their kayaks, essentially assigning our partners. Andre and Genevieve are in one kayak. Alice, despite standing right next to Oli during the entire safety talk, ends up with Louise. Oli and Marlene are in the third. I silently start panicking that I'm going to be in a double kayak, by myself, when Ben looks me right in the eye and says, "That leaves you and me."

"You're coming?"

"I'm the guide."

"Didn't you just say in the safety talk that we could all just explore?"

"I'm there in case something goes wrong. Don't worry, it'll be fun."

Of course.

Of course, I end up in the kayak, not with one of the exciting artists I could get closer with, share this experience with, not even with the man I'm crushing on, but with my ex-boyfriend.

I get in the front of the red kayak.

Oli approaches just as Ben is about to get in the back. "Hey, man. I was hoping to go with Zara."

My heart leaps, while my nerves fizzle. I shoot a look at Marlene, who's fiddling with her life vest, not paying us any attention. Thank God.

Ben's eyebrows shoot up to his beanie. "Really?"

"Yeah, I have some logistical questions for her. About the retreat."

Ben nods slowly but doesn't move away from our kayak.

Oli is undeterred. "Mind if we switch?"

"Sure. That's fine."

Ben heads toward Marlene, but not before throwing me a look I recognize well. It's a mix of puppy-dog pouting and red-hot longing. But maybe I'm reading into it. Maybe that's just his *things-are-going-a-different-way-than-I-planned* face.

Oli pushes us into the lake. After a few awkward strokes, we find a steady rhythm with our paddling, gliding through the water. The sun peeks behind charcoal clouds, lining them in gold.

Louise and Alice end up paddling straight into the dock, with screams and yelps. We turn to help them, but Ben gets there first. So, we turn our kayak back.

"What logistical question do you have?"

"Huh?" Oli says, his paddle slicing through the glassy water.

I laugh, turning a little in my seat to catch a glimpse of his face. The plains of his face are lit by the sparse golden sunbeams, his cheeks a little pink either from the fresh air or the exercise, and for a moment, I lose my train of thought.

He smiles. "Yes, Ms. Bytheway?"

I laugh, turning back around. "That's what you said back there to Ben."

"Ah yes—to Ben. That wouldn't happen to be Ben of Zara and Ben, would it?"

I focus on the ripples in the lake emanating from our boat. "It is."

"That's crazy. What are the odds...unless. Oh shit. Did you want to kayak with him? I didn't mean to cock block you."

That startles another laugh out of me. "No. No. It's not like that. This is just the only cabins near Fortune Falls. Marlene wanted rustic small town."

No response. I wonder what he thinks about me coming back here.

If I could see Oli as we talk, maybe I could read his facial expression. I spot a clearing on the other side of the lake and suddenly remember what's hidden over there. I glance around. Everyone is paddling in different areas, mostly content, except Alice and Louise, who are both scowling. No one is paying any attention to us. I don't think anyone will notice if we sneak away for a moment.

"Come on," I say as I dig my paddle into the water. "I want to show you something."

CHAPTER 14

THIRTY-TWO DAYS LEFT OF THE RETREAT

We paddle to the muddy shore then hop out and pull the kayak the rest of the way. I unzip my life vest, relishing the rush of cool air that seeps through my sweater. I leave the vest with my paddle on the boat then grab Oli's hand. His lips turn up at the corner in that delicious smirk that I want to kiss off his face.

"Come on."

I lead the way up the dirt trail flanked on either side by a mix of pine trees and some kind of tree with golden-yellow leaves drifting down with each gust of wind. We come to the familiar set of wooden stairs, still as rickety looking as I remember. It seems most of the renovations have stuck to the main lodge and cabins.

Oli holds my hand a little more snuggly once we're tucked away in the woods. "I didn't mean to overstep by asking about Ben. I was just curious." His cheeks turn an adorable shade of pink as he looks away and says, "And maybe a little jealous."

"There's no need to be." Besides the fact that we can't date, I think in my head but don't say. "Ben and I were over a long time ago."

"You wouldn't be able to tell that by the way he looks at you."

I'm stunned. Does Ben still have feelings for me? Impossible after what I did. I shake my head. There's no way. "That's just how he looks. He has that Northwest, beanie-wearing, bearded, plaid thing happening."

Oli holds up his shirt, a screaming green plaid, then points to his forest-green beanie.

I laugh. "But you don't have a beard."

We reach the top of the stairs. Oli pulls me close to him, his lips brushing my ear, sending heat straight to my thighs. "Do you like beards?"

He pulls back, and our lips are so close. His misty scent surrounds me, making me feel almost drunk.

"I like you." The words are out of my mouth before I have time to consider them. They're reckless. It's like his lips are a magnet—gravitational. I'm powerless against their pull. My eyes flutter closed just for a moment before I come to my senses. I can't lose my job. I move a step back just as a loud crack echoes through the air.

"Zara?"

Shit. It's Ben.

"I'm sure they're *fine*," sings Marlene.

Double shit.

A minute later, they come into view on the trail, and I head down the stairs, Oli following behind me. "We're here."

"Great." Ben looks suspiciously at Oli behind me. "We were worried something happened. Is everything alright with the kayak?"

"Yeah. I just wanted to show Oli the old pump house." I point up the stairs. "Is it still up there?"

"Yep." Ben sighs and offers me his hand as I get to the bottom step. I don't want to take it. I'm perfectly capable of navigating the bottom of a wooden staircase onto a dirt path by myself. But I also don't want to appear rude. So I take it quickly then drop it like a hot potato once I'm on firm ground. Looking briefly at Oli, he's giving me a look that seems to say, *SEE!*

Ben continues. "Kids still party out there. I never catch them. They must be getting in from the back roads, even though I've gated them all. I still find beer bottles out there and the whole thing is covered in graffiti. The little shits."

Marlene's eyes go wide.

Oli's smirk is more amused than offended. "What kind of graffiti?"

Ben crosses his arms. "I don't know. It all looks the same to me. Vandals damaging my property."

"Do you use the pump house?" Oli asks, his tone sincere.

Ben shakes his head as we all get our life vests back on at the shore. "No, all the equipment is gone. It's just a hollow cement shell."

Frown lines appear around Oli's lips. "What do you care, then, if they mark up the building?"

Ben stands taller, fire in his eyes. "Because it's not theirs."

Oli stares right back, not backing down. "Putting a concrete building in the middle of this beautiful forest could be seen as an act of vandalism. Maybe the artists are just trying to make it more colorful, more aesthetically pleasing."

Ben scoffs but starts to get his kayak ready to go back in the water. "I'm just glad they're not spray painting the lodge."

Oli nods but doesn't make a move to get in. "Mind if we go check it out? I'd like to see the property damage."

"Knock yourself out." Ben looks to me then to Marlene, who's already in her seat, vest zipped up, snug as a bug in a rug, waiting to be pushed into the water like a princess in a carriage. "I'll go with you. So you don't get lost."

I shake my head, unzipping my vest again. "I remember the way. We got it."

* * *

We head up the stairs again, this time with no hand holding, and head straight for our destination. About a quarter mile down the path is a clearing in the trees, with remnants of a fire pit and a small cement house. Where a door and windows would be are open holes. Moss covers the roof, so thick it hangs down in places.

"Whoa," Oli says, reaching out to touch a moss tendril. "This is some real *Lord of the Rings* shit."

I remember thinking something similar when my mom and I first moved here from the desert. Oli steps inside the doorway, takes his phone out, turning on the flashlight, and shines it around the dark cavern. It's like the small room swallows the light. I take out my phone and add my flashlight, but it's still dark and smells of damp leaves and dirt, more so than even outside.

On the walls is the graffiti Ben was talking about. Most of it is black scrawled letters, the only actual words I can make out are *fuck you*, and underneath it is a tiny *ok* in what looks like fine-tip Sharpie.

Oli turns around, taking each wall in. "I almost feel bad defending *this*."

I laugh. "It's not very attractive, that's for sure."

Oli is nodding, but clearly the wheels are turning in that handsome skull of his.

"We should head back before Ben sends a search party for us."

I turn to leave, feeling the smallest sting that Oli didn't want to pick up right where we left off before. Of course, we shouldn't. Marlene nearly caught us, and if she does, I can kiss this job goodbye.

THE AFTERNOONS ARE RESERVED for quiet contemplation and art making. Today, I'm in the mood for neither, but being the good student I am, I try. I get out my sketchbook and try to draw more on this idea of reflections, but again, I get absolutely nowhere. Why is this so hard? I see the vision for the painting so clearly in my head. Why can't I put it on paper?

Putting away my sketchbook, I get out a canvas and put it on the easel provided. Maybe I should just start. Less planning, more doing. The light in the little cabin is something to be desired, though, so I drag the whole thing out on the porch. Getting out my paints, I set those up on the porch as well, dragging out one of the bedside tables to put everything on. Slipping in my headphones, I put on a classical music mix to zone out. An instrumental version of "Wildest Dreams" comes on, and I inhale deeply.

Let's do this.

I push paint on my palette, mixing, adding some white here and a smidge of red there until I have a beautiful peachy color, perfect for the undercoat. Taking a large brush, I paint it on the stark white canvas in broad strokes, feeling the magic of turning nothing into something deep in my chest.

Once three canvases are done—the undercoat at least—I go about the meticulous task of washing my brushes and cleaning up my paints. The undercoat will have to dry before I go on to the next step. I really should have a rough idea sketched before I paint.

I check my phone that I essentially ignored while I was painting. There's a text from Marlene. Shit.

Marlene: Let's check in. Meet me at the lodge at 3pm.

I check the time. It's five after three. Shit. Shit, shit, shit.

Tugging on my boots, I'm out the door before the left one is fully on my foot. The sky is already dark, the clouds having rolled in again, but it's dry for now.

When I get to the lodge, I'm out of breath. Marlene is sitting by the fire, a steaming mug in her hand.

"Sorry, I'm late. I—"

She holds up a hand. "You have to stop apologizing. It's stealing your power, not that you have any in this situation, but still."

I hesitate before taking a seat across from her.

"So..." She crosses and uncrosses her thin legs angling them less toward the fire and more toward me. "How do you think it's going?"

"It's off to a great start."

Marlene smiles, but there's worry in her eyes, making my stomach fizzle uncomfortably.

"What do you think?"

She sighs. "A canoe ride is not what I expected from *the* OG."

It was a kayak, but I'm pretty sure that information wouldn't be helpful. "What were you expecting?"

Marlene gingerly sips her drink then sets it down with a frown. "Something more dynamic than convening with nature."

"I think it was more about being in tune with your surroundings and making art based on that relationship. We just happen to be in nature."

Marlene is staring into the fire. "These artists could do that on their own. Will you talk to him? He seems to like you."

My chest burns. "I…"

Have we been obvious? Does she know there's something going on with us? I study her face, but it gives nothing away, nothing that might say *I know you're crushing on our star artist and have been thinking of little else since you kissed on the train.*

Marlene continues. "He could show us how to spray paint something, or take us when he puts up his next piece. That would be exciting. Talk to him."

"I'd love to talk to him."

Which is true.

"Good, good. Make sure to keep it professional. I think he may have a little crush on you. Don't let that go anywhere."

"Of course."

Fuck.

CHAPTER 15
THIRTY-ONE DAYS LEFT OF THE RETREAT

The next morning, we all meet up after breakfast. Oli's eyes are bright, and he has a pack on his back. He addresses the group. "We're going for a hike to get a feel for our surroundings."

The group is not as excited as Oli looks. Genevieve is whispering to Andre. Alice is fiddling with her camera; out of everyone, she seems the most go with the flow. Marlene catches my eye and mouths, *Did you talk to him?*

Moving closer to her, I whisper, "I haven't had an opportunity yet."

"No time like the present," she says through gritted teeth.

"Why don't we all go on this hike and then I'll talk to him about making everything less...outdoorsy this afternoon."

I'm not sure what Marlene expected when we booked cabins in a *forest*?

"Fine." Then louder to the rest of the group, she says, "Have a great time. I'll see you all at lunch."

Without a moment's hesitation, she's back to the lodge, taking the stairs with swift movements.

We head to the trails, the air crisp and cool, only wispy white clouds in the sky this morning. The trees get denser, the sun pushing through them, illuminating the yellow leaves. Alice stops twisting her lens this way and that, directing it at one. Andre and Genevieve are meandering slowly, quietly whispering to one another. Louise is bringing up the rear. I hang back so she's not alone.

"You don't have to wait for me, dear."

I shrug. "I like this pace."

Louise smiles, her gold tooth flashing in the sun.

"How was your quiet contemplation time yesterday?"

Louise levels her clear gaze in my direction. "How was yours?"

The paint gliding on the canvas felt good, even if I didn't accomplish anything much at all. "It went surprisingly well."

Oli stops up ahead at a viewpoint, a small wooden railing overlooking the lake below. The group waits while Louise and I make our way there.

Oli is beaming when we get there. "Isn't this amazing?"

Alice says an emphatic, "Yes!"

While the others murmur.

"A couple miles further is Fortune Falls." My heart rate spikes as Oli continues. "The waterfall the town is named for."

That's the destination today? Fortune Falls? I haven't been back there since that day so long ago with Ben.

Louise shakes her head, leaning a little on the wood railing. "I'm going to head back from here. These old legs have had enough hill today."

Genevieve says, "We have a call in half an hour with our lawyer, so we'll head back, too."

No. This is exactly what Marlene was talking about.

"I'll go back with them," I say, not really wanting to leave Alice and Oli to go frolic off to the waterfall on their own, but what choice do I have? I should walk Louise back, and I definitely have no desire to see those falls again.

Oli's smile falls from his face. "Alright."

He catches my gaze, and I can't quite read the look in his eye. It looks a little sad, wistful, maybe.

To my surprise, Alice turns with the group. "I got a lot of shots of the falls on my first day here. I think I'll head the other way today. I'll walk Louise back if you want, Zara."

Louise huffs. "I do not need 'walking back.' I'm not a dog."

Louise is still muttering as she and Alice make their way down the trail.

A spark returns to Oli's eyes, and he looks to me with a tilt of his head. "What do you say?"

Fifteen minutes later, it feels like we are trudging straight up the side of a mountain. I don't remember the way here being so steep, although we mostly walked it from the opposite way, from the parking lot, which is a lot closer.

Oli points out a little red mushroom with white spots growing in some leaves. "It's perfect. Like something out of a storybook."

His enthusiasm is infectious, but I still have the dark cloud of having to talk to him on Marlene's orders hanging over my head. I clear my throat. "Oli…"

A slow smile spreads across his face as his name comes out of my mouth, and suddenly, I'm too warm in my black sweater. I can picture his name slipping past my lips in an altogether different context. The look in his eyes as he turns to face me tells me he might be thinking the same thing. "Zara Bytheway…"

"Stop." I hold up a hand. "You can't look at me like that right now."

"How am I looking at you?" he asks, still with that lazy smile that tells me he knows exactly how.

His strong jaw is covered in a light dusting of stubble, the plains of his sharp cheekbones highlighted by the sun dappling through the trees. He's gorgeous. I can't tell him that so far his artist retreat sucks when he's looking at me with his eyes smoldering. I motion to his face. "Like that. Like I'm a piece of chocolate cake."

He takes a step closer, one hand brushing my hip, his voice low and husky. "Far more delicious from what I remember."

I should take a step back, put some space between us, but I don't. It's like my feet won't move. Instead, I inhale deeply his spicy scent, surrounding me along with a strong mix of pine, dirt, and sunshine.

"Oli, you have to stop with the nature stuff."

He quirks his head to the side, his expression changing in an instant. No longer soft and sweet. I want to take back my words. "What do you mean?"

I sigh, taking that step back. The light around us darkens. Off the steep ravine, over the lake, black clouds are rolling in. I keep walking up the path. Maybe this conversation will be easier with more activity and less eye contact. "Marlene would like less nature content and more graffiti stuff."

Oli grumbles next to me. "More graffiti stuff, huh?"

"Yes. I think those were her exact words."

"Too bad for Marlene, she's not running this retreat."

"Except she sort of is."

"Right. But she hired me to provide the lessons. And a huge part of my work is becoming familiar with the environment you're in. Otherwise, how would you know how to respond to it? You can't make art in a vacuum…"

The rush of water makes it hard to hear the last thing Oli says. We turn a corner and make our way over the old stone bridge, and there it is, in all its raging glory, Fortune Falls.

The waterfall isn't tremendously tall, but it is wide. Water rushes over the rocks framed by trees with sparse yellow leaves. The water flows over a boulder at the bottom, splashing on and running off into the pool below. Oli leans against the side of the bridge, looking out at the falls.

I do the same, the moss on the stone bridge soft under my fingertips as I run my hand over the edge before leaning an elbow on it. I forgot how much I love the falls.

"It's amazing," Oli shouts over the water.

"It is. When my mom and I first moved here"—Oli leans in closer, and despite the sharp rise in my heart rate, I keep talking— "it was the summer, and I didn't know anyone. She had to work all the time, so I rode my bike a lot. Mostly around the neighborhood. One day I rode farther and I saw a sign on the street that said Fortune Falls with an arrow. I followed them until I ended up here. After that, I came back anytime I could."

"I would, too."

"It's where I met Ben." And where he proposed, I think but don't say.

Oli nods once and looks back out at the water. "How can Marlene think this is lame?"

"Some people just don't get it."

Oli covers my hand with his, and we take it in without words. After a few minutes, he turns to me. "Okay. No more nature stuff."

"Thank you."

"But, if you have any time, can we still explore a bit?"

The corners of my mouth turn up, and the word slips easily off my tongue. "Yes."

This time I don't want to take it back, either.

AFTER A WHILE, clouds move in and a drizzle comes down, so we head back to the trail. Despite wearing a sweater that is more absorbent than repellent, I don't mind. It feels nice to be surrounded by the sound of rushing water, to revisit a place I love and have avoided for years.

"Thank you for coming with me, even if all this nature stuff is stupid." Oli gives me a half smile.

I laugh. "It's not. It's just..." I shake my head. "Not what Marlene was expecting."

"Got it. Don't worry. I have a plan for tomorrow that will hopefully satisfy her."

There is no satisfying her, I think. "Have you always loved nature?"

"When I was a kid, my mom would take me on these long nature hikes. It was an inexpensive way to get out of the house when my dad was in a foul mood—I realized that later. But at the time, it was magical. Just me and her and the trees. Out there, I could just be myself."

Oli's looking up toward the canopy we're walking under, the leaves still clinging to the branches in brilliant hues of yellow and red, mixed with the deep forest green of the pines. Upon closer inspection, Oli isn't just taking in the grandeur of the forest. He's trying not to cry. I stop in my tracks, grabbing for his hand.

"Oli?"

He wipes underneath his eyes; a couple tears having rolled out despite his attempt to blink them away. "She would've loved it here. It's been years since she passed, but whenever I'm out in the trees, I feel close to her."

"I'm so sorry."

He squeezes my hand then drops it and continues walking. I fall into step next to him.

"Can I ask—"

"Cancer. Breast cancer. She fought a long time. She got thinner, the sparkle in her eye dulled. It was like watching her disappear...her light dim. And in the end..."

My heart breaks for him. "My mom and I aren't close...but I still can't imagine—"

"Why?"

For a second I think he means, why can't I imagine losing my mother, but then I realize he means why aren't we close.

"She got pregnant young. She was only sixteen. A mom at seventeen. It made growing up challenging, for both of us."

Oli steps a little closer to me, our fingers brushing as we keep walking down the trail.

"When she left, she started a new life. She ended up marrying that guy, they have a little girl."

"Sisters," Oli says with a smile.

Sisters. But I haven't even met her.

There's a long beat of silence, then heat floods my cheeks. "I'm sorry. I've made this all about me, and you were talking about your mom."

Oli turns to me, his eyes warm and filled with fire. "Don't apologize to me for sharing. I want to know you, everything about you. I want to know what your favorite food was in second grade. I want to know what you think about when you lie in your bed at night staring at the ceiling. I want to know what made you."

We lean in. His skin is slick from the drizzle. His lips are so close to mine I can feel the heat of his breath on my mouth. I want to crawl inside him. If I just leaned a bit further in, our lips would touch.

But we can't.

I move away, my eyes unwavering from the trail. "We should go back."

Oli nods but doesn't say anything. A few minutes into our descent, there's a figure heading up the trail. As he gets closer, I see it's Ben, a deep frown etched in his brow. "Marlene was worried about you two out here in the rain. Thought you might've got lost. It's been, what, ten years since you've been to the falls?"

CHAPTER 16
TWENTY-SIX DAYS LEFT OF THE RETREAT

The next day, there is no nature program, in fact, there is no scheduled activity at all. Oli tells the group it is a day to make, to think, to be alone. Basically, all day quiet contemplation time. And the next day. By the third day, it feels intentional, and by the fourth, Marlene is livid.

On Halloween, however, Oli tells us all to meet at the lodge at 10 p.m. sharp. Marlene seems giddy as she gives me instruction to have the SUV ready. During the day, I make sure it has gas and the inside is all clean. At a quarter till, one by one the artists trickle into the lodge, including, to my surprise, a very attractive older man with salt and pepper hair dressed in black.

I recognize him from his picture in the file. "Miguel?"

"Ahh, yes. You must be Ashford?"

I'm so confused. "When did you arrive?"

"Just yesterday. Been getting settled."

"You should've texted. I could've picked you up."

"No need. Brought my motorcycle, and a nice young man showed me to my cabin."

I smile, but my muscles tense. I feel like I haven't done my job.

Oli is the last to enter the lodge, in a black beanie, holding a stack of stickers in one hand and a brown paper bag in the other.

"Your partner from the other day with the kayaks is going to be your partner tonight," he says while he hands out the stickers, one to each pair. He gives me mine. It's smooth vinyl, a large silhouette of the girl he uses in a lot of his pieces. "We're going to go to town, and you'll find a place to put your sticker. Think about how it relates to the environment, but also be conscious of where you're putting it. For instance, you wouldn't want to put it on someone's car. Great places to look are things owned by the government and not the community. Fire hydrants, electric boxes, telephone poles, the backs of stop signs. Take a picture. We'll all meet back at the van when we're done."

There are excited smiles around the group. Marlene is beaming, squeezing Miguel's hand.

We all pile in the car, and I drive to Main Street.

Oli shakes his head. "We can't park somewhere where people will see us."

I turn onto a side street and drive all the way to the water. I pull into an empty community lot for the beach. The asphalt is so covered in windswept sand I can hardly make out the lines to park. Beyond, dark waves crash one after another. I can just make out Oli's smile in the dim light from the moon. "Perfect."

He turns to the group and opens a plain brown bag, handing out black cat masks. "Take these if you like. Since it's Halloween, it won't look out of place. We'll meet back here when you're done. If someone sees you putting up the sticker, run!"

There are giggles, but Oli speaks again. "I'm serious, it's not paint, but it's flyposting and you can get in a lot of trouble."

The car gets very quiet, and I catch some solemn nods.

"Don't take too long. If you're not back in an hour we'll know something is wrong."

Oli and I wait while all the others file out of the car, and I pick up the sticker again, feeling the smooth vinyl between my fingers. Oli catches my eye, his face lit by the moon and the small lamp-post in the parking lot.

"You ready?" he asks, handing me the kitty mask.

My lips turn up at the corners as I put it on, the cool plastic soothing on my face.

"Let's go."

We get out of the SUV, leaving it unlocked for the others, and walk through the lot, the sand on the cement louder than I expected, but no match for the roar of the waves.

"You have an advantage." Oli brushes my fingers. "You know this town."

I do. I know this town better than I know anywhere. My mind scans through Main Street, trying to see it all through Oli's eyes. Where would he put this girl in the fifties dress?

We start walking down Main Street, but it's too exposed. I grab Oli's hand. "This way."

I pull him along, ducking down a side street and into the alley. Dumpsters, electric boxes, just about everything Oli listed in the car are lined up in the dark alley, but nothing looks right. There's a fire escape. Maybe the sticker could wrap around one of the ladder posts. I touch the rough metal, the paint on it peeling—everything rusting in the sea air. It's not right either, though.

Oli turns his head this way and that, the little cat mask glinting in the moonlight. "It's secluded back here. Very safe."

"Safe?" I laugh. "Is that your way of calling me a chicken?"

He shrugs. "If the beak fits."

My mouth is agape. "Oli!"

He holds a finger to his lips. "Shhh."

I roll my eyes, and then it comes to me. I know the perfect place. I take off at run, my shoes smacking against the concrete, and Oli's footsteps match mine. He lets out a small whoop, and I look back, his face is lit up like a kid's on Christmas morning. I run through the alleys then down a side street and up a hill. I slow to a walk as the hill gets steeper. Even on this dark night, the view of the ocean is spectacular. There's a large sign at the top of a rickety set of wooden stairs that leads down to the beach. There are seven diamonds, four on top and three beneath, each with a different warning and a little person. *Beware of sneaker waves, stay off the logs, beware of rip tides.*

On the top, one spot is blank, like when they made the sign they forgot one essential danger of the beach. Kids used to tag it, or sign their names. *Andrea and Sam forever, Ryan was here,* that kind of thing. Right now, there's just the faded remnants of past tags.

I peel the back of the sticker, lift up onto my toes, and try to place it in the empty spot. It's too high. I jump a little and hear a deep chuckle behind me.

"Need a hand there, shorty?"

Spinning on my heel, I catch the twinkle in Oli's eye. "Who you calling shorty?"

I hand him the sticker, but he shakes his head. "You should do it. I'll just give you a boost."

Oli takes me by the shoulders, turning me around to face the sign again. Goosebumps travel up my arms as his hand travels to my waist.

"Ready?" he asks.

"Yes," I breathe out as his grip on my waist tightens and heat rushes between my thighs.

"One, two."

Before he says three, I'm in the air. He's bent down a little, and my legs move instinctively. He lifts me onto his shoulders, and it occurs to me, I don't think I've ever sat on someone's shoulders.

It takes a second for us to find our balance, and once we do, Oli rests his hands lightly on my shins.

"You good up there?" he asks.

I laugh. "I think so."

He moves us forward, and my abdomen tightens with the motion. My thighs squeeze, too, and I'm suddenly very aware of my core nestled in closely to the back of Oli's head.

"You ready?"

Shaking myself out of the dirty thoughts, I place the sticker in the empty spot. I call down. "Do you have a pen?"

He hands me a black paint pen. I draw a diamond around the girl, roughly the same size as the others. Underneath I write, *Dreamers Welcome.*

"All done."

He bends down, and I gingerly step off his shoulders. I hand the pen back to Oli, his lips turned deliciously up at the corners. He says softly, "Nice."

Getting my phone out, I take a picture. The sound of a car engine on the street closest to us sends adrenaline shooting to my toes. As the car turns the corner, the first thing I see is the lights on top.

Oli grabs my hand and pulls me behind a nearby tree. He has his back to the tree and his hands are on my arms holding me in place in front of him. We listen as the car slowly drives by. Oli's body is warm, his breath hot and minty. A few minutes pass with no other sound except the roar of the waves and the soft pulse of our breaths mingling. Oli drops his hands from my arms.

"That was close," I say as I move back onto the path. "Want to walk back on the beach?"

Oli frowns. "Yeah. Halloween might not have been the best night. There're always more cops out."

We walk down the rickety steps carefully, some of the planks held together more by hope than wood grain at this point. Oli takes off his mask, shoving it in his back pocket. I do the same, pushing mine up like a headband. The sand is hard from the tide, but it's out now. Crabs scurry in the moonlight. Oli kicks off his shoes, pausing to balance as he takes off each sock.

"It'll be freezing."

He shrugs. "I like to feel the sand under my feet."

Suddenly, I have an overwhelming need to feel what he's feeling. I kick off my boots, almost losing my balance, but Oli holds my arm, steadying me. I tuck my socks into my boots. The sand is ice cold under my feet but smooth. It's refreshing. A jolt to the system. It makes me more alert, all my other senses heightened: the soft fabric of my sweater, the crisp ocean air with a tang of seaweed, Oli.

We walk down the sand, so close that every now and then our fingers brush, sending shivers down my spine. The rhythm of our steps matches the steady in and out of the tide.

"How did you get into graffiti?" I ask, hopping over a bit of broken crab as I do.

Oli hops over nothing.

I shoot him a look, unable to help my grin as I ask, "Are you copying me?"

"Are you copying me?" He laughs. "Sorry. It just looked fun. What were you asking?"

"I was just curious how you became an international graffiti superstar?"

He laughs, the sound disappearing instantly into the waves. "Right. Good question. Not sure, to be honest."

"How did you get into graffiti?"

"It came into my life after my mom died. My friends were home for Christmas. We all went out drinking. Someone brought some spray paint, and we went to this abandoned building right outside town. It wasn't the first time I tagged something, but it was the first time I got lost in it. I spent hours on it. It calmed me in a way nothing else had before or since. There was a peace in it."

He pauses for a moment, and we both listen to the waves roll in and out. Then he keeps talking.

"The guys got bored, stopped helping. They were listening to music in the truck when the sirens started. At first, I thought it was just some song they put on. I don't blame them for taking off."

"They left?"

Oli shrugs. "I heard them calling, and I kept spraying. Even when my dad got there with lights flashing, I was still finishing the piece. He arrested me."

"No."

Oli's fingers brush mine again. "It was probably better than the alternative."

"Were you charged?"

He nods, looking at me, his blue-gray eyes lit by the moonlight. "And convicted of criminal mischief. I had to pay a fine and do some community service. As soon as it was done, I left and haven't been back since."

"And you kept making graffiti?"

"I had to. I felt like it chose me, you know? There's something magical about bringing light on a forgotten part of the city, or making an eyesore into something beautiful. Something that makes someone feel connected."

He stares at me as the last word comes out of his mouth, and I can feel it all the way down to my toes.

"I got better at not getting caught."

By the time we make it to the car, I'm shivering all over. We get in, and I turn over the engine, blasting the heat. I brush off my feet and put my shoes back on then hold my hands up to the vent, the air coming out starting to warm up. Oli fiddles with the radio until he finds a song he likes and turns it up.

"We Fell in Love in October" fills the car. My eyes flick to him. His are looking right back at me. My breath catches in my throat; the air in the car feels thick. The moment stretches like a stray thread on a sweater, I want to tug it, but I know if I do, the whole thing could fall apart.

Instead, I look toward the ocean and ask, "So, how did you go from getting arrested to secret identity, art star?"

Oli lets out a long breath turning his attention toward the waves as well. "That's a great question. Luck."

"Luck? Really, that's it?"

He puts his shoes back on, tying the laces taught. "I had a couple good ideas. They hit at the right time. My buddy was a photographer, and he got a job at *Vice*. He took pictures of some of my stuff, then they started an OG watch. It all kinda took off from there."

I let out a long sigh, picturing what it must feel like to obtain success like that. To see your work in magazines and actually be able to make a living off of it. "Must be nice."

Oli's brow furrows. "It was at first."

"Why just a first?"

"It sucks being Batman. Like when I met you on the train, I felt like I wasn't being totally honest with you. I wasn't. I couldn't tell you who I was or what I actually did for a living. Or like this retreat, my lawyer would be furious if he knew this is what I was doing, even with the NDAs. He thinks I'm on a tropical vacation. Only a handful of people know me, really know me, and they've been the same seven people for the past decade. I love that my work resonates with so many, but at the same time, I'd love to make something where I could actually show my face."

"Have you ever thought about..." I stop myself, not sure my idea makes any sense.

He puts a hand on my leg, and warmth spreads to my chest. "Thought about what?"

I shake my head. "It's silly, but I guess starting a second career? One where you could attend an opening for your work?"

"If the art looked anything like my other stuff, people would know..."

"They'd speculate. But maybe that wouldn't be all bad. They'd have to prove it, right?"

Oli opens his mouth, then closes it again as the back door opens and Louise and Alice jump in the car, slamming the door behind them. Louise is breathing hard. Alice's cheeks are rosy.

"That was...." Louise starts.

"Incredible!" Alice finishes, and they both dissolve into maniacal giggles.

The rest of the mission goes off without a hitch. Everyone comes back to the car happy, adrenaline pumping. Marlene is over the moon about the shift in the retreat.

When we get back to camp, we swap sticker stories over the fire pit with s'mores. Marlene's eyes just about pop out of her head when Oli hands out the sticks each with a marshmallow. But even she roasts one and smears it on a graham cracker.

The marshmallows are squishy, the moon is high and bright, and for one brief and shining moment everything feels right.

CHAPTER 17
TWENTY-ONE DAYS LEFT OF THE RETREAT

There are no workshops this week or talks scheduled, just quiet contemplation time, all day. It's the fifth day, and I'm losing my mind.

We are having our first group critique, so everyone needs something to present by then. Even me, apparently.

Everyday, I've tried to get back into the zone. Recapture the feeling of the smooth paint across the canvas. But they don't need another undercoat, so now it's time to decide what's actually going to be the painting. I'm paralyzed.

The canvases look impossibly blank.

I want to find Oli, talk to him more. Our time at the waterfall and walking on the beach felt good. Soothing. Maybe I should head to Oli's cabin? Knock on his door.

But this time is supposed to be uninterrupted. It's something Marlene built into the program, and I'm not sure I should break it. Time to work is a hallmark of each of the retreats but not quite so much of it. If this is Oli's plan to satisfy her, he's missing the mark by about a thousand feet.

I try sketching my idea again. The lines are forced and jagged. Not at all what I'm picturing. It's a mess.

My phone buzzes, and I thank the heavens for the distraction.

Oli: How's it going?

Me: Funny you should ask—Terrible!

Oli: Terrible how?

I sigh and flop back on my bed. Thinking of how to describe what I'm experiencing.

Me: I have this idea...

Oli: The reflections?

Me: YES! But every time I try to sketch it it's not what I picture. It feels flat, and derivative, and stupid.

I hit send and immediately regret it. Oli's work flashes in my mind, piece after piece like a slideshow. What am I doing complaining to him about what a shitty artist I am? He wouldn't understand. He's full of ideas, and all of them work. No, not just work, they're amazing. My phone buzzes in my hand, pulling me out of my spiral.

Oli: Let's get out of here.

Me: Um, excuse you! You are the one that set the schedule. This is quiet contemplation time. ALL WEEK apparently.

Oli: We can contemplate at the beach.

We figure out logistics. I'll get the car then drive it down the road a bit. He'll meet me from the trail, so we won't be seen sneaking off together. The plan works flawlessly, and we're on our way to the beach.

"Should we pull up GPS?"

I shake my head. "I know the way." I could drive to Short Sands with my eyes closed.

"Do you want to talk about your paintings?"

"No." I turn up the music, Fleet Foxes playing, making the slate-gray day feel more ethereal and less gloomy.

We head down the highway, eventually taking an exit that leads us into another forest. Winding roads are lined with thick trees covered in moss. The road goes up and up and up to a parking lot on a cliff. There's a short rock wall separating us from the beach. Just rocks and ocean below.

I put the car into park, getting out first, and Oli follows.

Wishing I'd thought to bring a thicker coat, I cross my arms, wrapping my sweater tight around my torso. Oli comes to stand next to me.

"Wow, I thought that other beach was pretty, but look at this," he says, his blue-gray eyes fixed on the horizon, nearly the same color.

My lips turn up. "Come on."

I lead the way down the muddy path, planks of wood dotted throughout like a staircase. Half nature, half man. The foliage around the path is thick, the ocean just coming into view at the opening at the bottom. It is a small cove. The beginning and end are both visible. On one side is a massive hill covered in pine trees. On the other side is a rocky mountain that dips its toe out into the ocean. In between is sand, rocks, and a small creek.

We step out onto the firm beach, the sand compacted from the tide and the rain. Oli takes off his shoes and socks.

"You're nuts." I laugh.

"I've been told that a time or two." He shrugs. "Have to feel the sand under my feet. It's a thing."

Sighing, I take mine off as well, the sand hard under the soft soles of my bare feet. I feel more alive, more in my body than I have for a long time. Probably since that night on the train.

Oli grabs my hand, the warmth from his skin a welcome contrast to the cold, misty ocean air. The gray waves roll in and out in a soothing rhythm. A few surfers dot the waves, but not many today. We walk the length of beach, toward the rocky side, where I know there are some caves to explore, our fingers intertwined. I don't remember ever holding hands so much with someone before. Did Ben and I hold hands this much? I don't think so. But with Oli, it's like his skin is magnetic. Also this feels....allowed. Like we're not crossing the line as much. And it's nice, comforting.

If I'm being honest, though, what I'd really love is for him to throw me down on the beach and ravage me *From Here To Eternity* style. Although with how compacted the sand is, I might break something with the throwdown. I gaze up at Oli, his eyes sparkling as he takes in the beach. It'd be worth it.

We explore the tide pools. Touching a purple starfish, feeling the wet prickly skin under my fingertips, I catch sight of my reflection in the pool, and I suck in a breath.

"Here. This."

I point to the pool, and Oli rushes over from where he was dipping his toes into the ocean like a madman.

"What?" Oli looks over my shoulder, his reflection filling the pool, too. I watch his brow wrinkle in the water. "The starfish?"

"No. The reflection."

He squats so he's right next to me, heat radiating off his body. "Beautiful."

I turn to face him, and he does the same, our eyes lock and time slows. The ocean waves crashing behind him, mist settling in over the waves. His eyes scan my face, his soft lips parting ever so slightly. Want pulses through me. Oli reaches a hand out, tucking a stray hair behind my ear.

Grabbing his hand, I bring it to my lips, on instinct. He leans in, his lips coming close to mine, so close I can feel the heat of his breath. A cold gust of wind smacks me in the face. I stand, coming to my senses. We can't do this. I need my job, and this is a dangerous game we are playing.

"Oli...we can't. I..."

His face falls, all the mirth sucked out. "I know."

AFTER A BIT more exploring at the beach, I can't feel my fingers. It's like the temperature has dropped suddenly. Rubbing them together and blowing isn't cutting it anymore. The fog is rolling in heavy, so thick, in fact, that if I take ten steps back, I can't even see the ocean.

Oli wraps his hand around mine. "Oof, you're freezing. Let's go. Know anywhere we could get a hot drink?"

"Yes I do," I say through teeth chattering.

We drive to the closest place, my headlights doing nothing to help visibility in this thick haze. It's like driving into a cloud. The sun isn't visible anymore, and I'm not sure if it's set already or if the fog is blocking it out. We should head back soon, but we have time for one quick drink.

Oli enters the Vern and heads straight to the bar. "Two hot toddies please."

I grab Oli's arm, whispering, "I have to drive."

Deep lines form around the bartender's mouth. The same guy that was working here last time. What was his name? He says, "This fog is going to freeze, probably already has. Black ice all over the roads. Best not to drive."

"First frost of the season," an older gentleman wearing lived-in denim overalls and puffy flannel chimes in. "Interstate's already closed. Lots of roads are shut down, too. Should clear up tomorrow or the next day."

"Shit," I say under my breath. "What about the road up to Camp Ironwood?"

The old man spins his beer glass. "Nah, that's always the first one they close in weather like this. Too steep. Kyle here is right. Stay off the roads."

Shit. Shit. Shit. What if Marlene notices we're gone?

Oli asks, "Anywhere to stay nearby?"

Kyle says, "Fortune Falls Inn is right down the street. Still want those drinks?"

Oli looks at me, and I nod.

The bartender gets to work on heating the water, while I get out my phone. I start to write a text to Marlene.

Me: Got stuck in town running some errands. Roads closed.

Should I tell her Oli's with me? They're going to notice he's not at dinner. I will. I have to.

I delete my first message and rewrite.

Me: Oli needed some things in town, but now we're stuck

because of the weather. The road is closed. We'll be back in the morning.

The bar is sleepy today, which makes sense with how the weather has turned. We take our drinks and snag the table closest to the fireplace. The warm liquid, tart with lemon and smooth with whiskey, warms my chest and my fingers as I wrap my hands around it.

I set my glass down but don't remove my hands. "This was a good idea."

Oli smiles. "I'm full of them."

My phone lights up with a text on the table.

Marlene: K

That's it. That's all it says. *K.* Is she pissed? Does she think we were sneaking off to be together, which in fairness, we were, but it's not like we were making out.

I'm still staring at the text as if more information will present itself from the one letter response if I look at it hard enough.

Oli places a hand over mine and the phone. "We can't change it."

I look up into his slate-gray eyes. His words sink in like the tide in the sand. We can't change it. How many hours of my life have I wished things were different? Wished I could've known my dad. Wished my mom was more interested in me. Wished I was different, smarter, funnier, anything that might change things. But for all my wishing and worrying, nothing ever changed. I could stare at this phone all night and Marlene's response would remain the same.

Lightly, I touch the button on the side of my phone, turning it off. A rush of excitement pulses through me, like I just jumped off a cliff. I can't remember the last time I turned off my phone. Maybe never.

Laughter bubbles up in my chest, coming out as a giggle.

Oli laughs, too.

I put my phone away.

"No work?"

I shake my head. "I'm all yours."

The smile that spreads slowly across Oli's soft lips sends shivers down my spine. It's devilish. "What am I going to do with you?"

My cheeks warm, possibly from the booze, or the fire, but most likely from Oli's intense gaze.

After our first round, we order another, taking them over to the dartboard.

"I've never really played."

Oli quirks an eyebrow up. "A small town girl like you?"

I laugh, but my stomach sinks. Is he serious? Is that how he sees me?

"Don't worry, it's easy enough." Oli walks toward the board, plucking all the darts off. He puts them in his front pocket but keeps one in his hand. "Step a little closer."

I step in the worn part of the wood floor where it looks like people have been standing for decades to throw darts, right up to the faded blue line.

Oli hands me the dart. I aim at the board and, before I can overthink it, quickly throw. The dart sails across the room, but not quite far enough to hit the target, or the board at all.

"Whoa there, Tex."

I shrug. "Your turn."

He shakes his head. "Let's try that again."

He walks closer to me, his leather and spice scent more intoxicating than my hot toddy. Handing me another dart, he places his hands on my shoulders. They tense under his touch, but he gives a little squeeze and my muscles relax. "First you have to loosen up. For someone two drinks in, having a great time with a handsome man at a bar, you're very tense."

A small smile plays on my lips. "I think you mean someone stranded because of freezing fog."

"Semantics. Do you want me to give you a few tips? Or would that be too mansplainy?"

I love that he asked. That he cares if I even want to learn this silly game. I don't really, at all, but I want him to keep touching me. In a soft voice I say, "Show me how to play."

Oli's Adam apple bobs hard, and his pupils flare. He faces me toward the dart board, standing behind me, moving his hand down to my hips, and my skin tingles at his touch. "You want to keep balanced and face right at the board. A lot of power comes from your hips."

The way he's touching them right now, I feel those words deeply.

After directing me how to position my feet, he brings one hand to my arm holding the dart and gently brings it up. "Make your arm a right angle."

He runs his hand from my wrist to my shoulder, sending goosebumps in his wake. He takes a step back, and it's like a cold wind seeps into the bar.

"Focus and then throw with the belief that you will make your target."

Closing my eyes, I take a breath. *I will make my target.*

I throw. Oil whoops as the dart connects with the board. It's not a bullseye, but it's certainly a lot closer than the first dart. I turn, my cheeks aching from my wide smile. "I did it. I made the board."

Oli's face is as excited as mine feels. "You're a natural."

He picks me up and swings me around. I'm laughing when he puts me down.

"What are we celebrating? Did y'all just get engaged?"

My good mood plummets just as quickly as it rose. I know that voice. When I look up, my fears are confirmed. Standing there with a glass of bourbon is Bridget.

"No," I say. "I just made a good shot."

She looks past me toward the dart board where the one and only dart sits in one of the white triangles, not at all close to the bullseye.

"Is that what we're calling that?" She laughs at her own joke then keeps talking. "Is this who's taking care of you these days?"

My mouth fills with saliva. I take a hearty sip of my drink to try to wash this sick feeling down, too large a sip. The lemon juice hits me wrong in the back of the throat, and I start coughing. I hold up a hand.

"Hon, are you okay? You can't chug toddies."

"I'm fine," I choke out and silently excuse myself to the bathroom.

Once in the bathroom, I take a long look in the mirror. My reflection is a little cloudy, like they're using the wrong products to clean it, but other than that, it looks like me. My shiny black hair is hanging loose, my cheeks are pink, possibly from my coughing fit, but I look healthy. Nothing Bridget says can hurt me. I don't need her, or this town. I take care of myself, and always have, no matter what she says.

When I head back out, I feel better, more confident, but I still don't want to spend any more time with Bridget fucking Masterson than I have to.

I put a hand on Oli's arm, interrupting whatever Bridget was just saying. "We should get going, they have strict check-in times at the Inn."

Which isn't a lie.

Oli nods. "Cool, yeah let me just grab our tab. Nice meeting you, Bridget."

Bridget's smile is so wide she looks like a cartoon cat. "Yes. So nice to meet you. Hopefully we'll see you in February."

Oli heads to the bar. I turn to follow him, but Bridget catches my arm. "I was hoping we could talk."

Not wanting her to know she affects me at all, I suppress a sigh. "We have to go. Maybe another time."

Turning to leave, I feel her eyes on me the whole way out.

CHAPTER 18

The blast of cold air that greets me as I enter the night is arctic. "Fuck," I exclaim as another gust stings my cheeks.

Oli flips up his collar and hunches his shoulders to his ears. "It's so cold. How far is the Inn?"

"Just a couple blocks."

We trudge ahead, our hands in our pockets, our heads dipped against the wind. It's too cold even for talking. I want to ask him what Bridget meant by *See you in February*. At the same time, I really don't want to.

I pull my phone out to check the GPS, to make sure we're headed the right way, but the map won't pull up. Any service I was getting is completely gone now. From the bar to the Inn is only a couple blocks from what I remember. We turn toward the water, but this fog is so thick I can hardly see the streets ahead.

Once we get to the second break in the sidewalk, I take us to the left. The lantern hanging out front of Fortune Falls Inn is a beacon.

We hurry in the door to a quiet lobby. The strong scent of pumpkin and cinnamon fills the space. There is a fire in the hearth and a small silver bell with a sign: *Ring for Service*.

Oli presses the bell, and a ding echoes out. Mrs. Pepper comes out before the sound is even done. The floral dress is gone, replaced by a two-piece knit lounge set and curlers.

Her face softens when she sees me. "Ah, you again. Well, you should know check-in cut off is 6 p.m."

I check my watch, it's nearly eight. "Sorry."

She places her fingers on the keyboard to bring her computer to life. "Is the reservation under your name? It was Ashford, right?"

"Yes." I'm impressed by her recall. "But we don't have a reservation. We got caught in the weather, and we're hoping you had something available."

"It *is* nasty out there." She clacks a few keys.

Oli clears his throat. "We were hoping you had two rooms."

We were? I mean, of course, we should be in separate rooms. It'll be much easier to have everything be professional. If I'm honest, it wasn't what I was hoping for.

Mrs. Pepper keeps clacking. "Two? You're out of luck there."

Even though it shouldn't, my heart leaps.

"I have one queen room left in the whole place." She makes a few more clicks and with a dramatic flourish to last keystroke, looks away from the monitor and smiles. She hands me the key with a red tassel for a chain.

"It's the same room as before, dear, do you remember the way?"

I nod, and Mrs. Pepper smiles, bustling back down the hall. "I'm missing *Survivor*."

I lead the way up the tiled stairs, past the second floor fireplace, down the long hall to the last room. I flick on the switch, which turns on the bedside lamp and the lamp in the corner by one of the wingback chairs, washing the room in a soft amber glow. It's just as pretty as I remember, except the bed looks smaller than it did before.

The fire isn't lit this time, and the room is cold. There is a large stack of wood next to it. Oli rubs his hands together, blowing, then spots the firewood. Kneeling, he starts throwing logs in.

I sit on the loveseat next to the fireplace. "Can I help?"

He smiles. "I got it. What's the deal with Bridget?"

Wrapping the throw blanket from the back of the couch onto my shoulders, I consider how to answer that question. "I could ask you the same. What was with all that see you in February stuff?"

"She invited me to a wedding. Said you were going, or if you weren't, I should make sure you do."

I feel like an idiot. Of course, the wedding. Oli gets the fire lit and goes to inspect the snacks. He holds up a bottle of wine and raises his eyebrows to me.

"Yes, please."

He pours us each a glass and sits next to me. I move the blanket from my shoulders, placing it over both our laps, as he scooches closer, and I instantly feel the warmth from his body. Sipping the rich Cabernet, I let my mind linger on the strong earthy notes as I begin to speak.

"When I was in high school, I had this painting that I was really proud of. It was a self-portrait of places. I painted everywhere I ever lived, one on top of the other. The next essentially erasing the last. Leftover was a mass of colorful layers, but it had a nice texture."

Oli smiles. "Sounds cool."

I look up at him, the fire highlighting the plains of his cheeks, his eyes intently focused on me.

"I thought so at the time. I entered it in the Fortune Falls annual art contest. It was judged by the mayor, a librarian, and that guy from Everclear."

Oli laughs. "No! Seriously? Shit, what was that guy's name? Alex?"

I stretch out my legs a little. Oli moves them onto his lap, and it feels as natural as breathing. Sitting here in front of the fire, my legs draped over him.

"Art Alexsis," I say.

"That's it."

"I met him when I won."

"You won? Congratulations!"

I frown, taking another sip. "I was living with Ben and his family at the time." I explain all about my mom moving. How she moved and I stayed. Oli listens intently, his eyes focused on my face. "Ben's dad worked in the mayor's office. There was a rumor that went around school that I was only dating Ben for his money and connections. It was an old rumor, and it hadn't bothered me in years. But it started going around again, this time they said the only reason I won the art contest was because of Ben's dad's relationship with the mayor."

"Seriously? How old were you?"

"Seventeen."

Oli sighs. "That's brutal."

"It didn't stay just in our high school either. Several complaints were made, by some influential people. They took it back."

"Took what back?"

"Me winning the contest. They said the votes were tallied incorrectly. They gave the win to the runner-up."

"Bridget?"

"I'm pretty sure she was behind all the rumors. But I could never prove it. What does it matter where it started? People believed it. It didn't stop at the art contest. I got Facebook messages from fake accounts telling me to crawl back to the gutter. Someone spray painted *Gold Digger* on my locker."

Oli's jaw is tight. "I fucking hate when people use spray paint for evil."

I laugh. He runs a hand on my thigh, and I feel the motion deep in my chest.

"That's terrible."

"It was. It felt like the whole world was against me. But it wasn't just that."

Oli waits patiently; he doesn't try to fill the space with chatter. Maybe that's why I admit to him something I've never told anyone before. "Part of me agreed with them."

"Agreed?"

"When I first met Ben, it was...well, I was only fourteen. I'd just moved to this new town, and I was flattered. And he was cute. But if I'm being honest, there was no thunderclap."

Oli nods.

"We started dating, and I thought, *this is great, he's sweet and cute and funny.* But if I'm honest with myself, I thought of him more as a friend for a lot longer than I thought of him as anything else. I should have broken up with him long before I did."

"Just because you were unsure of your feelings for him doesn't mean you were using him."

I know what he's saying is true, but I still feel terrible.

"Is that why you haven't been back?"

"Yeah, when I left, I just packed up all my stuff and drove away. I didn't tell anyone. I left the ring on Ben's pillow with a note. There's no coming back from that."

Oli runs a hand on my leg leaving goosebumps in his wake. "I get that. There weren't any long goodbyes when I left either."

"No?"

"Mom was gone. The last words my Dad spoke to me was reading me my rights. My friends didn't understand my new graffiti compulsion. There was nothing left for me there."

"Where did you go?"

He looks off into the fire, moving his hand down to my foot, rubbing circles in my soles. "Moved around a lot. Brooklyn, Seattle, Detroit."

I'm intently listening, but the feeling of his hands rubbing into the soft pads of my feet is so good. But also intense. He hits a sensitive spot, and I let out a small moan as a reaction.

His eyes snap to my face, hungry. He presses the spot again, and I suck in a breath. "Do you like that, Zara?"

"Yes," I breathe out, the sensation traveling all the way to my core.

Slowly, he moves his hand from my foot, up my calf. "What about this?"

I nod, not taking my eyes off his stubbled jaw, his smoldering eyes.

His hand continues its path up my thigh, stopping near the top. "What about this?"

His hand is so close to where I want him to touch me, but so maddeningly far away. I take his fingers in mine moving them further up, and he lets out a small animal-like grunt, then leaps up as if I'm on fire.

He holds his hands up, pacing in front of the fire. "I don't want to get you in trouble. You've made it very clear we can't..." He motions between the two of us. "That we shouldn't...."

He's right. We shouldn't. But who would find out if we did?

"That is what I said, but—"

"But?" His breath comes out quick, and he shakes his head. "I need a minute."

He heads to the bathroom then storms back out seconds later. "Is that *the* tub?"

"Huh?"

He whips out his phone, pulling up the picture I sent him when I stayed here before, my bare legs poking out of the bubbles. "From this picture?"

"Oh, um." I can feel my cheeks heat. "Yes."

"Okay, so the bathroom is not a safe space."

I laugh. "Safe?"

"Yeah, there's apparently nowhere in this room where I'm not turned on by you. Should we go for a walk?"

Crossing the room, I take his hands in mine, his palms warm. "Do you think it will help?"

I tilt my face to his.

His pupils swell. "No. I'm turned on by you everywhere."

He leans down, bringing his lips to mine. It's like the first sip of hot chocolate after a long day in the snow. It melts my insides. My core is liquid gold. He moves his hands to the small of my back, and I wrap mine around his neck, deepening our kiss. How have we not been doing this the entire time?

Moving his hands down, he cups my ass then lifts me up.

I wrap my legs around his waist, gasping, and kiss his neck. "What's your plan?"

Oli breathes out heavily, leaning his neck back, giving me a better angle. "We can make it up as we go."

He walks me over to the bed, tossing me as lightly as if I were a feather. I laugh as I bounce a little on the soft mattress. Oli unbuttons his flannel, and the giggle dies in my throat. His chest is chiseled, his abs taught. I scooch to the end of the bed and run my fingers down his perfect torso, feeling the gooseflesh my trail creates.

Oli tugs at the bottom of my sweater. I move my arms, letting him pull it off, feeling a slight chill as the cool air hits my back. Oli throws my sweater across the room and runs a finger under my black bra strap. He moves the strap off one shoulder then the next. My bra is still held in place. I'm about to help when Oli gets on his knees, so his face is nearly level with my breasts. He reaches behind my back, unhooking my bra, the flimsy fabric falling in my lap as he does, my breasts spilling out, nipples hard. Oli runs a hand lightly over one breast then the other. He takes a handful and brings his mouth to my nipple, hot and wet. He flicks his tongue, and I gasp.

"Oh, fuck."

He groans in response. With a light touch, he lays me down on the bed, walking his fingers down to my jeans. "Can I take these off?"

"Yes. Please."

The slow unbuttoning of my jeans threatens to undo me. The zipper going down echoes in my ears, sending shivers to my toes. He yanks the jeans off, taking my underwear with them, and tosses them both aside. He spreads my legs, running a light finger right where I want him.

"You're so wet."

He pushes one finger in, and I cry out, clenching around him.

"More."

His grunt as he sticks another finger inside me is the hottest sound I've ever heard. "Greedy girl." He moves his fingers slowly. "How's that?"

It's divine. But I need more. I could consume him whole. "More," I cry out.

"Fuck, Zara." He slowly pulls out and sticks three fingers inside, making me gasp in pleasure. Heat travels up my core as I clench. He moves slowly, watching me as I writhe under his touch.

"I need you, Oli."

Oli moves quick. He's across the room and then back in a flash, his pants gone and a condom in his hand.

"Do you always have a condom?"

His cheeks turn a rosy shade of pink. "If I know I might spend time with you…"

"That's very presumptuous," I say, sitting up.

"I prefer hopeful."

He rolls the condom on as I watch. Once it's all the way rolled on, I pull him down on the bed and climb on top of him, lowering myself gently on the length of him, as his eyes flutter close. I go slow, lifting and lowering, over and over, consistent as the tide. Oli's hands find my breasts. He squeezes as I sink onto him as deep as I can handle.

We melt together until we're nothing more than skin and sweat. Gasps and grunts. Lips and thighs. He's on top of me, thrusting deep inside, my legs wrapped around his back, when stars release in my chest, my whole body tenses around him, and I feel him release, too. The swell, and the pause. We lay next to each other, panting. Spent.

"Please tell me you brought more than one condom," I say, still a little breathless.

Oli props his head up on his elbow, an adorable smile spreading across his face. "I have three more."

"Very hopeful."

"What can I say? I'm an optimist."

He leans down and brings his lips to mine, salty with our mingled sweat.

CHAPTER 19
TWENTY DAYS LEFT OF THE RETREAT

The gray morning light filters through the gauzy curtains, while Oli snores lightly next to me. I wriggle out of his grasp, padding lightly across the room, peeking out the window. The fog has dissipated, and the world is covered in sparkles. An icy coating covers the road, the car windows shimmering with it. Beyond, the waves crash undeterred by the ice. It's beautiful.

I check my phone. No texts from anyone, and my battery is at twelve percent. Perfect. Quickly, I get dressed. I should see about the roads and maybe a charger. I shut the door lightly as I slip out so as not to wake Oli. I head down stairs to the lobby, where Mrs. Pepper is reading a book in a chair by the fire. She looks up as I traverse the last step.

"Ah, dear. Did you sleep well?"

"Yes, thank you."

She holds up her mug. "Coffee's hot in the dining room. There's some pumpkin muffins out, too."

"Thanks. I was wondering, have you heard anything about the roads?"

Mrs. Pepper's lips turn down into a stern frown. "I'm afraid most are still closed. Ice is supposed to clear up tomorrow, though."

I sigh. I'm elated and deflated at the same time. Is Marlene going to be pissed? But what can we do, really? Nothing. Inhaling deeply, I close my eyes for a moment and tell myself to just enjoy it.

"Do you know where I might get a charger for my phone?"

Mrs. Pepper points to the left. "There's a little general store down the street about two blocks away. They have some stuff like that. Not sure they're open today, but you could check."

I wrap my sweater closer around my torso. "Thanks. I'll go see."

"Not in that you won't." Mrs. Pepper sets her Susan Mallery book down on the table next to her coffee, suddenly all business. "Where is your coat?"

"It's only the beginning of November. I didn't think it would be this cold."

Mrs. Pepper opens a small coat closet. "You never know what the weather's going to do on the coast."

She pulls out a massive white fur coat with a giant fuzzy collar and a sash belt. It's amazing. I reach out and touch the fur. She hands it to me, and I put it on quickly running my cheek along the collar, the soft pelt making my skin feel expensive. "This coat is intense."

Mrs. Pepper laughs. "So was my mother. It was hers, you're welcome to borrow it. It's a fake but a good one."

"Thank you."

She smiles, heading back to her book. "Can't have my guests freezing to death."

Outside, the icy wind that greets me stings my cheeks. I scrunch lower into the collar of the coat, carefully walking down the road, keeping my eyes peeled for the general store. Every time I try to walk a bit faster, my boot slips precariously. I pass an antique store (closed), a wine shop (also closed), and a plant store (closed with all the lights off). After the third block, I'm about to give up and head back, when I see the small white sandwich board with black paint on the top that says *open*. The chalkboard in the middle has a drawing of a penguin with icicles coming off his beak. Underneath, in block letters, it says *Have An Ice Day*.

I open the door, little bells jingling as I do, and grab a shopping basket by the front. The man at the counter gives me a silent nod. I wander the aisles. There is a snack aisle with Cheez-Its, Triscuits, or Chicken in a Biscuits. I didn't even know they still made that cracker. Honestly, I'm not sure they still do. It's quite possible this box of crackers has been sitting on this shelf since the late nineties. There is a small section on the end of an aisle with electronics and a charger for my iPhone. Thanking the universe, I throw it in the basket and keep browsing.

There's a craft aisle with yarn, embroidery floss, seed beads, and a small paint set that comes with a leather-bound sketchbook, and a small set of watercolors. It's beautiful. I pick it up on an impulse, along with a pack of their nice ink pens.

The personal hygiene aisle does not disappoint. Along with a couple toothbrushes, I get a pack of condoms, since we went through the four we had. If we have to stay, we might as well take advantage of our alone time. Flashes of last night fill my mind, Oli's mouth on my nipple, his hands on my wrists, his—

"Zara?"

Whipping around, I'm so startled, I drop the black-and-gold box of Magnum condoms on the floor.

"Mrs. Willard."

I bend to grab the box, but she's quicker, and I register as her eyes widen and her cheeks turn a light shade of pink. She hands it to me without making eye contact. "I didn't realize you were back. Have you seen Ben?"

Her eyes meet mine, and there is a hopeful expression on her face that crushes me and makes me forget about how mortified I am for a second. Only for a second. I put the condoms in my basket and quickly cover them with the watercolor set. "I have. Actually, I'm staying at the cabins with an artist's retreat."

"That's wonderful. You know I..." Mrs. Willard fixes the seam of her gloves. "I always wanted to reach out and see how you were doing. But I didn't want to overstep."

Her eyes meet mine again, and the sting of shame I feel for leaving this kind, gentle woman without so much as a goodbye is a swift slap to the face.

"I'm sorry…" The words tumble out before I can arrange them artfully. "For all of it, but especially for the way I left."

She waves me away. "Honey. It's fine. You were so young. Water under the bridge."

Silence surrounds us. What do I say to the woman who welcomed me into her home, who I thought would be family someday? It seems Mrs. Willard doesn't know either, because she pats her sides and says, "Well, I should go. Just needed some flour, I have a batch of cookies waiting." She grasps my arm, her grip firm. "It was nice to see you, honey."

"You too," I say, and it's only a little bit of a lie.

Once my basket is filled with essentials and some absolute non-essentials that there was no way I was leaving the store without, I check out, my credit card visibly shuddering at the small town, *only-tiny-store-open-in-an-ice-storm* markup.

Oli is up, sort of, when I return to the room. The radio in the corner is playing classical music. The curtains are open, the cool light filtering into the room, mixing with the amber glow from the fireplace, bathing him in light and shadows. My fingers itch for the brushes in my bag. Oli's in bed, his hair wet, the covers around his waist, his bare chest exposed, reading Dave Eggers's *You Shall Know Our Velocity!* Without thinking, I reach into my pocket, pull out my phone, and snap a picture. He raises his eyebrow at me quizzically.

Smirking, he moves the blanket further down, exposing his abs, that he's totally flexing. "See something you like?"

"Mmm-hmm." I throw my bags down and shrug off the coat

before crawling into bed. I plant a soft kiss on his lips. Pulling back, I hop back onto the hardwood floors, too excited to show him the stuff I got.

He groans. "I wasn't done kissing you."

"But look what I found us!"

I throw a beanie in his direction then put the matching one on my head. It's a bright-orange knit hat with a s'more embroidered on the front underneath in cursive is stitched *S'moregon.*

Oli laughs. "Amazing." He puts his on, too, his dark hair poking out the sides at adorably odd angles.

"And that's not all…"

I empty the bags onto the bed, and Oli sits forward, digging through the cheap knit gloves, snacks, wine, toothpaste, and brushes. He holds up the watercolor set. "Ooh."

Then the box of condoms, and his voice deepens an octave as he says, "Ooooh."

I laugh. "The roads are still closed…so we have to stay another night."

The smile that spreads across his face is massive. You'd think I just told him he was nominated for a Turner Prize.

He pulls me down on the bed and rolls over me, brushing my hair off my face. He kisses me deeply and starts to pull my sweater up. I run my lips along his neck whispering into his ear, "We need coffee first."

He laughs. "How about coffee after?"

"I'm in desperate need of a shower, too. You're all squeaky clean, and I'm filthy."

He growls and dives into my neck. "I like you filthy."

I laugh. "It's not balanced."

He sighs then sits up, sorting through the debris of my general store run. He holds up a bottle of wine. "This is the only beverage I see."

"Mrs. Pepper said there's coffee in the dining room."

Oli nods and reluctantly gets out of bed, slipping into his jeans. "Mrs. Pepper in the dining room with the coffee."

I smile and watch as he buttons up his flannel as sexy as any strip tease.

"I'll get the caffeine, while you shower."

"I can come," I say getting off the bed.

He crosses the short distance between us, grabbing me by the hip bones and bringing me flush to his body. "Oh, you will."

I laugh.

"You foraged all this stuff, the least I can do is get the coffee." He presses his lips to mine, his kiss so long and deep you'd think he was shipping off to war and not just heading down stairs at a bed and breakfast. It sends shivers all the way down to my toes and makes me rethink the whole coffee thing.

He leaves me breathless and wanting more. "I'll be right back."

"You better," I sigh out.

Once he's out the door, I switch the station to something a little lighter. I find the top forty station and crank it up. T Swift fills the air. I dance my way out of my clothes all the way into the shower. The warm water doesn't get quite as warm as I like, so I make it super quick. By the time I hop out, Oli still isn't back yet.

After drying off, I wrap the soft towel around my body, tucking it in at my chest. Doubt fills my mind. We shouldn't be indulging this little fling. We're going to have to go back to hands-off as soon as this ice clears up. And won't it be harder? Poor choice of words. I bite my lip, flashing to Oli on top of me. It's fine. We'll get it out of our system then be back to complete professionals tomorrow.

I wander over to stoke the fire, and the song changes to "Classic" by MKTO. Bubbles of joy fill my chest. I haven't heard this song in years, not since high school. I sway a bit, the beat infectious, as I wander to the window, looking at the ice still sparkling on every surface.

My feet are moving, too, when Oli walks in holding two mugs of coffee in one hand, muffins tucked under his chin. "Dance party."

I laugh, feeling my cheeks flame at getting caught dancing in a towel to a pop song, and an old one at that.

But Oli looks genuinely happy. He sets the coffee down, quickly pushes the table over on the fluffy shag rug, and holds his hand out to me. "May I have this dance?"

"Yes."

I place my hand in his, and he puts his other on the small of my back, twirling me around the makeshift dance floor. I follow his lead as best I can. His feet are swift, and he's performing some complicated salsa-like moves.

"What the fuck?" I say, through laughter. "Is there anything you don't know how to do?"

He smiles. "My mom was an avid *Dancing With the Stars* fan. I may have practiced some of the routines in the living room."

I can picture it, Oli with gangly limbs dancing in front of the television.

He spins me, and the world blurs, soft whites and the amber glow of the fire. The song changes to a slow song with an interesting guitar strumming and a slow piano. I don't recognize it, but I don't hate it. Oli pulls me close, slowing down the tempo. He brings both hands to the small of my back, the pressure firm and gentle at the same time. I wrap my hands around his neck.

The singer croons "Come Away With Me" as we sway.

"I like this outfit," he says, tugging lightly at the fabric of the towel.

"Oh, this old thing?"

"It's very modern."

The corner or my lips tugs up. "It is. Maybe too modern. Just not quite me."

I bring my hand to the expert tuck I have in the towel, and slowly pull it out. The rest of the fabric falls away, the cool air making my nipples instantly hard, or maybe it's the way Oli is looking at me—his pupils so wide his eyes are practically black.

Dropping the towel dramatically to the floor, I stand there for a beat, completely naked, then with a smirk, I look pointedly at the bedside table. "Mmm. Coffee."

"Not so fast." Oli places his hands on me, one on each shoulder.

He leans in so his soft lips touch my ear as he whispers roughly, "Can I touch you?"

"Yes," I sigh out.

He moves his hands, slowly, deliberately down. Inch by inch. Goosebumps appear in the wake of his touch. He pauses at my breasts, cupping them. A moan falls from my lips as he gives my left nipple a hard pinch.

"You like that?"

"Yes."

"You like a little pain with your pleasure?" He squeezes a little harder, and my core clenches at the sensation.

"Yes."

He moves his hand to the small of my back, keeping the other firmly on my breast and leading me in much the same way he did while we were dancing, he backs us up until his legs are flush against the loveseat. Bringing his mouth down to my breast, he puts my nipple in his mouth, still tender from his pinch. He sucks lightly, and I have to tighten my thighs to stay upright. He keeps moving down, kissing and licking on the way, until he's sitting on the couch.

Looking up at me with his slate-gray eyes, he says, "Spread your legs."

The rush of want that shoots to the pit of my stomach is so intense all I can do is exactly what he's asked. Moving my legs, I stand with each foot about six inches apart.

"You're going to need to be wider than that, my greedy girl."

I bite my lip and move my legs wider.

Starting at my knee, Oli runs a hand up the inside of my thigh so lightly, I can't help but sigh. I want to push into him. I want to feel the pressure of him. But he's teasing me with his soft touch. He runs a finger through the center of me.

"You're so fucking wet."

"Yes," I breathe out, not sure how long I can take the teasing. And as if he knows, Oli takes his finger and pushes it inside.

I cry out. He works his magic, finding just the right spot until I'm a puddle of want and need. Hardly able to stand anymore.

He tugs off his sweater, and as he does, I kneel down, undoing his pants and yanking them down. The condoms are mercifully nearby. I grab one, tearing the package open with my teeth as Oli takes off the rest of his clothes. Just as slowly as he teased me, I roll the condom on, his eyes fluttering closed.

Once that's on, I straddle him, hovering just above him. I take my hand, guiding him to just the right spot, then lower so slow it's painful. Inch by inch. A grunt escapes Oli, and he buries his face in my breasts.

"Oh, fuck."

I lift off and do it again, so slow. Such a sharp contact to the hammering of my heart.

Oli's jaw clenches. "Zara."

My name on his mouth makes me lose all my calculated control. No more teasing. I ride him like the sun may not rise tomorrow. He grabs my hips, bringing me down deeper on him, and my muscles clench.

"I'm close," he says through pants. "Touch yourself."

I obey, but I don't even need to. Just him, alone, is threatening to push me over the edge. The added stimulation is all it takes. "Oli. I'm going to...."

The words get lost in the scream that tears through me. I feel him swell under me, every muscle of his flexed, grabbing my ass on top of him, as stars explode in my veins.

I lay my head on his shoulder as he traces his fingers lightly along my back. His heart is pumping hard in his chest, and I can feel the vibrations in mine. I search for words, something to say, to express how amazing that was, how intense. But there are none. So I close my eyes and listen to the crackle of the fire, to "Stick

Season" playing over the radio, to Oli's heartbeat. I feel the smooth skin of his shoulder on my cheek and just breathe.

CHAPTER 20

The coffee is so rich and delicious it's even good cold. Oli doctored it just the way I like without even asking.

He had to step out to make a phone call. Something about his agent.

The shag carpet actually makes the floor quite cozy, but to make it cozier, I place the comforter down on the ground, too. I've selected one of the books from the shelf, wrapped myself in the throw blanket, and am lounging on my belly in my little nest by the fire, coffee within reach. The book I grabbed is quite good: it's about a woman who goes to a hotel to kill herself, but there's a wedding happening and she decides not to.

I'm so absorbed, Oli startles me when he comes in. The sound of him rubbing a hand over his face, his scruff on his soft palm, is a siren song. I want to run my teeth along his jaw. When I look up, his face is drawn, his mouth a set line. I don't know what that phone call was about, but it doesn't look like it went well.

"Everything all right?" I ask, propping myself up on my elbow.

Oli's eyes find me in my little blanket nest. His whole face changes. The frown lines disappear, his eyes soften, crinkling at the corner, and a small smile plays at his lips. "You're so beautiful."

My cheeks warm under his gaze.

He raises a hand in the air. "Don't move."

I do move a little, just getting myself a bit more artfully arranged for the picture I'm sure he's going to take. But then I hear running water.

"What are you doing?"

He comes and sits next to me. "I want to paint you."

"Okay."

He opens the little watercolor set, getting out the brush and dipping in the water as I turn my attention back to my book. Oli is not the first artist I've dated, and this is not the first painting I've sat for. In the movies it's very romantic, very fevered and *Titanic*-esque. In practice, it's usually quite dull and takes forever.

Then I feel the cool, wet bristles of the brush on my back.

I laugh. "What are you doing?"

He smiles, that slightly crooked grin. "I'm painting *you*."

And by the way he emphasizes the last word, and the soft brush between my shoulder blades, I now understand what he means.

"As in I'm the canvas?"

"Yes. Hold still."

I lay my head on my hand, elbow bent, and close my eyes, focusing on the sensation of the brush gliding across my skin. It's soft and wet. Smooth, yet firm at times. A lot like Oli. It's delicious.

After about fifteen minutes, Oli moves away. "It's done."

"Wow, that was fast."

He lies on his stomach next to me on the floor. "In my line of work, you kind of have to be."

"Right. Can't dally with the po-po breathing down your neck."

He laughs, and the sound of it goes straight to my heart. "I don't think they like being called po-po."

"Really?"

Oli shrugs. "Can't be sure, but I don't think so."

"Will you take a picture and show me?"

He grabs his phone out of his back pocket and rises to his knees, snapping a picture then handing me his phone. He's painted me in soft pinks and purples, with the occasional pop of yellow, like the highlight on my cheek. "It's gorgeous."

"How could it not be, given the subject matter?"

It's a cheesy line, but it works. I rise to my knees, letting the blanket fall around me, the cool air hitting my naked body, and Oli's eyes widen.

He grabs my hips, fiddling with the waistband of my black thong, the only clothes I'm wearing, as I unbutton his shirt, slowly. One button at a time.

As I'm rolling the sleeves off his broad shoulders, he leans in for a kiss, but I back up. "Not so fast. It's my turn to paint you."

"Yes, mam."

I move to the side so he can lie down then get my paints set up. Lifting a leg over, I straddle him, sitting on his back. He groans, reaching back and grabbing a fistful of my ass.

"Maybe you could paint me after…"

"Nope." I swat his hand away. "You'll just have to wait."

The glow from the fireplace rests softly on Oli's high cheek and strong jaw, almost as if I set up lights in a studio for a proper portrait. I dip the brush, starting with the pale colors and moving onto the shadows. Every now and then, Oli lets out a soft sigh. The third time he does it, I ask, "Do you like the feel?"

"Mmm. Hmm. It's soothing. Being art for once instead of having to make it. And the brush tickles."

I giggle, but his words hit me. There is so much pressure to create. I've put so much pressure on myself to crank out paintings, to perform for the BFA board, to get this show and that. It is nice to just let go.

It takes me twice as long, but finally, my painting is done. I move off of Oli's back and assess my work. For working with a sighing, wiggling canvas, it's actually not bad. Moving across the room to where my phone is charging on the dresser, I catch Oli in the mirror getting up from the floor. He comes up behind me, placing his large hands on my hips and pulls me into him. Under the rough denim, he's hard as a rock.

I nuzzle my backside into him, but whine, "We need a picture."

"I need you." He hooks a finger under each side of the straps of my thong and tugs down. I move my feet, stepping out of the underwear all the way. He places my hands on the solid wood of the dresser deliberately, palms down, and catches my eye in the mirror. "Don't move."

He's all fire and lust. His muscles clenched, his jaw set, and I breathe out, "Yes."

Placing one hand over mine, he takes his other hand and unbuckles his belt. The zip of his zipper sends a shot of lust down the center of me.

He moves away, and I watch him in the mirror, stepping out of his pants tearing open a condom packet with his teeth, and I could climax just from watching him move. I want to tear my teeth into him.

He walks back slowly. He's impossibly hard, watching me watching him.

Running a smooth hand over my back, he takes his hard length and smacks my ass with it. I cry out. It doesn't hurt, but the feel of his meaty flesh against me is so intense.

"Do you like that?"

"Yes."

He does it again. My hands move, clutching the edge of the dresser. "I said don't move." He places my hand back where it was and gives my ass a loud smack. "Got it?"

"Yes," I say, relishing the tingle left by his hand.

He runs his hands up my back then wraps them around to my breasts, watching as he squeezes them in the mirror. He moves one hand away and whispers in my ear, "Are you ready for me?"

"Always."

He grunts as he thrusts inside me, my entire body clenching around him. Over and over, he pushes inside me. I soften, letting him in deeper and deeper, as we both watch in the reflection.

My legs start to shake, and he pulls out, lifting me up and setting me on the dresser. I reach for him, hungry, feeling empty at the absence of him inside me. I get him snugly against me. He pushes back in as I suck in a breath. Each thrust goes deeper until I am full. I am consumed by him.

His teeth skate across my breasts, and he runs his hands up my back. The sweat, his skin, his fingers on my spine, his mouth on my nipple. It all swirls around me as the pressure builds and builds until I erupt, clenching so tight around him that he cries out gripping my ass in his strong hands.

My muscles are limp, and Oli is panting heavily, his body still. He pulls out gently and lifts me off the dresser, bringing me into his body, wrapping his arms around me.

"Did we just come at the same time?" I ask with a lazy smile spreading across my lips.

He smirks. "Unless you were faking?"

I laugh. "If I was that good an actress, I wouldn't be working for Marlene. I'd be accepting my third Oscar."

He takes my hand, leading me into the bathroom. "Do you think Meryl Streep fakes it?"

"Pssh," I say, as he turns on the shower. "Have you seen her? She doesn't have to."

Oli runs his hand through the water, and my face falls.

"What about our paintings?"

He shrugs. "Nothing lasts forever."

A chill passes through me, like my body just registered that it's naked, that it's icy outside, that the fire is dying.

I nod. "Let me take a picture first."

"Okay."

I run on tiptoes to grab my phone. I've missed a call from Marlene. Even without listening to the voicemails, the world seeps in. The snow globe cracks—all the glitter sinking to the bottom and running out.

Oli's back is a little smudged from our *after-painting-activities*. I take a deep breath and hold it as I press the button. The voicemail icon is nagging at me. Oli steps under the running water, blues and oranges swirling down the drain. I hold up my phone.

"I'll be just a minute."

Pressing my ear to the receiver, I listen to Marlene.

"Ashford, call me back."

That's it. That's all it says, and she sent it last night. Fuck.

Quickly, I throw a blanket over my shoulders, like she'll be able to see my nakedness through my voice somehow. She answers on the first ring...this can't be good.

"Ashford, what's going on?"

"Nothing. Everything is good here, just waiting out the ice. Last I checked, the road on the way up the mountain is still closed."

"Benji—"

Benji? Oof, I'm sure he loves that.

"—just got back from town. He said it's fine."

Shit.

"That's great. I'll get Oli and we'll head back."

"Wonderful. The gallery can cover the cost of the rooms."

Rooms.

Shitty, shit, shit, shit.

"Um, that's great. There was actually..."

"Genevieve is coming this way, I have to run. See you soon."

I'm frozen with the phone in my hand. What is Marlene going to do when she sees there is only one room to reimburse? Wait. She won't. I handle all that stuff. She should never have to see the bill at all.

Oli comes out of the bathroom wrapped in a towel, a lazy smile on his face. "Where'd you go?"

"We have to leave. The roads are open. Marlene called. She wants us back."

Oli's smile drops. "Okay."

"I'll shower, and we'll get on the road."

Oli picks up his discarded clothes. His back glistens with water droplets from the shower, the painting completely washed away. His words ring in my head as I let the warm water of the shower wash over me, colors swirling at my feet.

Nothing lasts forever.

CHAPTER 21

The drive back is quiet. On the way out, I practically begged Mrs. Pepper to charge me for two rooms. She agreed, eventually, even though she said it seemed really dishonest.

I make the turn up the hill into the trees, while Oli sighs. "Are you going to get in trouble?"

"No. I don't think so."

"That's good." Oli moves his hand over to my leg, sending tingles down my thighs. "I had a great time."

I smile, thinking about it. "Me too."

Once we're back at the campsite, it's business as usual. Oli heads off to his cabin. I check a few things at the lodge. Marlene and Miguel are having coffee by the fire, deep in conversation, so deep, in fact, that thankfully Marlene glances in my direction but doesn't make a move to talk about my absence. *Our* absence.

Heading back out the door, I'm about to head off to my cabin, when Ben calls out my name.

"Got stuck in town, huh?"

I turn on the dirt trail. Ben's in a red flannel, his beanie tight around his ears. "Yeah, they closed the main road up here, I guess."

He frowns, "My mom said she ran into you."

"Yeah." My mind flashes to Mrs. Willard catching me holding a box of Magnums, but she wouldn't tell Ben that, would she? "I had to pick up a toothbrush."

Ben nods, but there's an odd look in his eye.

I look away first. "Well, I have some work I need to get done."

"Zara, can we talk?"

"Sure." I smile, but it feels false on my face.

"Great. Let's go to Stonehouse tomorrow for breakfast."

"Breakfast? Can't we talk right here?"

Ben rubs a hand over the scruff on his face, definitely more than stubble. Is he growing a beard?

"I'd prefer to talk in private."

I suppress a sigh. I don't want to say yes, but I already said yes. "What time?"

"Eight."

I cross my arms and try for a friendly smile. "Okay, see you then."

Turning, I make a beeline to my cabin, but not before running into Louise about halfway there. She grabs me by both arms.

"Zara! I'm making work again, and I think it's actually good."

"That's amazing."

Louise's smile is megawatt. "It is! It really is. That night when we graffitied opened something up in me."

Her eyes are so bright they're practically glowing.

"That's great!"

She clasps my hands, her smile so wide it's infectious. "How's your painting going?"

I think of the painting on Oli's back. "I did make one interesting piece."

"Wonderful. I can't wait to see it."

I walk back to my cabin. I handle some emails from gallery clients and a few from artists interested in showing at the gallery. Then I go out to the porch, where my canvas is still set up. The vast blankness of the flat undercoat stares back at me accusatory.

There's a tickle in the back of my throat and pressure building behind my eyes.

Sleep. That's what I need. I'll be able to handle it all after a little nap.

WHEN I WAKE UP, it's already getting dark outside. My head feels worse. It pounds behind my eyes, and my nose is stuffy. It's probably just exhaustion. I'm absolutely not sick. I can't be. There's too much to do.

I grab my phone. It's after four, and there're a couple of texts, the first from a few hours ago.

Oli: I miss you.

Then from twenty minutes ago.

Oli: Is that too cheesy?

Adjusting the brightness on my phone, trying to see if it'll help my head, I text back.

Me: I adore cheesy. Sorry I fell asleep. Not feeling great.

Putting my phone away, I hide my head under the covers again. The warmth on my head makes my eyelids flutter close.

A knock at the door wakes me up. This time, the windows are completely dark, just a small reflection of the moon on the water outside. I wrap my sweater tighter around my torso, but shiver anyway, and head to the door.

Oli is standing there with a bag in one hand and a bouquet of marigolds in the other. He has a smile on his face, but it immediately falls when he sees me. "You don't look so good."

I head back to the bed, crawling under the covers. "Such a sweet talker."

"No." He sets his stuff down. "You always look great...I just mean."

"I get it. I'm sick." I throw myself down on the soft pillows. I can't deny it any longer, the snot filling my head won't let me. I really am sick. "How are you *not* sick?"

Oli shrugs at my little kitchenette counter as he puts the flowers in a pitcher and fiddles with some stuff in the bag he brought. "I never get sick."

My mind circles around clever responses to that. Some witty banter. Some snarky comment. But all I can come up with is sticking my tongue out and making a raspberry noise.

Oli laughs, and it feels like that was the right call. He brings over a steaming bowl of pho.

I sit up, the sweet and spicy steam from the soup soothing something in my forehead. "Where did you get this?"

Oli smiles. "I borrowed Miguel's motorcycle. Rode all the way to Seaside."

Picturing Oli on a motorcycle riding down the highway, the wind in his hair and the waves rolling in the distance, warms me almost more than the soup. "You didn't?"

"I did."

I hold the warm soup bowl in my hands and breathe in deeply. "How did you know I was sick?"

"You texted me you weren't feeling great."

"Oh, right. I did."

I take another deep breath of the soup fumes.

Oli laughs. "Are you just going to huff the pho, or are you going to eat it?"

"Don't rush the process."

"Fair enough." Oli brings the chair over by the bed, slipping his boots off. He sits and props his feet up on the edge of the bed. "Under normal circumstances, I would find us something to watch, but the internet isn't strong enough for streaming so..." He pulls out his phone. "I am going to read to you."

I feel a smile tug around my lips even as I take a bite of noodles. "That is so grandpa in *The Princess Bride* of you."

He shakes his head. "Never seen it."

"What?" I nearly drop my bowl. "How is that even possible? It's going on the list." Even as I say it, even in my fevered state, I know this is a dangerous game we're playing. Implying there is a list. Making plans for a future we can't actually share unless I want to find a new job. I bring my focus back to the present, to this room, to this bed, to my soup, to this handsome man that's going to read to me. "What are you going to read?"

"You get to pick. I have a couple downloaded. There's *The Woman in Cabin Ten*, *Basquiat: The Life and Death of an Art Star*, or *Another Roadside Attraction*."

The last one lights up my chest. My favorite book, the one he bought on the train, is on his phone. "Did you read it? The Tom Robbins book?"

He smiles. "I did. You're right. We should all give up. No better art will ever be made than that hot dog painting that was never really painted."

Swallowing my sip of broth, I say, "It's true." I don't want him to be bored. It's so sweet of him to bring me soup, and offer to entertain me. "Which one haven't you read?"

"I haven't read the mystery yet."

"Mystery it is." I tuck into more noodles, my headache easing a bit.

His voice is deep and smooth as he reads, "In my dream, the girl was drifting, far, far below...."

Sometime after I finish the pho, I lay my head down on the cool pillow. Oli reads about Lo accepting an invite to a very fancy cruise as I fall asleep again. When I wake up, the room is still dark, the world quiet. Oli is sleeping next to me in all his clothes on top of the covers, one of his hands resting near mine, the other still holding his phone.

Taking the phone out of his hand, I put it on the bedside table, but not before I notice he has a notification of a missed text.

Tyler: Everything's all set. Are you sure about this?

My headache is back, stabbing behind my eyes. I try not to

think about what that might mean as I close my eyes and let sleep crash over me once again.

———

COFFEE WAKES ME UP, the sound of the ancient coffee maker clicking and whirring more than the smell, which I can barely make out through my congestion.

"Mmm." I stretch a little, my muscles still feeling achy.

Oli turns, his strong jaw lit by the overcast light trickling in through the window. "How are you feeling?"

"Terrible."

"I'm sorry."

I shrug and pick up my phone, noticing that Oli's is gone from the bedside table. It's eight thirty-seven, and I have a missed call, and five texts. "Shit."

"What is it?"

My headache pricks at the base of my skull. Before I can answer Oli, there's a knock on my door.

Oli looks at me, his eyes wide. He mouths, *Who is it?*

I don't answer, although I have a pretty good idea. The knock comes again, and Oli heads into the bathroom, closing the door lightly. I wrap my sweater around myself tighter and get out of bed, every muscle protesting. The sound of the hinges squeaking as I swing it open slices through my skull, and the brightness of the gray day makes my eyes close reflexively.

"We were supposed to meet half an—" Ben stops mid-sentence, his brows scrunching when he sees me. His face fills with concern. "Oof, you don't look good."

I suppress a sigh and am about to say, *so I've heard*, when I stop myself. Instead, I just nod, the motion sending ripples of pain through my body. "I'm sick."

"Is that why you stood me up?"

"I'm sorry, Ben, I just forgot." A cold wind blows right into my little cabin and against my bare legs, sending a visible shiver through my body.

Ben pushes his way in, guiding me by the shoulders. "You need to get back into bed."

I do, but I really don't want Ben to find Oli. Words won't form to protest, though. I crawl under the covers as Ben's eyes travel around the room, lingering on the take-out bag on the counter.

"Can I get you anything?"

"No, I just need sleep."

"Can I get a rain check on our talk for when you're feeling better?"

I inhale a large breath through my mouth. Too large. A cough spasms in my chest. Once I have my breath back, I say, "What is there to talk about?"

He sits on the edge of the bed. "Fate?"

"Fate?" My stomach clenches.

"Yeah. Fate. Like how we met at the waterfall that day. And here we are. Thrown back together. It's fate. I think we owe it to ourselves and to each other to explore the reason why?"

My eyes water, and I don't know if it's from my cold or this conversation. "There's no such thing as fate. People just bump around into each other. It's random and stupid and honestly never works out. We met at the waterfall because we were both there. My boss insisted on the retreat here because I was talking about growing up here. And your family owns half the town so, it's not that weird that if we were to hold a retreat anywhere in Fortune Falls, I'd have to deal with you."

"Deal with me?"

"You know what I mean. Look, I don't want to be a bitch, but what's done is done. We were over so long ago. Let's not dig it all up now."

Ben's eyes fill with so much sorrow, I almost want to take it all back. He asks, "But why?"

I roll on my side, burying myself in the covers. "Because my head is going to explode."

"Why did you leave in the first place? We were so good together."

"We were kids. You asked me to marry you. I didn't want that to be my whole life. I wanted to explore the world and make my mark. I didn't want to be a wife at eighteen."

Ben shakes his head. "I said we could have a long engagement."

"Life isn't a Jane Austen novel."

"I don't know who that is."

"*Pride and Prejudice*."

He scoffs. "Sounds half right."

"Do you know what people were saying?" I say, softly.

Ben rubs a hand over his hat, taking it off and holding it in his lap. "People are always going to talk…"

"They said I was with you just for your money. That I won that art contest because of your dad's connections. They called me little orphan Zarrie."

"They were bitches. That shouldn't change how we felt about one another. How we feel."

I sit up, the effort taking all my strength, and lean against the headboard.

Ben reaches out and tucks a strand of my hair behind my ear. It's a familiar gesture, one he's done a thousand times. When we started dating when I was fourteen, I thought it was so sweet. I felt so cared for. As time went on, the gesture felt more possessive, proprietary, like I was one of these cabins, or one of his family's properties that needs tending. Now the gesture just feels hollow.

I reach for his hand and squeeze it briefly in mine then set it in his lap. "Ben, I really am sorry for the way I handled things. Or, more accurately, didn't. I shouldn't have just left the ring and a note. I should've talked to you about everything. Honestly, I was worried you'd talk me out of it and I needed to leave. Can you forgive me?"

Ben's eyes are soft as he reaches for my hand again. "Yes." His eyes flutter down and then snap back up to mine. "Do you think we could go on a date? When this is all over? See if anything is still there."

My stomach twists. I don't want to reject him again. Rejecting him and still being stuck here for the next couple weeks sounds awful. But I also don't want to get his hopes up. So I opt for the truth, but not the whole truth. "I'm actually seeing someone."

Ben drops my hand like it's on fire. "I didn't know. Is it serious?"

Is it? I mean, honestly, it can't be, but Ben doesn't need to know that. A lump forms in my throat, and I swallow it down. "It is."

He places his hat back on his head. "Who is he?"

I squeeze the tissue wadded in my hand. "You don't know him."

Ben stands, walks to the door. "That makes sense. I mean look at you. Even sick, you're gorgeous and so smart." His foot reaches out and kicks Oli's boots sitting by the door. Shit. "Nice boots."

"They're…"

But Ben is out the door before I can explain.

Oli waits a few minutes then comes out of the bathroom. The smile on his face is bright. He swoops me in his arms, spinning me, and my already dizzy head scrambles. I pull back and attempt a smile. "That was a close one, but I think he bought it."

A frown quickly replaces the smile on Oli's face. "Bought it?"

"Yeah." I sit down, my head still spinning. "I'm not sure how much you heard. I had to tell him we were serious so he'd leave."

"Yeah, sure." He nods as he heads straight for his boots and starts lacing them up. "I should let you rest."

His eyes won't meet mine. I'm trying to figure out why, but my head burns and I can't completely remember everything I've said.

"Oli…"

He gives me a quick kiss on the cheek. "Text me if you need anything."

I lie back on the pillows and sink into sleep like a stone at the bottom of the lake.

CHAPTER 22
EIGHTEEN DAYS LEFT OF THE RETREAT

In the morning, my headache is gone. I'm still a little stuffy, but my muscles don't have that achy need to stretch feeling anymore. The lake has a mist hanging over it, like a sleepy cloud too tired to be all the way up in the sky.

Despite the chill, I make my coffee and take it out onto the porch, watching the sun rise over the water. The pine trees shiver in the wind. The other trees are nearly bare, just a few golden and red leaves blowing this way and that, clinging on for dear life.

Today is the group's first critique, and I have absolutely nothing to show. But that's fine. I'm here to work. I can participate, but that doesn't mean I have to. In fact, it might be unprofessional to insert myself. At least that's what I tell myself as I try to sketch my painting with no luck.

One of the sketches seems promising enough to try. I lay the paint on the canvas; it looks more like a straight self-portrait than the reflection I'm going for. Frustration builds in my chest, and I paint over it in large strokes of light pink until it's essentially a blank canvas again. All my progress wiped away.

An hour later and no closer to having anything done, I give up. After a hot shower, I take extra time with my outfit and makeup. I may have no art to show, but I'm going to look good.

Tucking my sketchbook in my bag, I make my way to the lodge, the crisp morning air stinging my cheeks.

Miguel is sitting on the steps to the lodge, coffee in hand, dressed in chocolate leather pants and a brown suede jacket. "Ah, good morning, Zara. How are you feeling?"

"Better," I say wearily. "Does everyone know I was sick?"

Miguel sips his coffee, steam rising off in great wafts. "Small camp, word travels fast."

It makes me uncomfortable. What else does everyone know? But I slap on a professional smile. "I'm feeling much better now, thanks for your concern. I'm going to grab some of that coffee."

Inside, Louise and Alice are chatting by the fire with plates of food like old friends. Louise looks up. "You've rejoined the living."

I sniff, despite feeling much better. "I have. You two look cozy."

"We were discussing the collab," Louise says, her eyes bright.

"Pull up a chair and sit with us," Alice says.

"Sure. Let me just grab some coffee first."

I make my way to the carafe, grabbing a mug just as Marlene comes out the swinging doors from the kitchen. "Ashford. Thank God you're feeling better. I was worried I'd have to send you home."

My brows knit together reflexively. I sent Marlene a text saying I was sick, but she didn't check on me the whole time. "I'm fine. It was just a cold."

"Benji said you were in bad shape."

Benji. Shit. What else did Benji say?

"Much better now."

"Good. Everything is all set for the critique in the great room."

Weddings use the great room for dancing. I've seen small summer camps put on their talent shows there. It'll be perfect for our critique.

I check my watch, there's about an hour until the start time. "Is everyone's art set up?"

"It's very informal, so the artists are bringing their own work and hanging it or propping it up. Did you bring your piece, or do you need to go back for it?"

"I wasn't going to take up the group's time with my work."

Marlene's lips smash into a tight line. "In order for it to be a truly creative and safe space, everyone must participate. My work is already in there."

My eyes go wide. Marlene is showing? I haven't seen her art in person...ever. I've only seen what I've found in old art magazines on the internet. She never brings it into the gallery or talks about it. It hits me, I'm actually going to need to show something to these people. Something more than just sketches.

"I'll just go get it."

Marlene nods as I quickly walk out the door, the panic in my chest turning my brisk walk into a jog. By the time I make it inside my cabin, I'm out of breath and in a spiral, complete with terrifying heart palpitations.

I take a massive inhale, too big for my still recovering lungs, and end up in a coughing fit. Opening the door to the porch, the cold air shocking my lungs back into submission, I stare at the blank canvas.

One hour. The paint will still be wet, but I'm not showing Louise fucking Walker an undercoat.

First, I get out my sketchbook. Then I connect to my little Bluetooth speaker and crank it up. Losing myself in the music, I sketch out my idea. Working quickly, I lay down the underpainting. The time flies, and before I know it, I'm gingerly carrying my art to the lodge, and hoping they don't mind that it's wafting paint fumes.

When I get there, everyone is walking around the room, sizing up each other's pieces. I prop mine on an open patch of wall and fall into step behind Alice. Oli is deep in thought, crouched and peering at a large pencil drawing on a whitewashed piece of wood. I try to catch his eye, but he's too engrossed in what looks to be a drawing of a leaf pile.

Marlene clears her throat. "We'll take about fifteen minutes looking at everyone's work. Then we'll go one by one: giving thoughts, offering criticism, and asking the artists questions."

I head over to the leaf pile drawing, but as I do, Oli moves on to the next piece. He gives me a small smile as he does, but it's not the free and easy smiles he usually gives me. This one is guarded. It looks like it costs him. I can't figure out what is going on with him. Did I say something when I was sick that offended him?

Kneeling to get a better view of the wooden board in front of me, I'm drawn in by the intricate lines of the leaves, some falling delicately from the sky. The lines are all so interesting. As I lean in, squinting, I see that it's not just a leaf. On each one is a small but detailed vagina in the veins of the foliage.

I do a double take and get even closer. They are unmistakable. There's no name on the piece, and I wonder whose it could be? Maybe Alice. But then I move on to the next piece: an open laptop with a photograph displayed on it. This must be Alice's. It's a portrait of Louise, the lake covered in fog behind her. Her eyes the same dark blue as the foreboding clouds and golden leaves in the distance off-setting the whole thing.

Could the vagina leaves be Louise's?

Marlene claps her hands and motions to one of the large tables. "Once you've looked at everyone's piece, come take a seat and we'll begin the discussion."

Quickly, I move through the rest of the pieces. On a nearby table, there's a small clay sculpture of a man crawling, his back half covered in a blanket. The intricate folds of the fabric cascading into a pool on the wood of the table is reminiscent of Ancient Greek sculpture. While the figure of the man is so hyper-realistic it has an extremely modern feel. It's delicate. This piece has to be Miguel's, since he's the only sculptor.

There's an abstract painting, the color and the brush strokes bold. Then there's a small charcoal drawing of a woman's face in profile that turns into an abstract array of texture and line. I'm not entirely sure which one is Andre and Genevieve's, Louise's, or

Marlene's. And I don't see anything that looks like Oli's anywhere.

We all find a seat at the table, and Marlene clasps her hands. "I think we should start with the leaf drawing. I have to say, I find it extremely interesting."

Louise sits forward in her chair. "I've been calling it *Wet Leaves*."

"Ooh, erotic," Marlene coos.

I'm pleased that it's Louise's. We talk about hers for a while. She says she's in her O'Keeffe phase and is into exploring different mediums other than paint.

The bold abstract painting is Andre's. They are going to project it at an abandoned drive-in movie theater in Santa Fe. I contribute where I can, just so I don't come across as dumb, or worse, meek. But I feel a little overwhelmed and nervous about what these people will have to say about mine.

The charcoal drawing is Marlene's. It's soft and feminine, no trace of the hard-as-nails gallery owner I work with every day; it's the most surprising so far.

My work is next. The room feels stuffy suddenly, the heat from the fireplace stifling. I haven't even had the chance to assess mine. Looking at it now, I can see it's not right. Lightly sketched out in graphite over the pink base is my reflection in the train window. Or I'm attempting to make it look like a reflection, anyway. The real challenge of that will come later in the details. It's unfinished, obviously, but it's not even a good start. The colors are all wrong, even for a base coat, and the composition is too in-your-face.

Miguel speaks first. "It's hard to know where it's going from what is on the canvas."

Marlene's hand is at her chin, her brow furrowed.

"I'm not sure about the face being so off to the side in the frame," Alice says softly. "But I agree with Miguel. It might work. It's just too soon to say."

"I think it needs more," Oli says, looking right at me when he does.

"Interesting," Marlene says. "More what, exactly?"

"More vulnerability. It's a reflection of the artist, but right now, and I know it's just a start, it feels surface level."

The words sting. I open my mouth to defend my poor sapling of a painting, but then immediately close it. We aren't supposed to argue or defend.

He keeps going. "It seems there was a cellphone in the reference photo, the painting might be more interesting with that included."

I thought Oli got what I was trying to do, but clearly I was dead wrong. It's not about cell phone selfies. What I'm trying to express—the kind of introspection and existential spiral I'm trying to capture—is timeless.

There are murmurs of agreement, but Genevieve speaks up. "How can you tell it's a reflection?"

Oli falters, looking at me, then back at the painting. "The streaks in the corner."

"Hmm."

Mine is the last piece in the room, there's no sign of Oli's. Is he not putting any work in this critique? Wanting to move on from my work, I ask, "Oli, where is your art?"

The corners of his mouth turn up just the slightest bit. "We have to go for a little walk."

"A walk or a hike?" Genevieve asks, stretching her leg out from under the table revealing her very high-heeled boots.

"It's a bit of a trek."

A deep crease forms between Marlene's brows. "We'll take a small break so everyone can get the proper attire."

I leave the room quickly, heading right out the door and gulping fresh air. There's a light drizzle dusting the steps in a thin sheen of water.

Marlene comes out, followed by the others. She lets out a heavy sigh. "Oli, how far is it?"

Oli shrugs, buttoning his raincoat. "About a mile or so."

Genevieve looks at him like he lost his mind.

"We're going to have to wait until the weather clears to see it in person," Marlene says. "I don't want anyone else getting sick. You don't have any photos we could critique?"

Oli shakes his head. "I could go take some, though."

"Perfect, take some photos and we'll look at them over drinks tonight."

"Sounds good. I'll go now. Anyone is welcome to come see it in person."

There are murmurs of *no, we'll see the pictures,* and *work to do.* I look into Oli's slate-gray eyes. Even though his critique still stings, I want to be near him. I want to see his work. And more than anything, I want to shake this feeling that he's mad at me.

"I'm game," I say.

His eyes spark. "Let's go."

CHAPTER 23

Borrowing two of the lodge's slickers, we head out on the trail. The rain is light but relentless, coating everything in an ethereal shine. Oli is quiet, always staying a few feet away, despite my attempts to get closer. At one particularly narrow part of the trail, our fingers brush, and I swear he flinches. It's too much.

I stop. "What is going on?"

Oli's eyes stay focused on the path. "We're walking to my piece."

"No, I mean with us? Did I do something? You seem pissed."

Oli shifts his gaze to the tree behind me, to the lake, everywhere but at me.

I raise and lower my hands. "Oli! You made me come five times the other day, now you can't even look at me. Tell me what's wrong."

There's a snap of a twig on the trail, and I freeze, the blood draining from my face.

More sounds of footsteps approaching, my eyes flutter closed, and despite my utter and complete lack of religion, I pray whoever it is they didn't hear me shouting about having sex with Oli.

"There you are," Louise says, putting a hand on her knee and catching her breath. "I want to see the art, too."

Oli hurries over, offering Louise his arm. She takes it and we continue our walk.

"So, your drawing was…" I search for the right word, but all that comes to mind is, "interesting."

Louise barks out a laugh. "You mean *The Season of the Slit*?"

The tips of Oli's ears turn pink, and I nearly choke on my laughter. "You are not calling it that?"

Louise giggles. "I have been."

"The details in the drawings are amazing," I say. "What made you switch subject matter?"

Louise shrugs. "I've always wanted to do something more provocative, a little tongue-in-cheek. I didn't because I worried what people would say. When we put those stickers up in town, I realized it doesn't matter what I do. If I want to make a comment on the nature of sexuality for a woman my age, no one is going to give a shit."

Oli is smiling. "Rad."

I nod, but I'm not sure she's right. I can picture the *Artforum* article. It might not be bad, but it will definitely make a splash, and people will talk. I can hear the whispers at the gallery now, the hairs on the back of my neck bristling. "Is it going to be a series?"

She shrugs. "I haven't figured it all out yet. It's still in an exploratory stage."

"We're nearly there," Oli says.

The trail narrows as we go up a slight hill, planks of wood dug into the earth to help us keep our footing. At the top of the incline, a massive tree sits off to the side, completely covered in yellow leaves. What's odd and striking about it is that it's a pine tree.

I step closer, running my hand along one of the brittle leaves, careful to keep my pressure light so the whole thing doesn't crumble beneath my fingertips.

Every branch has golden leaves sewn to the boughs.

Louise pulls her phone out, snapping pictures, but I'm stunned still. It's so different from his usual work. It feels softer. More vulnerable.

Louise stands back, her phone down now. "This." She points to one of the leaves. "This is how I've felt for years. Pretending to be something I'm not."

Oli lets out a heavy breath. "Same."

The tree is gorgeous, but also ridiculous. Trying to mold itself into something that will never work. It's how I felt before I left Fortune Falls. If I'm being honest with myself, it's how I still feel. A painter that doesn't paint. Fetching glasses of wine for assholes in a gallery I want to show in, not work in. I thought leaving Fortune Falls would fix things. And while the struggle has distracted me, I still haven't found my place.

Oli has illustrated so beautifully how I feel. How he feels, too, it seems.

"Did you sew on every leaf?" I ask, looking up and remembering when he was on the train and said he wished he could fly. It's no wonder. How did he even reach some of the taller branches?

"I did."

"When?"

Oli looks up at the tree, the yellow of the leaves reflected in his eyes. "I started last week." He flexes and relaxes his hand. "It felt good to complete something challenging, all on my own."

We head back down the trail, Oli helping Louise and chatting quietly. His tall frame dwarfs her, his strong arm holding her up on the steeper parts of the trail. Watching him take care of her turns me on more than I care to admit. We walk with her all the way back to her cabin. Once she heads inside, Oli turns his eyes on me. "Want to come over to my place?"

There's not a second's hesitation. "Yes."

We walk to his cabin—his and Louise's are probably the furthest from each other—as the drizzle that's followed us around all day turns into a torrential downpour. He grabs my hand, and we run, feet sliding on the trail and kicking up mud. Rain streams down my face, soaking into my hair and my leggings. The feel of Oli's slick hand in mine warms my chest despite the icy shock of the water.

Not even slowing down up the porch stairs, Oli runs inside, pulling me along with him. Once my body is fully inside, the door shuts behind me. The rain is even louder in the small cabin, echoing off the small skylight. Oli lets my hand drop. I glance around the room, taking in his space. Scrap paper with scribbled sketches hang on the walls near the desk by the window. Leaves and thread cover the work area. Before I can look further, Oli brings my attention back to him, pushing me lightly against the door, running his hands down my wet face. He brings his lips to mine, kissing me deeply. My body floods with a rush of warmth, and I moan into his mouth.

Oli's hands are busy, and I picture them meticulously sewing each leaf as he removes my coat and unbuttons my shirt slowly, one by one.

His hands don't stop. He moves right on to the waistband of my wet leggings, I kick off my boots as he slowly slides the tights down my legs, his hands caressing my calf as he works them off my feet.

I lean back against the door, closing my eyes, feeling his hot breath on my thighs. His thumbs hook under the bands of my underwear, and I expect to feel him pull those down, too, but a snap shocks my eyes open.

Oli's face is full of mischief as he tosses the ripped thong over his shoulder. "It was in my way."

"We can't have that," I say with a smirk.

I watch as he brings his mouth to me, the sensation soft and overwhelming. Light swirls, tiny sucks, as his other hand inches his way up my thigh, between my legs, his fingers so close to where I want them, I cry out, "Yes."

He traces the edges of me, teasing, his mouth still performing miracles. His face pulls back, and he stands, pressing me into the door, the wood cold and rough against my ass as his finger traces the edge of me. Watching my face, his eyes practically black, he slides his finger inside so slow I think my legs might buckle. He pulls his finger out, running it through the middle of me, and whispers, his breath hot on my ear, "Season of the slit."

I laugh, taking his fingers and putting them back snugly where I want them. "She doesn't know the half of it."

Pressure builds in my core as he pushes his fingers inside, his lips on my neck, his voice gruff. "I've wanted you like this all day."

His free hand moves over my breast, moving my bra aside until cold air hits the left, then the right. His mouth is hot on my nipple. The pressure is light at first, then he sucks hard, thrusting with his other hand, and I cry out.

My hands find him, and I stroke him over his jeans. "You're so hard."

"That's all for you."

"I want it now."

Oli backs up slightly, moving his hands to my ass, and I walk him backward toward his bed. I push him onto it and stretch my arms up lazily. His eyes rake over me as I reach behind my back, unhooking the clasp of my bra and letting it fall to the ground. I stand before him, completely naked, letting him look at me. "Take off your shirt."

He quickly pulls it over his head, his taut abs flexing as he does.

I bite my lip, and his pupils flare. "And your pants."

He undoes the button on his jeans. I clench in anticipation. He stands so close I can feel the heat radiating off his body, but not close enough to feel him, and takes his pants all the way off. His eyes are smoldering as they stare into mine.

Slowly, I walk over to my bag and pull out a condom. I roll it on the length of him as his Adam's apple bobs. I push him back onto the bed and turn around, giving him a nice view as I lower slowly onto him. He grabs my hips, his fingers rough as he helps guide me deeper. I move back and forth as he reaches around with one hand, swirling in just the right place.

My plan had been to go achingly slow, to make him beg for it, but his touch is sending me over the edge, and I let the wave carry me, rising and falling with it, moving up and down mimicking its pressure, until my legs are shaking and Oli cries out my name.

After we both clean up, Oli adds more wood to the fire. I lie on my side, my muscles limp in the most delicious way. Oli climbs into bed next to me. He runs a finger on my collarbone, starting at my throat and making his way out to my shoulder, his touch sending goosebumps down my arms.

His voice is soft as his eyes follow the motion of his hand. "Sorry about this morning."

"What was that about? Is it because I told Ben I was seeing someone? I meant you, and I just said it so I'd have an excuse not to go on a date with him."

"You need an excuse?"

"I…" I shake my head. It must be so nice to be a man. To not worry how your rejection of an offer like that will be taken. To not constantly contort yourself to please someone else. "While we're staying here at the retreat, yeah. I need an excuse."

Oli sighs, as he lies back on the pillow, his arms moving to cradle his head behind him, his eyes on the ceiling. "It's—" He pauses so long, his eyes focused on the skylight, that I worry for a second he's not going to continue. His gaze moves to my face. "Do you really not believe in fate?"

"What?" My brain searches our conversations, trying to pick up the thread, but I have no idea what he's talking about. In all honesty, though, I don't. Still, where is this coming from? "Why do you ask?"

"It's something you said to Ben, while I was hiding in the bathroom."

I remember now. "No. I don't."

"How can you not? How can you explain all the coincidences

that happen in life? How can you explain us meeting on the train?"

I sit up and move off the bed, grabbing one of Oli's flannels strewn on a nearby chair. Buttoning the top buttons, the fabric soft on my bare breasts, I turn to find him watching me.

"How am I supposed to talk to you when you look like that?"

I laugh and twirl, the flannel swishing around my thighs. "Oh, this old thing."

"Come on, Zara, I'm serious, though."

I sit back on the bed, crisscrossing my legs. "If fate exists and everything is supposed to happen the way it's happened, then how can you explain my dad leaving? How can you explain—" I was about to say the death of his mom, but I don't want to poke a wound that's not mine. "How can you explain all the vicious rumors about me in high school? How can you explain natural disasters and starving children? If it's all random, it makes a lot more sense."

Oli says, "You take comfort in the randomness."

I nod, because it's true. I do.

"I take comfort in the idea that the universe has my back."

"Isn't that a self-help book?"

Oli's smirk is so delicious I want to kiss it off his face. "Maybe… But there's a lot of truth to it. If it's all random, then it all feels so cruel.

"There was…" Oli traces a freckle on my knee, not meeting my eye. "You also said it was serious. Between us. Then you said it was an act."

My stomach plummets, like I'm on an elevator that lost the brakes. "It was just part of the excuse. You know we can't actually do this in real life."

This connection between us is so strong. To me it feels precious —important, even. But this thing between us can end as quickly as it started, quicker even. We aren't even supposed to be dating. We can't keep up these secret rendezvous when we go back. I don't even know where he lives. And if I want to keep my job at the gallery, which I do, I can't date him for real. Getting off the bed, I tug on my leggings, still a little wet, and cringe at the feeling.

He bites his lip. "Your job. I get it. The way my life is set up, the whole secret identity thing, it makes relationships hard. But I love being with you. What were you hoping for, with all this? What are you looking for?"

It would be so easy. To fall on this bed right now and cover him in kisses. To say we can try it. Maybe we could talk to Marlene. Maybe it wouldn't cost me my job. But it would just be prolonging the inevitable. Eventually, he will leave. Everyone does.

I grab my bra off the ground and shove it into the waistband of the leggings. "At the moment, the only thing I'm looking for is that broken thong."

Oli hops off the bed, stepping into some boxers, and comes over to me, grasping each of my arms in his hands. "You don't have to go."

I look deep into his slate-gray eyes, and the hope that's nestled deep inside me sparks. I can't squash that, like I did with Ben. And I can't give into it either. We can't date in secret until he leaves. I give him a kiss on the cheek and take a big step back. "I do."

CHAPTER 24
TEN DAYS LEFT OF THE RETREAT

Over the next week, I throw myself into my painting. It's not that I avoid Oli necessarily, but I don't seek him out either. I want to be more prepared for our next group critique, since there's only a few left before we leave. And I'm not sure what Oli and I are supposed to do. I feel like we're on the precipice of something that if we keep going, barreling forward like there are absolutely no consequences to our actions, it won't end well. For me especially.

With a blanket on my lap, I'm working on the flesh tones of the painting, Spotify playing a *made for you* playlist. The peach on the palette runs out. I grab the white paint tube to make some more, but as I try to squeeze the last bit out, nothing comes. I roll the little metal tube, like trying to force out the last of the toothpaste, but it doesn't work either. When I lived here before, there was a small art store in town. I was there nearly every day, wandering the aisles, drooling over all the materials and dreaming of all the things I could make with them. Hopefully, it's still there.

Throwing on my coat, hat and scarf, I head to the lodge, keys in hand. Alice runs down the steps as I open the driver's side door, her blonde hair billowing behind her.

Her eyes are a bit wild when she asks, "Are you going to town?"

"Yes. Do you—"

Before I can finish, Alice jumps in the passenger side. She's fully buckled, hands in her lap and waiting for us to leave, as I shut my door.

I turn the key in the ignition, the car purrs to life, and I glance at Alice. She's biting her lip and wringing her hands in her lap. I ask, "Is everything okay?"

"Yes. Yep. Just need a few things, that's all."

The drive to town is quick. I park near the general store.

"I'll leave the car unlocked and we can meet back here, if you want?"

"Is there a coffee shop nearby?" Alice says, her hands still fiddling.

"Umm. Let's see. There's a bookstore down the street with a café inside, I think. Story Club Books."

"Let's meet there," Alice says over her shoulder, hurrying into the general store.

I walk down the street to the art store, the air filled with the salty tang of the ocean, my feet remembering the way more than my mind. Nan's Art Stuff is still there and looks exactly the same. Same big gold cursive letters painted on the window, a little worse for wear. As I open the door, bells jingle, and the sound is also exactly the same.

"Welcome in," calls a voice.

When I come around the large display of Klutz kits, two women come into view, leaning on the counter knitting with chunky, hot-pink yarn, one with silver hair, one with white, catching the overhead lights making them look like they are glowing.

The silver-haired one looks up with a smile, her eyes peeking out from behind her heavy wall of bangs. "Need help finding anything?"

I shake my head and start browsing as the two women chat.

Most of what they say goes without me noticing as I run my hand over beautiful brushes that I don't really need. Then one of them says, "I just know they're OG."

"You're nuts," the other says. "Why would OG put stickers up in our dinky little town."

"Hey, Fortune Falls may be little, but it is not dinky."

"People were pretty upset about them either way. Don't see how it would matter if it's OG or not."

My stomach twists, and I pop around the shelf and say without thinking, "They're upset about some stickers?"

The silver-haired woman nods, needles clacking away. "Private property, respect, all that jazz."

"Huh," I say. "Don't they just peel off, though?"

She shrugs. "People like to get upset about things they don't understand. Art will always be a target. What are you here for today? Let me come help."

"No. I'm good." I wave and duck back into the aisle, picking up the white paint I need and a few other things that I don't, still thinking about what the woman said. Why would people care if there were some absolutely stunning stickers strategically placed on what before were complete eyesores?

After handing the women my money, I head to the bookstore. I turn the corner, and my gaze is drawn toward the water, the clouds a dark gray, the sun trying to push through making a golden lining around them. It's gorgeous and makes me want to keep going, head straight for the beach and stroll along the shore. Maybe Alice would like to go for a walk.

I climb the steps to the bookstore, each one painted like a different book, and open the red door. I noticed when I was in town before, but the transformation this store has undergone since I lived here is really something. What used to be musty and stuffy is now light and airy with the smells of pumpkin spice permeating the space. The café in the corner is buzzing, a couple sitting at one of the circular tables holding hands across their lattes, a mother with a toddler, a massive cookie crumbling out of his mouth, but no sign of Alice.

I order a black coffee to go, but then the cozy atmosphere makes me rethink my choice. "Actually, can you make that a mocha please, with extra whip cream?"

The chestnut-haired woman behind the counter with stunning blue eyes smiles like we're sharing a secret. "Absolutely."

Once I have my drink in hand, I take a seat at a table by the window. Alice comes out of a door in the back marked restroom, her fringed purse clutched tightly in her hands. I stand to wave, and she sits across from me.

"Can I buy you a coffee?" I ask.

"Sure. A triple Americano," Alice replies, her eyes focused out the window on the waves in the distance.

I stand to get it for her, but her hand flies to my arm, her eyes wide.

"Shit. I can't have that."

"Okay," I say slowly.

"A tea. Anything herbal."

"Sure." It's later in the day, maybe she won't sleep if she has caffeine now. Or is there another reason she might be avoiding coffee suddenly?

When I bring a peppermint tea back to the table, Alice mutters her thanks, still staring out the window.

"Do you feel like going for a walk on the beach? The—"

"Yep," she says, standing, grabbing the tea. "Moving is a great idea."

We walk down the block past the tall grass that separates the concrete world from the beach. The sand shifts under my boots as we walk along the shore, the waves crashing with such force it feels like the ground should give out.

Alice puts her hand in her purse and pulls it out again. She repeats the motion every few minutes like she's checking if something is still there.

"Alice, are you okay?"

She crosses her arms tightly, stopping, her bright-blue eyes brimming with tears. "I fucked up."

I'm not the best with crying, unless it's mine. Actually, even when it's mine. "I'm sure whatever it is, we can fix it."

"I think I'm pregnant."

My eyebrows rise all the way up to the bottom of my baby bangs. "Oh."

Alice is pregnant? How? I mean, I know how. But who? She said before this she was at a female commune. So it must be someone at the retreat. My stomach turns uneasily as for a split second I wonder if she might be fooling around with Oli. I quickly push the thought away. There's no way. Not only is he not like that, he wouldn't have had time.

"This was not in my plan. I'm on the pill."

I immediately fly into problem solving mode. "Look there's no reason to spiral until you're sure. When was your last period?"

"Five weeks ago."

"Five weeks. That's not too bad. You could just be late."

She shakes her head. "I'm on the pill. I'm literally never late."

"Let's go get you a pregnancy test and find out."

Alice starts walking again. "That's what I got at the store."

"Perfect. We'll head back to the cabins and take it. Then you can make a plan—"

"I already took it."

"What did it say?"

Tears roll down Alice's face at a rapid pace. "I can't look."

I stop and put a hand on her arm, leading her to a large fallen log. We both sit, staring at the waves. She hands me her purse, her finger-nails flecked with paint. That's unusual for her. Her hands are usually photographer-clean. Maybe she's been trying new mediums, too.

"Will you look and let me know what it says?"

The suede is soft in my hand as I open the flap. My fingers find the plastic stick, and I pull it out. In the little window, I make out one dark-pink line and a second light-pink line. Right next to the results, in case there was any confusion, is a key. *Not pregnant—one line. Pregnant—two lines.*

Alice is searching my face, her eyes moving rapidly.

"You're pregnant."

She rips the test out of my hand and a laugh escapes her, small at first then louder, until it turns into a small sob. "Fuck,'" she says quietly.

We sit in silence for a few minutes until Alice stands and chucks the test toward the sea, screaming, "Fuck!"

"Alice." I run after the test before a wave can take it.

When I head back, Alice is shaking her head and walking back and forth in front of the log. She puts a hand up. "I don't want to see that."

"We can throw it away, but I don't want some sea creature choking on it."

Alice stops pacing, her eyes filling with tears. "I didn't even think of the animals. I'm going to be a terrible mother."

I put my hands on Alice's thin arms. "If this is what you want, I'm sure you'll be a great mother. But if this is not what you want, it's still early."

She collapses onto my shoulder.

I wrap my arms around her and smooth her hair down her back. "You don't have to decide now. Have you eaten?"

Her voice is muffled as she says, "No."

"Let's get some food. Everything is more manageable after French fries."

We head to the Vern and take two open seats at the bar. There're a few people playing pool, but other than that the bar is pretty empty today, the soft murmur of the news droning on the television hanging in the corner. I order a basket of fries and a Diet Coke. Alice orders soda water with lemon, and I wonder if that means she wants to keep the baby? I'm dying to ask who the father is, but I also don't want to overstep. Doing the math, though, if her last period was five weeks ago then she probably got pregnant three weeks ago, which is just about when the retreat started.

Alice excuses herself to the restroom to clean up, and I sip my soda water, telling myself Alice's love life is none of my business. The news shifts to a picture of one of OG's early pieces. The bartender sets the fries in front of me. "Thanks. Hey, could you turn this up?"

With a nod, he cranks it up with the remote. The shiny-haired newscaster is mid-sentence.

"OG has become a household name through pieces like this and this." The screen shifts to some of his more famous works. "But the pieces that were unveiled today in New York, Detroit, Los Angeles, San Francisco, Portland, Seattle and a number of small towns along the coast might go down as his most talked about."

The camera pans to a derelict building in downtown LA, on the side of it is a small painting of the little girl in a fifties dress that Oli always uses in his art. She has a can of spray paint in her hand. There is a large faux crack in the facade of the building, and painted in the middle is a beach in a hyper-realistic style. It pans to the next one that's on the side of another abandoned building in what looks like SE Portland. The girl is the same, but the painting in the middle of the crack is of a river running through some scattered trees.

Alice comes out of the bathroom and sits next to me quietly. The screen scrolls to more and more, all across the country. Then it scrolls to a very familiar building. It's the abandoned warehouse up the road, on the edge of Fortune Falls. Painted between the cracks is a mossy forest.

The bartender stares at the screen. "Shit."

"What?" Alice asks me.

"That one's in town," I say. "It's Ben's family's property."

CHAPTER 25

The news shifts to another story, but the bar is full of chatter about the piece on Ben's property. When did Oli paint it? Who did he paint it with? Did some of his team come to town? They must have, there's no way it was a one-person job. But why wouldn't he tell me? Or ask me to help?

We drive back to the cabins in silence. Alice seems lost in thought, and I am as well. Why wouldn't he at least tell me what was going on?

When I get out of the car, Marlene comes running down the stairs, her phone held high in her hand. "Have you seen this?"

I know she means the graffiti, but I glance at the tiny screen just to confirm. It's the one closest to us lit up on her phone. "I just saw it on the news."

Ben steps out of the lodge, rubbing a hand over his face.

Marlene lowers her phone and her voice. "Walk with me."

We head down the trail, but I can feel Ben's eyes on us the whole time.

"Did you know about this?" Marlene's eyes search my face.

I shake my head. "No."

She huffs out an exasperated breath, it comes out as a visible white puff of air in the chilly afternoon. "Why wouldn't he tell us?

We're at a retreat. He's the artist we're supposed to be learning from, and he does this massive piece without a word to any of us. No inside scoop. No asking us for assistance. Meanwhile, *here* he's fiddling with fucking leaves."

It makes sense that she's upset. Being included in a history-making piece like this, well, it would've been extraordinary. But instead, we're still on the outside looking in.

"Talk to him."

A headache starts to pound in the base of my skull. "What am I supposed to say?"

"Ask him when his next big piece like this is and make sure he includes us. The retreat ends in two weeks. Maybe we could do one as the send-off. The grand finale."

Marlene knows as well as I do that he only does a large-scale piece like this once a year or so, and one on this scale in so many cities across the country, well, it's never been done.

Marlene takes me by the shoulder and directs me toward Oli's cabin, giving me a little nudge. "Go, now. We have to have something to tell the other artists."

TRUDGING down the trail toward Oli's cabin, I go over possibilities of what I might say. By the time I reach his door, the sun starting its descent below the menacing clouds, I'm no closer to figuring it out.

I knock lightly but get no answer. So, I take a deep breath, close my eyes, and knock a little louder just as the rain begins to fall. I hear rustling inside, but am still surprised when the door swings open and Oli stands before me in low-hanging gray sweats and nothing else. His hair is mussed. He's blinking like he just woke up, with a sleepy lazy smile on his face.

"Hey, I was just dreaming about you."

I laugh. "I bet you say that to all the girls."

His eyes narrow, and his sleepy smile morphs into a frown. "I really don't." He moves his body to the side. "Come in."

I step in the cozy cabin. The leaves are gone off his little desk, and in their place are patches of moss. I scan the room for evidence of the latest piece, but I don't see anything. "Were you napping?"

Oli sits on the edge of the bed. "Yeah. Late night."

He pats the bed next to him, but I shake my head and pace the room, still not sure how to handle this.

"What's up?"

I lean against the small counter that acts as a makeshift kitchen. "Your latest piece is impressive."

Oli squeezes the blanket under his hand. "Thanks."

"Why didn't you tell me about it?"

He shakes his head, his tousled hair falling on his forehead. "What?"

"I've told you all about my reflection painting—why wouldn't you talk to me about this? It's massive. How many cities are involved, even?"

"Twenty-three."

"Damn." Then under my breath, I mutter, "that's so cool." Because it is. If I didn't know Oli, if I wasn't feeling so betrayed by being left out, I'd be all over this. Sharing the pics. I'd be at the site right now taking my own pictures.

Oli crosses the space between us, the sound of the rain on the skylight echoing through the small cabin. He puts his hands on my hips and hoists me up on the counter. Instinctively, I open my legs so he can step in between them. He runs his hands down my back. "It's just work."

I rest my hands on his shoulders. "But it's not. It's a cultural phenomenon. It's your passion." He flinches when I say that word, and I ask, "Isn't it?"

Oli buries his head on my shoulder and mumbles into my neck, "You're my passion."

I laugh, but a pulse of want shoots to my thighs. He leans in and kisses me, and despite all the feelings I have about being forgotten, and my fear that at any moment he will leave me, my need for him overpowers it.

Oli tugs my cardigan off my shoulders and pulls my shirt up as I raise my hands high to help. Once my shirt is tossed across the room, he unclasps my bra, letting it fall to the ground, the cold air and his gaze instantly making my nipples hard.

"I have missed you," he says in a low voice before taking my breast in his mouth. His fingers slide under the waistband of my leggings, and I cry out as his cold finger finds just the right spot and starts to swirl.

He picks me up by the ass, my legs wrapped around his waist, and brings me to the bed. Slowly, he slides my leggings off, taking my underwear with them. He runs his hand down the length of my body, from collarbone to my calf, then gets up to grab a condom from the bedside drawer. He mumbles, "Gotta look in the bathroom."

I lie on his bed, waiting. Suddenly, feeling naked and exposed, I get under the covers, sitting up, drawing my knees in and pulling the comforter up to cover my chest. All the feelings I thought I could push aside come bubbling to the surface, making my throat feel tight.

Oli emerges from the bathroom, foil wrapper in hand. His triumphant expression falls when he sees me. "Zara."

I shake my head and feel like an absolute idiot as pressure pricks the back of my eyes. I will not cry. "I just... Why didn't you talk to me about it?"

He sits on the bed next to me and puts a tentative hand on my back. "I love art. I do. You're right, it's my passion. But if I'm totally honest, I'm more into the leaf piece I made than the one I helped put up last night."

"Helped? Isn't it your piece? Why wouldn't you let us in on it? You have a group of eager artists wanting to learn from you, to be exposed to this new medium, and you shut us all out."

Oli doesn't meet my eye as his hands move from my back to my lap.

The paint flecks on Alice's hands come to mind.

"Oh my god. You didn't shut us all out. You just shut *me* out."

"That's not entirely true."

I throw the blanket off and get up off the bed, hands on my hips, a burning in my stomach so hot I don't even register the chill. "Did Alice help?"

He nods, his lips in a firm line.

"Who else?" I demand. "Who else helped? Was it just me and Marlene left out?"

There's a knock at the door so loud it shakes the walls.

"Oliver Grant. Fortune Falls Sheriff department."

My mouth falls open as my hands fly to my breasts.

Oli hops off the bed, tossing me my leggings and underwear, as I dive across the room for my bra, but for the life of me, I can't find the shirt. Oli's already tugged his on.

A knock comes again. "Son, are you in there?"

Oli's already deep voice gets an octave lower as he says, "Just a second, officer."

I mouth, *Where the fuck is my shirt?*

Oli goes toward the small dresser and gets out a flannel, tossing it at me. He points to the bathroom. I take my armful of clothing and close the door, turning the knob so it doesn't make a sound as it latches.

I hear the front door open as I try to silently get dressed.

The voices are muffled, so I put my ear to the wood.

"Have you ever seen this building?"

"Yeah, the train drives past it on the way to Seattle."

"No other time than on the train."

There's a beat of silence.

The officer says, "You're going to need to come with us, son."

"Why?"

This time the silence stretches like hot glass, molten and dangerous. The tinny sounds of a phone speaker breaks it. I lie on the ground, peeking out the crack between the door and the floor. The sheriff is standing there in a Fortune Falls issued rain slicker, his hat dripping on the hardwood floor. Two uniformed men are on the porch behind him. He's holding a phone in Oli's direction, a video playing on it.

"Is this you, son?"

Oli's jaw clenches. "I want my lawyer."

"That can be arranged. Cuff 'im."

Cuff him?

I don't think—hopping up off the floor—I run out the door. "Is he under arrest?"

If the sheriff is surprised to have someone pop out of the bathroom, he doesn't show it on his face.

"He is."

The sheriff moves to the side. One of the other officers comes forward, swiftly moving Oli's hand behind his back and clicking the handcuffs. The officer lets him slip on his Vans as he mutters about Oli's right to remain silent.

Oli looks me in the eye, his gaze steady and calm. "It'll be fine. Tell Marlene to call my lawyer."

I follow them out to the porch. The rain falls in great sheets. I watch as they march Oli out the door, down the trail, and to the waiting cop car at the furthest part of the trail it will fit with lights flashing.

CHAPTER 26

After slipping back into my boots and shrugging on my sweater, I run to Marlene's cabin. The windows glow, and as I get closer, I can hear soft music playing and the sound of muffled voices. I don't want to knock. I don't want to interrupt but I have to.

Taking a deep breath, I close my eyes and rap on the door lightly. A minute passes. Marlene comes to the door, a large sweater on with bare legs, her bob uncharacteristically mussed. Her sharp eyes give me a once over. "Ashford, what is it?"

"I need the number of Oli's lawyer. He's been arrested."

"What?"

The door opens a little wider, but Marlene quickly closes it behind her all the way, stepping out onto the porch. Underneath her sweater, she's wearing what looks like a man's undershirt. Romantic music is playing from inside. Marlene has a man in there, and my guess is Miguel. With everything she said about not getting involved with the artists, I should be outraged. It seems neither of us listened to that rule. But right now, all that matters is getting help for Oli.

"I'm not sure. They had footage of him making the big piece at the warehouse in town."

Marlene's hand flies to her mouth with a gasp. "Video?"

I nod.

Marlene runs to her phone. "I'll call his lawyer, you go to the station and try to bail him out. Use the gallery card."

Yes. A plan. Perfect.

Stopping first at my cabin, I change into dry clothes, find my rain jacket, and grab my purse. The drive to town is slow, the windshield wipers hardly keeping up with the torrential rain. My thoughts swirl like paint running down the drain. Why wouldn't he include me in the project? I know I spent the last week sort of avoiding him, but he could've tried harder to get to me. He could've texted more, or come over. But he was clearly too busy planning this, with Alice.

Are they seeing each other? Is the baby his?

I turn up the radio, trying to drown out my thoughts. It doesn't work. The thoughts just pop up louder and louder, until I pull into the small parking lot at the station. Taking a moment to check my face in the mirror, my mascara is smudged under my eyes, and I wipe it away. I put my hair up in a ponytail and swipe a coat of lipstick on. I can do this. I can bail Oli out of jail.

The station is quiet until my boots clack on the tile floor. Golden light fills the room, illuminating the tan tile. If it wasn't a police station, it'd almost be cozy. There's a small wooden bench across from a desk with a little hanging sign that says reception.

There is not a person at the desk, but instead a little silver bell just like at the Inn. I so wish I was there, checking into a room, going to sink into a nice hot bath. And not here trying to bail out the man I'm what...seeing? Breaking up with? Was completely betrayed by, maybe on a bigger level than I'm even aware of?

I ding the bell, the sound echoing through the halls.

An older man in a brown uniform comes over to the desk. "How can I help you?"

"I need to bail out Oliver Grant."

"Ahhh." He runs a mouse back and forth over a foam pad. The

monitor that looks like it belongs in the last century illuminates his face and reflects on his glasses. "I don't see his name here."

"That's not possible. Is there another station in town?"

The man shakes his head. "Could be he's not processed yet. Have a seat." He motions to the bench. "I'll let you know when his name shows up."

The wooden bench is hard and cold, which so perfectly mirrors my mood I almost relish the wooden slats digging into my back. This is a disaster. All of it.

I get out my phone, scrolling to distract myself. Swiping past a serene woman walking a wooded path. That's what this time should've been for me. Quiet contemplation. Extreme productivity. Not falling in love.

The phone slips and falls to the bench as that last word repeats in my mind. Love? Am I in love with Oli? My body responds to him, and when I'm not with him, my mind is.

I turn my attention back to my phone, typing in the search bar OG. The first thing that comes up is a montage of his pieces. They're all so good. Dynamic and colorful, but there's something else to them. It's like a little piece of Oli is in each of them. It's pure magic. The next video that comes up is grainy, and I cover my mouth as I recognize it. It's the video that was on the sheriff's phone.

It shows Oli. Even in the low light, the video pixelating to compensate, its undeniably Oli, running in front of the camera, a giant bag at his side. He throws the bag down and yanks out a spray paint can, getting right to work. A figure next to him in a black beanie gets out a can as well. There are two more shady figures, but none of their faces ever come into focus like Oli's at the start of the video.

How is this out already? And who took it? The footage looks like it's taken from a far-off point. It's clear no one in the video knew this footage was being taken. Right? Unless one of them set it up and leaked it all over the internet.

The hours tick by. My eyes grow heavy. Eventually, using my

purse as a pillow, I curl up on the hard bench, just to be more comfortable.

A BOOMING LAUGH and the strong smell of coffee wakes me. I sit up, wiping my face, and the kink in my neck twinges in fierce protest.

Making my way over to the counter, I ring the ridiculous bell again. A different officer comes over to help me, this time a woman with a sensible light-brown bob and a steaming mug of coffee that makes my mouth water. "You're awake."

My cheeks heat, and I offer a small smile. "I'm just checking on my friend, his name is Oliver Grant."

She sets down her mug and starts typing, quick and furious. "Yeah, his lawyer showed up a while ago. Huh...Give me a second." She turns, taking her coffee with her. "Bob."

His lawyer already showed up? He must've walked right past me, and I slept through it.

The woman comes back a few moments later. "They should be leaving soon."

My brows scrunch together. "Did his lawyer post bail?"

The woman checks the screen again. "No charges were pressed."

"Oh."

The wooden double doors open, and a very polished looking man in a crisp suit walks out talking with an officer. Oli lags behind them, dark circles under his eyes, his jaw clenched so hard it looks like he might pull a muscle. I rush forward at the sight of him.

Once I'm closer, I hear the lawyer say, "We understand, officer. Thank you."

"Oli." Without thinking, I reach forward and wrap my arms around his waist. He does not return the hug, just stands there.

I let go and fall into step next to him as we all head out into the parking lot. The morning sky is pink and light blue, the air so cold our breath is visible. The lawyer is tapping on his phone with impressive speed.

I brush my hand against Oli's. "Do you want a ride?"

Oli shakes his head, still not meeting my eye. "No, I can get a ride with Nathan."

"Okay. They dropped the charges completely?" I ask, my brain having a hard time catching up.

Nathan puts his phone in his pocket. "They didn't have a leg to stand on. Aside from all the permits, that video could've been anyone. But in the spirit of keeping everything friendly, we have agreed to leave."

"Leave?"

"Yes. We'll pack up and head out." Nathan's phone lights up in his pocket. He holds up a finger. "I have to take this. Oli, I'll meet you in the car."

"You can't leave. What about the rest of the retreat?"

Oli looks physically pained. He sighs. "There's a clause in my contract about legal troubles. Plus, pretty sure someone breached the NDA. It's best for everyone if I go."

"What? Who? What about the critique today? What about everyone's work? They're so excited to show you. They're so excited to work with you on the collaboration. How can you let everyone down like this?"

"Me? I'm letting everyone down?" Oli raises his hands to the air. "What about you, Zara?"

Even though I have no idea what he's talking about, guilt sinks in my stomach. "Me?"

His jaw is clenched. "Yes. *You.* How did the cops get the video?"

I'm more in need of caffeine than I thought, because I am not keeping up with Oli's logic. I shake my head, wrapping my sweater tighter around my torso. "I have no idea."

"Really?" He laughs, but there's not a speck of joy in it. "How did you know Alice helped if you weren't there?"

It all makes sense now. It hits me like a physical blow. My mouth falls open. "You think I made the video? You think I put it all over the internet? You think I breached the NDA and sent it to the cops?"

My stomach is full of lead. My mouth is dry. How can Oli possibly think that? How could he think I would betray him on that level after what we shared?

"What I can't figure out is why? More publicity for the gallery? Did the news pay for the video?"

I shake my head, each of his words making my stomach sink lower and lower. How can he think I would do that? I thought we knew each other better than that, but now it seems we don't know each other at all. I look up into his eyes, more blue than gray in the morning light, and despite my best efforts, my own eyes brim with tears. It occurs to me maybe he thinks I'd break his trust like that because he's done the same to me.

Swallowing the tears down, I ask, "Are you sleeping with Alice?"

Oli takes a step back. "Is that why you followed us? Was it just jealousy?"

Nathan presses the horn for one quick beep.

"I have to go."

Oli's tall lanky figure makes quick strides toward Nathan's Tesla. He slams the door, and I feel it in my soul. My shoulders slump, but I force them back, head held high as I walk to my car in case Oli's watching. As soon as I'm alone, I crumple like a wadded-up tissue. The tears flow unbidden. How can I have misjudged him so utterly and completely?

CHAPTER 27
NINE DAYS LEFT IN THE RETREAT?

Once my tears have dried up, I grab a coffee to go from the bookstore café. I'm not ready to face Marlene. The thought of seeing Oli again right now makes me so nervous and angry I'm shaking. I take my coffee to my favorite beach, Short Sands.

The beach is empty, just a couple surfers out in the tide. I can't help but think of when I brought Oli here. His face lit up with excitement and his eyes so tender. So far from how he looked at me today.

How can he think I would do this? We've only known each other a short time, but I really thought he knew me better than that. It felt like we had a deep connection. Shit, just yesterday I thought we might be falling in love. And now he thinks I went behind his back and tried to fuck up his career, get him arrested, ruin his life.

The waves rolling in and out with rhythmic consistency doesn't do anything to ease my mind today. When I get back in the car to drive back to the cabins, I'm just as devastated as before. This gut-wrenching ache feels permanent. It feels like an unfortunate metamorphosis. I may never feel the same again.

When I park the car, Marlene runs out of the lodge like she

was sitting at the door waiting for me. And it's entirely possible she was. "Oli left. With his lawyer. They're gone. We need to get him back."

I suppress a sigh. "I'll look at our contract with him, but he said he has a clause about legal problems and breach of NDA."

Marlene's forehead smooths out, and her eyes close for what feels like a long time. "Fuck," she says, so quietly it's hardly audible. "This is a disaster."

Remaining silent seems the best option, so I nod solemnly.

"What are we going to do?" Marlene screeches. Apparently, silence was not the correct option.

"The group critique is in an hour, I think we should go ahead with it. We can explain that Oli had some personal business he needed to attend to."

Marlene bites her lip. "They paid a lot of money to be here. What if they all ask for refunds?"

I look off in the direction of Oli's cabin. I can't believe he's gone. I can't believe he'd leave it like this and not say goodbye.

Marlene flails her hands next to me. "Are you even listening?"

I sigh, unable to hold it in. My entire body sags with it. "If they ask for refunds, then we give them their money back. What else can we do? I'll grab my painting and set up the room for the critique."

Marlene is muttering something and stomping up the steps back into the lodge as I make my way down the trail.

The wind is bitter against my cheeks, and it feels like the weather may turn on us again. Only this time, there will be no cozy shacking up in hotel rooms, or painting each other's backs. Before I go to my cabin, I have to see for myself that he's really, truly gone.

Oli's cabin looks the same from the outside. String lights on the porch, a soft glow coming from inside. Maybe he didn't leave after all.

I open the door, the hinges creaking, my breath in my chest as

I take in the cabin. The lamp is on, but the room is empty. Bed made. Desk clear, all the moss that was on it before now neatly tucked into the trash. One sketch is left hanging on the wall. I cross the room, tears welling in my eyes as I see what the drawing is.

The hinges squeak, and I jump, grabbing the paper off the wall and shoving it in my pocket.

Alice, her hair hanging in long waves framing her pale face, covers her mouth as she looks at me.

My nerves turn to steel along with the tone in my voice. "He's gone."

She sighs.

I can't help myself. "I'm surprised you didn't go with him."

"Me?" Her hand drops to her chest. "Why would I? Should I leave? Are the cops looking for me, too?"

I shake my head. "No. I don't think so. I just meant, given your relationship with Oli..."

She laughs. "My relationship? You were the one sleeping with him."

My brain is stumbling, trying to keep up. "You knew Oli and I were..."

Alice quirks up an eyebrow, like she can't quite believe I'm even asking. "Um, yeah. Your googly eyes at each other and sneaking off at the same time was a tad obvious."

The blood rushes from my head, my nerves of steel dissolving. "Do you think everyone knows?"

Alice shrugs. "Anyone paying attention."

Alice turns to leave and then swings her body back abruptly. "Wait...Why did you think Oli and I had a relationship?"

My eyes flick to her stomach as a pure reaction, but I quickly look away. Not quick enough for Alice not to see it, though.

Her eyes go wide. "Oh my god. You think Oli is my baby daddy? How can you think that with how he looks at you?"

"But he took you to work on the graffiti piece."

"I just ran into him on his way out last night. He *had* to take me. I practically forced him." Alice shakes her head. "How could you think that of me? Of him?"

Alice storms off, each stair shuddering under the force of her footfalls. I've done things in my life I'm not proud of. Ran out on an engagement, left a loving group of people that had graciously let me stay in their home, left my best friend without saying good-bye. But I have never felt as bad about myself as I do right now. How could I think that of Oli? He must've been so hurt.

But he also thought some pretty terrible things about me.

His words at the bar when we were stranded ring through my head. *We can't change it.* It's all out there now.

Shit.

I head back to my cabin, grab my painting and hurry to the lodge. The critique starts soon, and I need to make sure things are set up.

Everything else will have to wait.

———

GENEVIEVE AND ANDRE are the first ones to set up their work at the critique. They have several paintings and some sketches of different ways they could use them for large-scale installations. When they notice me, Genevieve looks at me with so much genuine concern in her gaze, I instinctively take a step back.

"Are you okay?" she asks softly.

"I'm fine." I am absolutely not fine. But it's important they all think I am. "Why do you ask?"

"Dear, you have a little bit of mascara under your left eye." I swipe at it as she continues. "And of course we saw the news about Oli. Is he okay?"

"He's good. Fine. But he did have to leave to sort some things out."

I excuse myself to the bathroom, not waiting for Genevieve's response to the news. Staring at myself in the mirror, I fix the mascara smear under my eye, but it does little to help my appearance. Dark circles rim my brown eyes that have a lifeless quality to them this morning. Like my heartbreak is leaking out my irises. Or like I slept for very few hours on a stiff wooden bench. Or both.

Pulling out the scrap of paper from my pocket, I smooth it out. It's a delicate and intricately drawn sketch of the photo Oli took of me on the train. The lines of my face are confident, precise, and as much as pencil can look loving, this is it. It's intimacy in sketch form. Picturing him studying his phone, sketching this, breaks my heart all the more. How could I have accused him of sleeping with Alice? What is wrong with me?

There's a knock on the bathroom door, and Marlene's shrill voice follows. "Ashford, we need to start now."

Quickly, I splash some water on my face and am drying it as I open the door. "Ready."

Marlene's lips purse. "Are you sure about that? You don't want to freshen your makeup?"

All my makeup is back in my cabin. There's no time. "Nope. I'm good. Let's get started."

The critique begins with everyone looking at the work first. Miguel has presented a clay figure. A nude. Classic, beautiful, and the face is similar in a way to Marlene's. Did she sit for this? Them together in her cabin flashes through my mind. I was so focused on helping Oli, it didn't fully sink in, but something must be going on between them, despite Marlene's rules about not dating the artists.

Louise has another nature inspired drawing, this time an up close hyper-realistic rendering of tree bark. At first glance, it's very tame, almost boring. But when you peer in, there are figures in intimate arrangements hidden in the shapes of the bark.

Alice has presented a photo on her laptop again, this time of… I do a double take, but it is. It's a portrait of Miguel. Nude on the dock, hunched in on himself. Have they been spending time together, too? Or is it purely an artistic arrangement? Could he be… No. That's not possible. He's clearly seeing Marlene. Looking toward where he is in the room, I find him and Alice standing together appraising my painting, his hand on the small of her back. He wouldn't be sleeping with them both.

Marlene gets to the laptop and backs up like the screen is electrified. She claps her hands. "Okay, let's discuss."

Louise wags her finger in the air. "We have to wait for Oli."

Marlene shoots daggers in my direction.

I clear my throat and address the group. "Oli isn't coming."

Louise's cheeks fall, all the joy sucked out of her face. "What?"

"Some of you already know, Oli put up a large-scale piece and footage of him doing it was leaked to the press. He has to attend to some matters."

"When will he be back?" Louise asks.

I swallow hard. This can't be happening. I'm definitely going to lose my job over this. "He won't be."

There are frowns all around the room.

"But he's the artist-in-residence," Genevieve insists.

"Yes, this is true." I need to save this situation. "We all have such a special bond that Oli's helped us create. Let's carry it on. We can move each other's work forward and plan an amazing collaboration…"

"Oli won't be part of the collab?" Genevieve asks, her arms wrapped tightly around her chest.

I shake my head.

Genevieve and Andre whisper to each other, while Marlene gives me a pleading look to fix it. Solutions run through my mind. Could we get another artist? No, not in time and the fee we'd have to pay another artist wouldn't make it a sensible option. Could we get Oli to come back? Maybe.

Genevieve speaks up. "We're leaving."

"No," Marlene screams. "You can't"

"I assure you, we can," Andre says in his gravelly voice.

"Give me a day," I say with strength I do not feel.

All eyes turn to me, and I'm suddenly not so sure.

"If I can't get Oli to return, then you're all welcome to leave, with full refunds." What am I even saying? Full refunds. I want to scoop up the words and shove them back in my mouth. But it's already done. So, I smile confidently.

We finish the critique, but I can't focus. All I can think about is how am I going to get Oli to come back?

CHAPTER 28

As soon as the critique is over, Marlene grabs my arm, her eyes on fire. "What were you thinking? We can't give everyone full refunds."

"I know, trust me, I know. We won't have to," I say with confidence, despite the fact I have no idea if this will work.

Marlene's lips purse into a stern from "If we do, it's your job."

She walks off without a look back.

It shouldn't come as a surprise. And yet it still is. I nod once and head out the door, my heart hammering in my chest. Tilting my face into the falling rain, just to feel something other than this overwhelming sense of panic, I close my eyes.

The little golf cart engine approaches, but I still don't open my eyes.

"You okay?"

It's Ben, his face full of concern, and for a brief moment, I remember when we were close. When I used to tell him everything.

I shake my head. "Not really, no."

He gets out of the golf cart and offers me his hand. "Let's get out of here."

"I can't... I have to..."

"You look like you're about to snap. I've seen that look before and then no one heard from you for ten years. Nothing is so important it can't wait an hour. Come on."

We lock eyes, and I take his hand, his palm rough with calluses. "Okay."

He leads me to his truck and opens the door for me. I get in, feeling the smooth leather seats under my palms. What am I doing? I should be figuring out how to get Oli to come back, not going on a field trip with Ben.

He gets in and turns the engine, the cab filling with twangy guitar and a soulful singer lamenting on lost love. How more on the nose can you get, Universe?

Ben pulls out onto the dirt trail.

"Where are we going?"

His lips twitch up at the side. "Trivia night."

I groan. "No. I'm not in the mood to see a bunch of people right now. I can't."

"Come on. It'll be fun. Do you remember fun?" He smirks.

"Everyone will be talking about the graffiti. They'll all think I had something to do with it."

"Did you?" His eyes shift over to me quickly then back to the road.

Saying no almost feels disingenuous, because if Oli had asked me, I absolutely would've helped. But he didn't ask, so I tell the truth. "No."

Ben's smile is back. I want to curl up in my seat and disappear. He parks across the street, and we make our way into the Vern. The blast of warm air that greets me as I walk through the heavy wooden door is stifling. Friends instantly surround Ben.

Nick is at his side first, slapping him on the back. "Hey, man. I see you got my message. Nailed him."

Nick slurs every other word, clearly having been at the bar for a bit.

Ben shushes him and makes eyes in my direction. I quickly

look away so they won't catch me eavesdropping. Then my arm is yanked, and I'm wrapped in a soft hug.

"You're here!" Meg squeals. "You have to be on my team."

I follow her to her table, filled with some of the girls from her bridal party, and take the chair closest to Meg. I try pretending like I can fade into the background and the girls won't notice me, but no luck there.

Bridget leans forward. "Where's your boyfriend?"

I half smile and accept the beer Meg poured me from the pitcher. "I don't have a boyfriend."

"Ahh," Bridget sneers. "Now that he's a fugitive he's not your boyfriend? What happened to stand by your man and all that."

I take a large gulp of my beer and shoot daggers at Bridget. "He was never my man. I never said that."

Bridget laughs, so shrill it stabs behind my eyes. "That's true. Didn't stand by Ben either. Left him high and dry, ring in hand."

I stand, pushing my chair back with my legs, my blood boiling. That's it. I'm done. "Bridget, what is your problem with me? What did I ever do to you?"

Bridget stands, too. "I'm just sick of seeing you use people. Chew them up and spit them out."

Meg gets between us, her short stature not breaking our eye contact. "Come on. Let's all just sit."

"Who?" I demand. "Who did I chew up and spit out?"

She rolls her eyes as if the answer is so obvious it pains her to reply. "Ben. You should've seen him after you left. He was..."

Some of the fire leaves my chest in a puff of smoke. "I couldn't marry him. I didn't love him anymore. Wouldn't that have been worse?"

"Ladies," the bartender shouts. "Take it outside. Cool off."

Bridget storms off, stomping the whole way out the door.

I'm about to sit back down when the bartender pipes up. "You too! Y'all can come back when you're ready to be civil."

Meg shrugs. "It's like a Vern time-out."

Swigging down what's left of my beer, I head back out into the night, the cold air greeting me. Bridget is sitting on the sidewalk, her back against the building. I go over and sit next to her.

"We can go back in a couple minutes. Kyle always does this when it looks like there's going to be a fight."

We both sit in silence, the distant sound of the waves calming me some. "I didn't mean to hurt anyone by leaving. I was just a kid."

Bridget lets out a long low breath but doesn't say anything. After a couple minutes, she stands and brushes off her jeans. Her blue eyes look warm, a sight I'm not used to. She offers me a hand. I eye it wearily, worried she'll pull it back at the last second or fling me into the street.

As if reading my thoughts, she scoffs. "I'm trying here."

I take her hand and rise to my feet.

The air is crisp, the night so clear the sky is littered with stars. I search the sky for the moon and find it, nearly full, an amber orb dangling above us all. If Bridget can try, maybe I can, too.

Digging my phone out of my pocket, I type.

Me: Hey, can we talk?

Three dots appear then disappear.

The wind picks up as some clouds roll in. Looking at the clock, I tell myself I'll wait for two more minutes.

Three minutes later, there is still no reply.

I head back to the bar, packed for trivia night. There are too many people. It's crowded and loud. I'm just going to head out. Looking around, I spot Ben waiting at the bar, Nick at his side yammering in his ear. It's such a familiar sight from years past, a small smile spreads across my face, but as soon as I hear what he's saying, the corners of my lips feel heavy.

"Drinks on you," Nick slurs.

"I bought the last round."

Nick laughs. "You owe me, man, after that video I took. I got a Charlie horse crouching in the bush like that." He rubs his calf. "Still hurts."

Ben sighs, his eyes rolling up. "If you worked out every now and then, it wouldn't have been *so* hard."

The video. Nick took the video. Why? Why was he even there?

I step forward as they're ordering drinks.

Ben turns. "There you are. You want a red wine?"

Ignoring his question, I focus my attention on Nick. "You took the video?" Then Ben. "And you gave it to the cops."

Both of them look down at the bar.

"Why?"

Nick grabs his beer. "It's disrespectful."

"How did you even know he'd be there?"

"I . . . uh . . ." He looks at Ben, and it's like they're silently communicating, another old trick from high school, one I don't feel as much fondness for. It always made me feel left out. Like now. Nick takes his beer and disappears into the crowd.

Ben leans over the bar. "Kyle, can I get a large glass of red, too?"

"I'm not staying."

"Come on. Let's just play some trivia. Have a little fun. Loosen up."

"I don't want to. How did you know Oli would be there? Did you follow him?" If he did, then why didn't he just take the video? Then I remember Oli saying most of his large-scale pieces weren't technically illegal anymore, that he got permission to use the building ahead of time. The lawyer when he came out before said you couldn't see Oli clearly in the video but he also said *permits*. And now it all makes sense. "He got permission."

Ben sniffs loudly, looking away, he mutters, "Not mine."

"He got your family's permission. You knew when he'd be there. You didn't tell the cops that when you gave them the video, huh?"

"Nick took the video, and Nick gave it to the cops. I'm clean. NDA intact. Like I said, he didn't get my permission. His lawyer contacted Grandma. Of course, she'd love a mural on the old warehouse. She's always said it was an eyesore. But no one asked *me*."

That must've been how Oli got released so quickly once his lawyer got there.

"What was the point, then? You knew they weren't going to hold him."

Ben's eyes are warm, and he runs a hand over the top of my palm. "He's not the right guy for you."

My stomach clenches. Ben is still pulling this petty under-handed shit. Guiding my life in the direction he thinks it should go. Like in high school, his subtle suggestions on closer colleges, one with education programs, too, so I could think about teaching. Just think about it.

I pull my hand back. "That's not for you to decide."

Spinning on my heel, I walk away, right out the door, with absolutely no idea of how I'll get back to the cabins, but knowing without a doubt, I'm done taking any "help" from Ben.

Outside, I check my phone. There's one text.

Oli: I'm at the Inn. Same room.

CHAPTER 29

My mouth is a desert. I read and reread the text. I expected a phone call. I thought he went away, away. Off on a plane with his lawyer. Not just hanging out in our room. Shoving my hands in my pockets, I make the short walk to the Inn. Part of me wanting to run there, and part of me wanting to have the walk take as long as possible.

The front desk is empty, the little silver bell is on the counter, but I don't ring it. I know exactly where I'm going. I climb the stairs, my nerves rising with each step. The walk down the hall to the door at the end feels like a death march. Taking a deep breath, I close my eyes briefly. I can do this.

I knock.

There are muffled sounds, and then the door opens. Oli stands before me in a worn light-blue shirt, gray sweats, and bare feet. The sweats sit low on his hips, and I don't know how he does it, but he makes it all look better than a three-piece suit.

His eyes are warm as he looks into mine. Butterflies fill my chest, and heat rises to my cheeks. I lick my lips and say, "Hey."

The corner of his mouth quirks up. "Hey, yourself."

He moves aside. The room is bathed in an amber glow from the bedside lamp and the fire in the hearth. Oli's open laptop is on the couch. Oli hurries over, moving it to the coffee table. "I was just watching a movie."

He sits on the couch, and I take the other spot. "What movie?"

"*The Princess Bride.*"

My heart melts.

"Oli, I'm sorry I thought something might be going on with you and Alice. I..." This is harder than I thought. My heart is beating wildly. "I was jealous, and when I saw you took her to help on this huge piece, I felt left out. It was triggering."

Oli's face is pinched. "I didn't plan on taking her."

"I know. She told me." I take a deep breath. "I didn't follow you two, though. The video..."

Oli runs a hand over his face, the sound of the scruff and the crackle of the fire magnified in the quiet room. "I shouldn't have accused you of that. I—"

"You were under a lot of stress."

Oli looks at me. "I don't need you to make excuses for me. Just let me apologize."

I sigh. "I forgive you, okay?"

"But I didn't actually apologize."

"Fine. I'm sorry, too."

Oli moves closer to me on the couch, his spicy scent filling the air. He takes his hand and places a piece of hair behind my ear. In a low voice he says, "I'm sorry I accused you of taking the video. You said all that stuff about how this between us isn't serious. I thought maybe that was your way of making it okay. I've been burned by people close to me before, but I shouldn't have assumed the worst of you."

"I forgive you." I place my hand on his thigh and lean in closer, our lips inches apart. "Do you forgive me?"

He kisses me, and I melt. My limbs, that were solidified with stress, feel suddenly pliable. I crawl on him, my legs straddling either side of him, and he helps me take my sweater off then my shirt. He runs his large hands over my silk bra, moving his thumb over my nipple. I gasp at the contact. He pulls me in closer. I can feel his excitement underneath me. But do we have time for this now? If the others leave before we head back, I'm out of a job.

Oli kisses my neck as my thoughts swirl, muscles tightening again. Maybe we can pick this back up at the cabins. Once everyone has seen Oli is back.

"Oli?"

"Mmm," he answers into my collarbone, his mouth working its way down to my breasts. So close, I almost don't want to break the moment.

But I can't lose this job. I've worked too hard to get it. I let out a small sigh as my body shivers at his kisses, then I rip off the Band-Aid. "Can you come back to camp? Louise is devastated. They all are. They're going to leave."

Oli stops kissing me, his hands fall from my hips. He leans back and closes his eyes slowly. When he opens them, the hurt is palpable. "This is why you came here?"

I shake my head, but he's right. "It's part of it."

Oli moves me to the side and stands, his posture rigid. "You should leave now."

"Oli, I…" Shit. I'm messing this all up.

Oli turns away from me. "I'm going to take a shower. Please be gone by the time I get out."

He walks into the bathroom, closing the door without another look in my direction.

MIRACULOUSLY, one of the only Ubers in town is available and takes me back to the cabins. I head straight into the lodge, behind the bar, and pour myself a large glass of wine. I take it and sit by the fire, staring into the flames. I can't believe I fucked this up so badly. What was I thinking asking him to come back like that? In the middle of him kissing me. I shouldn't have asked him for something. I should've stayed present in the moment.

I'm not sure how long I sit there before Marlene comes into the lodge, her heeled boots clicking at a rapid staccato on the hardwood floors. "There you are. Where's Oli? Is he back in his cabin?"

I take a sip of my wine, tears welling behind my eyes. But I can't cry. Not now. "He's not coming back."

Marlene's eyes go wide as she starts to pace back and forth. "He has to."

"He won't." I turn my eyes back to the flames.

"This can't be. This is unacceptable."

She's right. It is.

"We'll have to issue refunds."

Inhaling, I push my shoulders back. "I can take care of it when we're back in Los Angeles."

Marlene frowns, crossing her arms tightly over her chest. "No, I'm afraid you won't. I was willing to look past you and Oli's little…" She waves her fingers. "Affair."

She knew? My mouth falls open, and she drops her arms, letting out a small humorless laugh.

"You two were not very discreet. But this…I can't look past this. You're fired, Ashford."

The words are not a surprise, but I'm stunned all the same. Years of grunt work for this one opportunity, and it's all gone up in flames.

"You can stay until our designated time in this backwoods hell is done, but once we're back…"

"No need." I shake my head. "I'll leave tonight."

She nods once. "I didn't want to have to do this."

I down the rest of my wine. "I understand. Thank you for the opportunity."

Setting my wine glass on the bar, I head out to my cabin to pack and figure out where I'm supposed to go with no car and very little options.

* * *

Packing is relatively easy, except for my wet painting. I take a sheet from the bed and wrap it around it. If Ben wants to charge the gallery for it, that's fine by me.

I scroll through my phone. I could try to call the Uber again. But where am I going to go? I can't go back to the Inn. I don't want Oli to think I'm following him, or not respecting his wishes.

I want nothing to do with Ben, plus he's probably still at trivia night. That's when an idea comes to me.

Dialing the phone before I can overthink it, I'm almost surprised when it picks up.

The speaker filled with voices, laughter, and clinks. "Zara, girl, where are you? You took off." Meg's voice is clear and full of joy.

"It's a long story. Hey, I hate to take you away from trivia night, but do you think there's any way you could come get me?"

"Honey, maybe two shots ago."

My heart sinks. Shit. I didn't think about the fact that she was drinking at the bar.

"That's okay…"

"Tommy's sober as a church bell. Probably home and in bed, but I'll call him. We can get you. Where are you?"

"At the cabins."

"See you in an hour by the lodge."

DESPITE THE COLD, I wait on the front steps. I don't want to go in and possibly run into Marlene again. My breath comes out in great puffs as I watch the reflections of the moon on the water.

I can't figure out how this all happened. Here I am left with nothing, just like I was ten years ago when I moved away from Fortune Falls. No job, no apartment, my painting is a disaster, and definitely no boyfriend.

"You look like your dog died," Louise says as she walks up the path, yanking me out of my thoughts.

"I don't have a dog."

Louise comes and sits next to me on the steps. "Maybe you should get one. I've heard they're delightful."

"I thought you were leaving."

She nods, the moonlight catching her hair. "I am. In the morning. It looks like you are, too." She motions toward my suitcase.

"I was fired."

Louise gasps. "You were?"

"This retreat was a disaster, and it's all my fault."

Louise shakes her head. "It wasn't a disaster. I'm making art I love again. It's a miracle."

"But you're leaving."

"Yes, well, that's true. But if Oli's not here, there's not much reason for me to sleep on that hard bed."

I know what she's saying makes perfect sense. They're all here for Oli. No Oli, no retreat.

She places a soft hand on my back. "Do you want me to talk to Marlene?"

Tears well in my eyes. "It won't help. It's fine. I'll find something else. Starbucks is always hiring, right?"

Louise smiles, her gold tooth flashing. "You know I'm going to be in the market for an assistant." But what she says next is drowned out by the sound of truck tires pulling up. Meg hops out the passenger side, and I stand slowly, feeling tired all the way down to my pinky toes.

"Hop in, honey bun!" She grabs my suitcase and tosses it in the back then throws the painting along with it. It hits the bed of the truck with a sickening thunk.

Louise stands and wraps her arms around me. "You're welcome to come see me anytime. I know it doesn't feel like it right now, but I really feel like all of this was meant to be. I'm going to email you."

Am I the only one not taken in by this fate scam?

I hug her back, though. She means well. "Take care, Louise."

CHAPTER 30

Meg chats the whole way to their house, down the backroads, through Main Street and all the way to the edge of town to a small blue house with a white picket fence about two blocks from the beach. She talks about trivia night, then the library, then their wedding.

As we pull into their driveway, she laughs. "This is it. Home sweet home."

I smile. The roses out front are not in bloom, but they are tall, and I can imagine how it must look in summer with the sun shining on the house. "It's beautiful, Meg."

"Thanks. We like it. Come on, I'll show you the inside."

She gives me the grand tour, which is pretty quick for the three-bedroom two bath ranch-style house. It's small but cozy. With original hardwood floors and a beautiful white brick fireplace in the living room.

She shows me the guest bedroom, and Tommy brings my stuff inside.

Meg fluffs the pillows and asks, "Do you want to go to bed? Or stay up for a bit? I could make tea, or I think I have some whiskey somewhere."

Tommy chuckles. "You don't need any more, darling. If your tongue gets any looser, it'll fall out."

She waves him away with a raspberry noise. Her face lights up. "I have hot chocolate."

"That sounds great."

Once we have two steaming mugs of hot chocolate and a fire roaring in the hearth, Tommy heads to bed while we settle in on the couch, staring at the flames.

"Want to talk about it?" Meg asks, tucking her feet under her legs.

Do I? Part of me does, but part of me thinks what's the point? It won't change anything. Where would I even start?

"I'm a good listener, when I can stop talking." She giggles. The sound so familiar, to sleepovers, and late-night drives along the coast, the windows down, ocean breeze whipping through our hair, the stereo blasting, that it hurts a little.

"It's all such a mess."

It all comes tumbling out. About meeting Oli on the train then finding out he was the artist-in-residence. About how hard I've worked for Marlene, inching my way into my current position, only to lose it in such a massive blaze of fire that I won't even have a reference. About how my art isn't going the way I had hoped. The painting is a mess, and I'll never make anything of real substance again.

"Was the big thing wrapped in the sheet the painting you were working on?"

"Yeah."

Meg makes an exaggerated face. "Sorry I chucked in the back of the truck like that."

"It's fine. Nothing could make it any worse than it is."

"Can I see it?"

No. That's what I want to say. But why? I've shared everything else with Meg. Why stop now?

"Sure." I set down my nearly empty mug and go get the painting.

I unwrap it carefully. The sheet is pressed into the wet paint in a few places, but other than that, there's no real damage. It's just how it was, my face in paint splotches, crafted around light and shadows.

Meg leans forward and looks at the painting. Really looks. Inspecting every inch with such intense interest, my insides squirm. She hates it. Even Meg can tell I'm a fraud. Not a real artist. I should hang up my apron. Burn my brushes. Maybe I should burn the painting itself.

A tear forms in the corner of Meg's eye. "It's beautiful."

"You think?" A pocket of warmth blooms in my chest.

"It's so...vulnerable. You were always good. You know I love your style. But this. The light." She points toward some of the streaks, the small reflection in my eye. "There's something about it. It's like looking at a piece of your soul."

There's a pause where we both look at the painting, and I try to see it through her eyes. Not looking at the flaws, or everything I did wrong, but looking at its potential. Maybe it's not as bad as I thought.

"You should keep going. Keep working on it."

I should, but I should also start looking for a new job and a new place to live. There's a lot of things I should do. Right now all I want is sleep. I stand. "Thanks for the hot chocolate. I'll be out of your hair in the morning."

Even as I say it, I have no idea where I'll go.

"You don't have to leave so soon. We have plenty of room. You can stay as long as you want."

"Thank you."

She wraps me in a tight hug, and tears well in the side of my eyes. I wash my face and brush my teeth, making it into bed before the tears start to fall. How am I back here? Relying on the kindness of friends for a place to stay. Is it me? Is it Fortune Falls?

I stare at the ceiling, my thoughts swirling, waiting for sleep to take me, but it doesn't come. Just more tears silently rolling down my face.

I SLEEP in the next day then go for a long walk. Meg and I watch *Gilmore Girls* in the evening, and it really does feel like a sleepover. We pass the days in much the same way. I keep waiting to feel better. For a plan to magically appear. But on the fourth day as I lie in bed with thoughts swarming like wasps, I'm no closer to an answer.

Bright light skitters through the wood blinds covering the window. I should have twisted them all the way closed last night. Somehow, I must've fallen asleep, although I have no memory of dozing off. It seems to be a pattern for me these days. That old *Sesame Street* tune comes to mind. Spiral myself to sleep. *And thank you, lamby.*

I get ready for the day feeling like death warmed over. I dress in black jeans and a black sweater, pulling my hair back in a high ponytail. Wandering into the kitchen, I follow the smell of the coffee. Bridget and Meg are sitting at the kitchen table moving tiny pieces of paper around a larger pink circle.

"No, Aunt Marge can't sit next to Grandma Carol. They'll end up throwing food, or worse."

Bridget moves a tiny scrap of paper.

Meg catches sight of me. "There you are. I hope we didn't wake you. Weddings are seriously a full-time job. Help yourself to some coffee."

I attempt a smile, but it feels like it gets stuck on my face somewhere along the way. Instead, I busy myself with the coffee.

Bridget clears her throat. "Where should we seat Viv?"

They can't mean Mom. How would they invite her? I haven't even spoken to her in nearly two years. We missed each other last Christmas, and the Christmas before. In all honesty, I let it go to voicemail.

"Hmmm, I'm not sure?"

"Zara, are you coming?" Meg asks.

I nod. "Yes. I'd love to. I'm planning on it."

"Do you want to sit next to your mom?" Bridget twirls the sparkly pink pen in her hand as she asks, like she's bored by her own question.

Meg's moving another tiny paper, not meeting my gaze.

"You invited *my* mom?"

She looks up, taking one glance at my face and raises her hands. "I didn't. But my mom did. Apparently, they're Facebook friends. I thought she might have told you. Your name was on the invite, too. I wasn't sure how else to get a hold of you."

"I can't believe you're talking to my mom. I don't even talk to her."

Meg stands, her voice soft but her eyes stern. "I didn't know that. It's not like you tried to stay in touch after you left."

How do I explain? While I'm trying to find the words, Meg grabs her mug. "I need some air."

Bridget shakes her head as Meg takes her mug out onto the porch.

Her smug expression is too much this morning. "What is your problem with me?"

She doesn't look up from her task. "Me? I have no problem. It seems like you're the one with all the problems."

I let out a long sigh, because she's not wrong. I am the one with all the problems. No job. Nowhere to live. Completely fucked up my one shot at a real relationship with someone I feel genuinely connected with.

Instead of saying any of that, I head to my room and pack up my stuff. I check my phone and thank goodness the Uber is available and will be here in five minutes.

Lugging all my stuff out on the porch, I sit next to Meg in a wooden rocking chair.

She eyes my things. "Taking off again?"

"I don't want to overstay my welcome."

Meg turns to me. "Is this like before? Am I not going to see you again for another ten years?"

"Meg, before I came here, my mom and I moved around a lot.

And we figured out it was easier to leave without saying good-bye. No tears. Less guilt. Just slip away into the night. So when I left after high school, that's how I knew I could do it. How I'd done it before. I didn't mean to hurt you. For me, it was the only way I knew. But I'm sorry. I should've found you."

Meg shakes her head. "I didn't know you'd lost touch with your mom. I wasn't trying to invite her behind your back or anything."

"I know." The Uber pulls and stops in front of the gate in the fence. "I'd still love to come to the wedding. If that's okay?"

Meg wraps her arms around me, squeezing me in a tight hug. "Bitch, you better."

THE RIDE IS QUICK. I get to the train station and am surprised by the massive line. I realize a lot of these people are probably going home for Thanksgiving. It's in a few days, and it would've marked the end of the retreat.

I sit on a bench near a window, not knowing where to go. Should I buy a ticket back to LA? I could stay with friends until I figure things out. Maybe a decade or so should about do it.

An older gentleman sits next to me and pulls out a book. I look out the window as the ocean rolls in the distance. My reflection looks nearly the same as when I took the train to Fortune Falls a few months ago and met an attractive man along the way. But I feel so different. I was so full of hope, and now what? All the things I felt hopeful for are gone.

A bird circles above a pine tree. At first, I think it's a seagull, but then upon closer inspection, the white head flashes. It's an eagle. Its massive wings are outstretched.

The man next to me points. "You don't see that every day."

I shake my head. "No."

The eagle dives, its talons out, and disappears behind the tree line.

The man asks, "Where are you headed?"

And for some reason, the only way my brain processes this question is with its existential meaning, and tears well in the corner of my eyes. I swipe at them with the edge of my sweater.

"Is it something I said?"

I shake my head. "I'm not really sure where I'm going or what I'm doing."

The man nods knowingly. "That's hard, but also exciting. The possibilities are endless. Where do you want to go?"

And suddenly, I know with complete certainty where that is.

CHAPTER 31

The cab pulls up to the small sage green house. Walking past a pink bike lying on the lawn, I take a deep breath as I climb the porch stairs. I knock and then step back, waiting.

A little girl answers, she must be around seven. Her long dark hair hangs in scraggly waves around her face, and her wide, clear brown eyes mirror my own. "Is your mom home?"

My breath catches in my throat as I hear her voice ringing through the entryway. "Baby, who is it?"

She places a hand on the door, her mouth falling open. "Oh my goodness gracious. Zara!"

"Hey, Mom."

She looks older than I remember, and for some ridiculous reason, that comes as a surprise. It's nothing drastic—a few more lines around her eyes, a few grays sprinkled through her hair. But it's not exactly what I pictured when I made this plan.

Tears well in her eyes, then in mine. She wraps me in a tight hug. She smells the same, rose and ginger.

"Come in."

"Mom?" the little girl asks.

And my mom's face changes. She swipes away the tears and

straightens up. "Baby, this is your sister, Zara. You met her once, remember?"

The girl wrinkles her nose in a way so similar to my mom it stings.

"Didn't you come visit?" my mom asks, her voice wavering. "When was it?"

"You were still pregnant." I offer as we both follow Mom into the kitchen. She picks up a potato and continues peeling. I remember it well. It was Christmastime. I ate Ramen for a month so I could afford the airline ticket, but then ended up having to take a Greyhound the rest of the way to Cloverdale anyway. So, it felt a little wasteful.

They were in this city, but instead of this house, they had a one-bedroom apartment. Mom was terribly nauseous the whole time. I was supposed to stay until New Year's Eve, but Christmas morning after Mom spent all day in the bathroom, Chris suggested she might be more comfortable without company. I traded in my ticket for an earlier flight, and that was the last time I saw my mom. Nearly eight years ago.

"That's nuts. This is Abby. Abby, this is your older sister, Zara."

"My sister? I have a sister?" Abby bounces on her heels, her hair bobbing up and down. Her words slice through me. I'm aware I'm not really a part of this life. Having a daughter more than twenty years older than the other isn't a great look. But the fact that Abby doesn't even know. It's a low blow.

I glance around the kitchen for any evidence of my existence. There're drawings on the fridge and framed family photos on the wall. I send a Christmas and birthday card every year, and I've sent a few paintings over the years as well. But they're nowhere to be seen, at least in the kitchen.

My mom laughs, it's bright but doesn't sound completely genuine. Not like the laugh she had when we watched *Clueless* and made muddy buddies. Or when we played slap jack and she cheated mercilessly. "Yes, of course, you have a sister. I've told you about Zara."

Abby shakes her head, her massive hair moving with the motion in a Muppet-like manner. "No. I'd remember, Mom." Abby turns her bright eyes on me. "Where do you live? How old are you? Are you married?"

Mom's eyes flick to the clock, one of those ones that has birds around the edge, then she looks out the kitchen window and points with the potato to a group of kids riding bikes. "Your friends just rode by. Better catch up before it gets dark."

"You told me to come help!" Her little mouth falls open in shock.

"Now I'm telling you to go play." She gives Abby a look. They are communicating without words. There're a few head jerks and lip purses from both sides. I look away. What am I even doing here? Why is this where I decided to go for…what? What was I expecting? Comfort? Home? Love?

Abby runs out of the kitchen, and Mom calls after her, "Come back before dark and stay on these two blocks."

I sit at the kitchen table and watch my mom meticulously peel the potato in her hand. She looks up every now and then toward the clock.

"How have you been?" she asks, breaking the awkward silence.

I shrug, trying to put on a brave face, but even the attempt hurts. I've never cried this much in my entire life. I thought I was all cried out, but apparently my body has years of pent-up emotions that insist on escaping through my eyes. Tears roll down my cheeks. Then suddenly, I'm racked with sobs.

My mom puts down the potato, hurrying to my side. "Zara. What is it? Are you sick? Are you pregnant?"

I shake my head. "No."

"Then what's going on?"

"I worked really hard at this job and I finally got a promotion and I fucked it up. I was fired. All my work was for nothing. I won't even get a reference now."

My mom sits in the chair next to me. "Is that all? You can find another job. You're so resourceful."

I shake my head. "That's not all."

Mom places a hand on mine, it feels dry but warm.

"I met a man. I...well... He's amazing."

"Okay. Now this is more my department. Tell me all about him." She rises and goes back to the potatoes.

"He's an artist. He's so talented and funny. And we have this..." I try to explain the feeling that I have when I'm around him and struggle to find the words.

My mom smiles. "Sounds like love to me."

Is it? I am in love with Oli? I search my body, the glow in the center of my chest even at the thought of him. The ache now that he's gone.

Shit. I am in love with Oli.

And it couldn't matter less.

"I fucked it all up, though."

"How?"

"It's a long story."

Mom holds up two potatoes. "Well, I have about ten hundred more of these to peel, so I have the time."

I move to the kitchen counter. "Want a hand?"

She nods. I tell her all about what happened as we peel potatoes. The whole story. She leans in and gasps, and by the time the water is at a rolling boil, the whole story is out and I'm no closer to feeling any better about any of it.

"Wow." She checks the clock again, maybe worried about when Abby will be back. "That's some love story. Do you want to know what I think?"

I'm afraid of answering yes, but too curious not to.

"I think you should go tell him how you feel. Apologize. You should be in his kitchen not mine!"

"I can't."

"Why not? What do you have to lose? You're already out of a job? You're already not together?"

She's right. What do I have to lose? But what would I say? I shake my head. "I don't even know where to find him."

"You said he loves that train, right? Start there."

Mom pops the boiled potatoes in a strainer then washes her hands. "I'll give you a ride."

"Now?"

"Yep." She grabs her coat, and I run after her. She already has my suitcase in her hand.

"Wait." But she's not listening. She's out the door. I grab my painting and follow her. "I was hoping we could catch up a little more."

She loads the suitcase in the back of her minivan as Abby rides by. "Go to Stephanie's, okay? I'll pick you up in half an hour."

Abby waves as she rides by in a pink blur. The sun is fading, day turning into night already and it's only four. Mom is in the driver's seat waiting. I climb in while placing the painting on my legs, next to my feet.

The engine purrs to life, and Mom backs out of the driveway.

"I was hoping we could catch up a little more."

"That's so sweet, but we don't have room."

I rub my arms, suddenly feeling chilled. "I thought I could stay at a hotel nearby."

"You could…" The light turns red, and Mom's mouth is set in a deep frown. "We're having company. Chris's family is coming this week for Thanksgiving. It'll be loud and crowded."

What's going on sinks in like acetone dissolving paint, revealing the truth. "They don't know about me."

A sound escapes her somewhere between a laugh and a scoff. "Of course, they do."

Her eyes are fixed on the road, her posture rigid. Even from this angle, I can tell she's lying. "No. They don't."

"It's just… If I tell them about you, I have to tell them the whole story. How I got knocked up at fifteen." Her eyes water.

"I'm not that person to them. The screw up. To them, I'm responsible. I'm a good mother."

She pulls up to the train station.

"I'm glad you can be that for someone," I say as the pieces of my heart that were left intact shatter one by one.

I get out without saying another word. Half expecting her to take it back. To invite me over for Thanksgiving. To say she's sorry. But she just mumbles, "Take care of yourself," before I close the door and she drives away.

CHAPTER 32

The train station is stuffy and perfumed. A woman in a puffy coat and perfectly curled hair tries to wrangle her toddler into the boarding line, but the child keeps wriggling its chubby fingers out of her grasp. A man waits behind them, tapping his foot in a camel-colored coat. I get in line behind him, not sure where to go. Then a thought occurs to me. And I send a text:

Me: Was that offer to visit genuine?

I stare at the phone for a full minute and rest my head in my hands. It was a stupid idea. The train reader board has many destinations to choose from. Maybe I should just close my eyes and point. After all my moving around as a kid, it's honestly the last thing I thought I'd do as an adult. Every time we moved somewhere new, not knowing where we were going or what kind of job my mom would find there, I told myself, *not me*. That won't be my life. But the apple doesn't fall far, I guess.

Closing my eyes, I take a deep breath and point, but my phone buzzes in my hand. I look down at it instead of the board.

Louise: I always have room for you, dear. As long as you don't mind company.

She sends the address next. It's in Oregon. I thought she lived in LA. I talk to the train attendant. There's a train headed that way in about an hour and there are three tickets left on the Sunshine Express. I purchase my ticket and wait.

EVERY PERSON that passes my seat, I look up, hoping to find Oli. One man notices me and asks if I want to get a drink in the dining car. I shake my head and turn my attention back to my book. I've read the same paragraph about fifty times. The story, the dark clouds folding into each other out the window, my heart—all of it feels hollow.

By the time I'm at the train station in Louise's town, I'm numb. I walk through the crowds, rolling my suitcase with the painting on the top, past happy families greeting one another, lovers embracing, past all of it and none of it can touch me.

I pull out my phone and am about to call a car, when a horn startles me. I look up, and Alice is waving out the side of a beat-up green pickup truck, more rust than metal.

"Get in! It's cold."

I throw my stuff in the back and get in the passenger seat, covered in a thick Mexican blanket. "How did you..."

"You gave Louise the train number. There's a tracking app. Figured you could use a ride."

"Thanks."

We drive out of the small downtown area, down a long winding road, the houses getting fewer and farther between. Past a field with horses, plaid blankets over their backs, the wind picking them up slightly at the edges. The sun casts its last rays of golden light as it dips below the hills.

"This is kind of far out there," I say, taking in the vast open spaces.

"Louise likes her privacy."

"I hope you don't mind me staying... I'm really sorry about what I said."

Alice waves me away. "Water under the bridge. Louise is nice enough to let me visit, too. Usually, I don't celebrate Thanksgiving. My parents split a long time ago, and after my grandma passed the rest of the family stopped getting together. It never bothered me, but this year, I found myself not wanting to be alone."

"Same. I actually tried to go home."

"Yeah? How'd that go?"

I shake my head. "Turns out, I went to the wrong place. I'm not sure where home is anymore."

Alice lets out a long sigh. "We have more in common than you think."

We pull up to a large blue house, with an even bigger red barn sitting a ways behind it. Louise comes out on the porch, wiping her hands on a towel. "Dinner is almost ready! Come in, come in."

Her smile is so bright and welcoming, it feels like a warm hug. I grab my things and climb the stairs. "Thank you so much for having me."

Louise puts a hand on my shoulder. "I'm thrilled you're here. Now we can open the wine." She motions her head at Alice who's walking inside. "That one's a party pooper."

"Not a party pooper, just pregnant."

Louise laughs, and whispers to me, "I like pissing her off."

She takes my coat and shows me to the dining room, where three homemade pizzas are laid out, the smell of the cheese, the basil, and pepperoni making my mouth water. We all sit and grab great slices, Louise pours me a glass of wine roughly the size of my head then one for herself and a sparkling cider for Alice. For a second, I think Louise might make a heartfelt toast, but she holds up her glass and says, "Let's eat!"

We dig in. The pizza is exquisite, the homemade dough is soft, and the cheese is gooey. After dinner, Alice heads for bed, saying the baby is making her extra tired, and Louise pours me a little more wine. We take it out back, and she turns the knob on a standing fire pit.

There's a blanket on one of the chairs, and I cover my lap, leaning back looking at the stars.

Louise taps my knee. "You know I wasn't joking about needing an assistant."

I take a hearty sip of wine then shake my head. "I don't want your pity job."

"Trust me. It's not. I don't feel sorry for you at all."

I nearly choke on my wine, laughing. "Not even a little bit?"

"Nope. You had a fine man and you fucked it up."

I scoff. "What do you know about it?"

She shrugs. "Things get around. Didn't you accuse him and..." She crooks her finger at the house. "Of making that baby."

"I...Well..." Shit. I did. I really low-key accused him of sleeping around. I sigh, looking back up at the stars. "Yeah. I did. In my defense, he also accused me of leaking that video on the internet."

"Is that defending yourself or attacking him?"

I let the question linger in the air with the smoke from the fire pit.

"Anyone can see you two are crazy about each other."

"Sometimes that's not enough."

"That's up for you two to decide." Louise rises to her feet. She puts a soft hand on my shoulder. "Think about the job."

"I will."

"And feel free to stay as long as you like. Don't push yourself so hard. Rest. You'll know when it's time to wash your face and get to work."

"Thank you, Louise. I..."

She waves me away and heads inside.

IN THE MORNING, I sleep in. The farm is quiet but not too quiet. There're sounds of goats munching in the yard, the rustling of wind through the pine trees, birds calling to one another in some language I don't understand.

I spend most of the day in bed. My limbs are heavy, and my heart feels like lead. I watch YouTube videos on my phone of kids running into haunted houses until night comes again. The next day, I do the same. Louise checks on me every now and then. Invites me on a hike to a nearby waterfall, but that's the last thing I want to see.

On the third day, I wake to the smell of sage and rosemary simmering.

I get dressed and head into the kitchen to find Alice tying rope around a turkey.

"Hey, I hope I didn't wake you."

I shake my head no, even though I'm not sure it's true. Louise walks out of the pantry holding some chicken stock. "Ahh there she is. Alice is insisting on a proper Thanksgiving."

"The baby wants turkey and stuffing. It's not me, I swear."

Louise laughs.

I wash my hands at the sink. "How can I help?"

We spend the next couple hours peeling and mashing sweet potatoes, basting the turkey, ripping bread, chopping celery. It feels good to have small manageable tasks that have an obvious endpoint. Louise even makes an apple pie from scratch, pointing out that the apples came from her trees.

We sit down to eat a little after four, and by five, we're snuggled up in Louise's basement family room with pie, hot mugs of tea, and snuggly blankets, *White Christmas* playing on the television.

It all feels wonderfully cozy. My muscles relax, my neck losing some of its stiffness, my shoulders descending from my ears. After they go to bed, I run myself a bubble bath, closing my eyes and feeling the bubbles pop around my legs. I think back to the text I sent Oli of my legs in the tub before I even knew who he was.

No. That's not true. I knew who he was, I just didn't know

what he did. But that's not the same thing. I don't know how I lost sight of Oli the man. How could I think he was sleeping with me and Alice? How could I accuse him of that? Was I trying to push him away?

That one hits home. If I push him away, he can't leave me.

That's no way to live. Never really opening up to anyone, despite my feelings for them.

I fiddle with my phone on the edge of the tub. Should I send him a text now?

What would I say?

Instead, I pick up the phone and google therapists in my network (network for now, anyway) and find a service that works over text.

The next morning, someone is moving around in the kitchen beneath my room at first light, and I get up, too. I head to the bathroom, shower, pull my hair up in a high ponytail, and get dressed. I can't find Louise at first, then I notice the light on in the red barn outside. Slipping into a pair of rubber boots by the door, I make my way out there.

I give the door a tentative knock, and Louise calls back, "Come in."

Pushing the white door open, I expect to see a hay-covered floor and horses in the stall, but what I find instead is nothing short of amazing. The floor is smooth, polished concrete; even through my rubber boots, I can feel the radiant heat. There are shelves filled with art supplies, two giant work tables, a couple of easels, a pottery wheel, and in the corner in the back, a small room with windows that looks like an office. On the walls are sketches, some rough, some more polished, and on the opposite wall are the drawings Louise displayed for our critiques.

Louise gives me one of her massive smiles. "It's nice to see you up."

I return her smile. "Time to wash my face and get to work."

"That's the spirit."

CHAPTER 33

Louise wasn't lying about needing an assistant. Her shelves, filled with supplies, have absolutely no organization whatsoever. The first thing I take care of is an inventory, then I organize and reorder some essentials she's low on or ran out of. That takes me the better part of the week. She works on some of her new drawings, chatting away while I organize. Every now and then, she looks to see what I've found buried in the back of the shelves. Literally, there is a glue that I think they outlawed in 1972.

In the evenings, we all make dinner. Alice loves to try new recipes, everything from chicken tortilla soup to Shepard's pie. We eat around the table, then head to the basement to watch more Christmas movies. Alice surprises me. When we first met, I never would have pictured her snuggled up on a couch with popcorn, snort laughing at *Four Christmases*, but I was wrong. I was wrong about a lot of things it seems.

Most nights, after everyone goes to bed, I work on my painting. Louise let me stake out a corner in her studio. It's coming along, the light and shadow forming the reflection. Once the first portrait is to a place I like, I move onto the next, but this one isn't a reflection. I paint from memory, and like my memory, it's slightly fuzzy, out of focus, shaped more by color than line. It feels good to get out of my own head, to not critique the idea before I've even put the brush to canvas and just paint.

After the great supply organization, Louise gives me access to her computer. She has about two hundred thousand unopened emails. Most are spam, but some are galleries interested in showing her work, a university interested in having her as a guest speaker, a book interested in featuring her work and...my breath catches in my throat, my coffee frozen midway to my mouth.

"Louise!"

She working on a drawing on one of the large worktables, her face inches away from the surface. "Hmmm," she says without looking up.

I run out of the little office. "PNWMOA wants to hold a retrospective of your work."

Louise still doesn't look up from her drawing, her wrinkled hand moving the pencil smoothly over the surface of the paper. "Hmmm."

Moving closer, I flail my arms out. "I'm not sure you heard me. The Pacific Northwest Museum of Art!"

Louise sets her pencil down and sighs. "Aren't retrospectives for after you're dead?"

"No. Andre and Genevieve had one."

Louise makes a fart noise. "They're practically dead. Genevieve didn't even want to do it. I don't know. I want to make work that's still relevant. If I accept a retrospective, people will think I'm done."

Louise's new series is gorgeous, funny, and *relevant*. I walk closer to the wall that now has about seven drawings. "What if they also show your new work?"

"Yes. Okay. I'm interested in that. But as a group show, with your work and Alice's."

I nearly choke on my own breath. "What?"

"I'll agree to the retrospective if they also give us a group show. We'll call it From the Farmhouse, or something clever. Not in the main museum, just in their affiliate gallery."

They do have a small gallery about a block away from the museum that shows less established artists (not that Louise and Alice are in that boat, just me). They might go for it. This isn't a terrible idea. In fact, it's brilliant.

"I'll send an email."

Louise turns back to her drawing, the corner of her lips turned up.

Over the course of December, twenty emails back and forth, and a video call with Louise, it's all set. Alice, Louise, and I have a group show that will open in September. They had an artist pull out and were looking to fill the slot. Louise's retrospective will go up the following June, including the work from the group show.

It's perfect. Almost like fate. I've been thinking a lot about how I ended up here with these two, amazing women. If everything hadn't tumbled like dominos, I'd still be struggling to please Marlene. Maybe there really is something to what Oli was saying about fate. Everything feels like it's falling into place.

Well, almost everything.

I haven't heard from Oli since the night I left his hotel room. On the news there was some speculation after the video came out that he is OG, but then another video came out a week or so later with a different crew putting up a piece in Brooklyn, so it blew over.

As I lie in my bed at night, I think about texting him. But I'm still not quite sure what to say. Working with my therapist has been helpful, and they have suggested I give it some space. The situation, him, us. Maybe space isn't always a bad thing. Maybe it doesn't have to be goodbye forever.

ON CHRISTMAS EVE, snow blankets the farm in a cold but cushy layer of fluff. The air smells fresh, clean, and a little bit like the mist scent that lingers on Oli's neck.

Louise, Alice, and I bundle up and run around in it like dogs.

Louise throws the first snowball, and then it's on. I try hiding behind a tractor, but Alice comes at me from the other side. We throw snowballs until we are covered in icy bits and breathless.

Once we've all changed into cozy clothes, not covered in wet snow, Louise turns on a classic Christmas playlist, which kicks off with Eartha Kit crooning "Santa Baby." I lip sync it into a spatula to the giggles and whoops of Louise and Alice as we bake cookies. Later in the day, once they've cooled, we decorate them like the true artists we are. There's a gingerbread Warhol, Basquiat, Frida Kahlo. My favorite is the one Alice painted of Picasso in a cubist style.

The next morning, Alice makes a feast of eggs, potatoes, sausage, and even homemade bread.

We sit around the dining room table, and I hold up my coffee. "Last month, well, not even just then, for quite a while, I've felt all alone. I spent Christmas Day at the movies, then Chinese food, by myself. I never thought... I just never expected..." Tears fill my eyes, and Alice gives a big sniff.

She waves her hand at me. "Stop. I have too many hormones right now for this mushy shit."

I laugh and tip my cup up. "Merry Christmas."

We clink glasses, the sound like a bell ringing in my chest.

That night, Louise turns in early, and Alice and I stay up with mugs of hot chocolate watching *The Holiday*. About halfway through the movie, I notice Alice's shoulders shaking. In the dim light from the screen, I can just make out tears streaming down her face.

I scoot over and put a hand on her shoulder. "Alice what is it?"

Alice wipes her face then places both hands on her belly. "I told the father today."

A gasp escapes me, and I quickly cover my mouth. I can't deny I've been dying to know who it is, but I haven't wanted to pry. I lower my hand. "What did he say?"

"He wants to be a part of the baby's life. That's good, right? It's just..." She sniffs. "It's stupid. Part of me was hoping he would make a declaration of love. But that's silly. We've only known each other a short while, and it was just a one-night thing." She laughs. "Okay, maybe a three-night thing. I haven't spoken to him since the end of the retreat. I mean, other than a few texts here and there."

"Alice, do you mind me asking who the father is?"

She swallows hard. "It's Miguel."

My eyes widen. I thought he was seeing Marlene. But maybe that wasn't his shirt she was wearing the day Oli got arrested.

"Miguel."

She dissolves into sobs again.

I put my arm around her. She lays her head on my shoulder, and I stroke her hair. "Alice, I'm proud of you. You were very brave today."

She sniffs. "I was."

"You were. And Miguel wants to be a part of the baby's life. That's wonderful news."

She lifts her head off my shoulder. "It is."

"And if there is something between you two, there's time. It'll grow."

Alice smiles and rubs a hand on her belly. "You're right. The best things grow with time."

She settles back on the couch sighing. "Can we rewind it? We missed the best part where Cameron Diaz has all the snacks."

I laugh and grab the remote.

IT'S ONLY the middle of January, but there's so much work to do before September, there's hardly time to stop and think. We fall into a routine. Louise makes the coffee in the morning, and then depending on the day, I join her doing Zumba. It's sweaty and ridiculous, but I find myself looking forward to it on Mondays, Wednesdays, and Fridays. Especially Fridays, because Alice usually makes a big breakfast after.

Winter has fully settled in. My belly is full of blueberry pancakes, and my legs feel energized from Zumba. I walk out to the barn to get to work on emails first, then I need to document some of Louise's work. Louise took off to speak at an elementary school career fair.

The frozen ground crunches under my feet as wisps of clouds roll by. When I open the door to the barn, the phone in the office is ringing. I run to catch it before it stops. A little breathless, I say, "Louise Walker Studio."

"Zara?"

I'm stiffer than the ground outside. "Oli?"

I don't know why I'm asking. His voice when he said my name sunk deep into my core. I know it's him.

"What are you doing at Louise's?"

"I'm her assistant."

"No more Gallery Six? That makes so much sense now."

"Why?"

"Just when I've asked Marlene about you, she's been so vague."

A small smile tickles my lips. He's asked about me. I bask in the glow of it. Once I regain my composure, I say, "Working with Louise has been great, and it comes with a place to stay. What about you? How have you been?"

This feels like small talk. I hate myself for asking. I just don't want to stop talking to him, and I don't know what else to say. Where to start?

"I've been…well…" He sighs.

I take the pause and jump in head first. "Oli, I'm sorry I accused you of sleeping with Alice. I don't know what I was thinking. That's not true. I was jealous you included her in this massive history-making art project, when I knew nothing about it."

"I don't know about history-making," he mutters.

"But I shouldn't have jumped to conclusions like that. And when I came to find you, it *was* because Marlene ordered me to.

But even if she hadn't, I would've wanted to talk to you. To work this out. What we have...our connection..." My stomach drops like I'm on a roller coaster, but I push past the nausea. "I was... I am... I know I said we weren't serious. That we couldn't be..."

"Zara—"

Someone yells in the background on his end of the line. The sound is too muffled to make out. I strain to try to hear whether it's a woman. I can't tell. Oli yells something back, but I can't make out what he says either. "I have to go. I just wanted to thank Louise for inviting me to the opening. I'll try to make it."

"I'll pass along the message."

"Thanks."

There's a long pause where he's still on the line, but neither of us says anything.

Oli clears his throat. "I'd really like to talk about this more. Right now, though. It's not the best time."

"Stupid time."

Oli laughs, and the sound fills my heart with silver-winged hope. There's more muffled talking.

"Take care, Zara." The line clicks off.

The rest of the day, I replay our conversation in my head, then our fights, then our kisses, touches, our late-night talks, and early morning snuggles. I should have told him I love him. It's the truth, and even if he doesn't feel the same, he should know. My fingers itch to text him, but that would be crazy. He just told me it wasn't a good time. I need to respect what he's saying.

Why would Louise invite him without talking to me about it first? At least tell me about it. I answer emails in a fog. I adjust lights and document her artwork in a haze of confusion, then anger. How dare Louise meddle like this? She should've talked to me.

By the time Louise gets back to the studio in the afternoon, I've worked myself into a frenzy.

"Lord help us if that's the future." She laughs as she hangs her coat on the rack near the door. "What the hell is Skibidi toilet?"

I turn my attention back to organizing the flat files. "You got a phone call."

"Anything interesting?"

"Oli. He's not sure he can make it to the opening, but he wanted to thank you for the invite." Now I look at her, study her face closely for a reaction.

She grabs a small stick of charcoal and works on the large drawing. "Hmmm. Did you two talk at all?"

It all makes sense. Why his invitation was clearly not sent by me, like all the others, and why he didn't email an RSVP.

"Are you trying to set us up?"

Louise keeps drawing but purses her lips.

"You are. You wanted him to call and get me. Why? Just leave it alone. I don't need your meddling."

"I wasn't meddling, per se. Just providing an opportunity. I care..."

"You care? About who? Yourself? You want a big international art star at your little—"

Louise stands and holds up her hand. "Zara, think hard about what you're about to say. Do you really want to push me away, too?"

I look into her dark-blue eyes, filled with love, and I let out a massive breath. I've been working so hard with my therapist, unpacking my tendency to push people away, to run, to extricate myself from relationships. Leave before they can. I thought I had come so far, but here I am, doing it again. My shoulders slump and tears fill the corners of my eyes.

"No," I say. The frenzied spiral of thoughts settling like a feather floating to the ground. "I don't want to push you away. I do wish you had talked to me about it."

Louise nods. "Okay. I see where you're coming from. But if I had, would you have talked me out of sending the invite?"

"Yes." I laugh. "Absolutely."

"Can't you two talk about it? I see you here, and you seem happy, but once in a while, you get this look."

She's right. I am happy here most of the time. Other times, I miss Oli so much it makes my skin ache.

Louise continues. "I just thought you both could use a little nudge."

A sound escapes me, somewhere between a laugh and a squawk. "Well, he didn't take the bait." A tear rolls down my cheek.

Louise wraps me in a tight hug. "You're not bait. And he's a bigger idiot than I thought."

I lean into her hug. "He's not an idiot. Maybe he just never felt the same for me as I did for him."

Louise lets me go, shaking her head as she goes back to her drawing. "If that's true and that boy doesn't love you, I'll eat this drawing."

CHAPTER 34

I keep expecting Oli to call back. Or text me. I check my phone non-stop. A week goes by with no word. Then two. I get back into the habit of leaving my phone in my room while I'm working.

Who does text with the regularity of trains pulling in and out of the station is Meg. One of her bridesmaids ran off with a married man. The most shocking thing about the story is that it wasn't Bridget. She asks if I can fill in.

"Meg, I don't know? What about the dress?"

"We still have Carly's, and you two are about the same size. We can just hem it a bit."

Of course, because everyone in the world is taller than me.

Meg is still talking. "Please. It'll be fun."

"Of course, I will. Do I have to do anything?"

"You have to come for the run through and the rehearsal dinner. You can stay at my place."

I shake my head, then remember we're on the phone and there's no way she can see that. "When is it? I'll book a room."

"The night before on Friday, February thirteenth. But maybe you could get here Thursday night so we can do a fitting of your dress in the morning."

I let out a long breath. "Okay, I'll book it right now."

Meg squeals on the other end of the phone. "One week! In a week, I'm getting married."

I laugh. "It's wild."

Louise lets me borrow a truck, for some reason she has three, one green, one black, and one silver. I asked her why, and she said she was in a truck phase and liked to drive the color that fit her mood that day. She thinks the green one is good luck, but I ask if I can take the black. It'll match most of my outfits, after all.

Driving up the highway along the coast toward Fortune Falls, I listen to Noah Kahan's "Stick Season." As I pass one naked tree after the next, the late afternoon sun spilling through their branches with not one leaf to snag on, his words make a lot of sense. It also makes me think of Oli. Being curled in his arms, the fire roaring, this song playing softly in the background.

By the time I get to Fortune Falls, it's only four but already dark. I check in with a smile from Mrs. Pepper.

"It's lovely to see you back again. Will your friend be joining you?"

"Nope." I swallow hard past the lump in my throat as I take the key. "Just me this time."

Sinking into the massive tub, I think about texting Oli. A repeat. A photo of my legs with a *wish you were here*. But I don't. Instead, I listen to an audiobook and lose myself in a tale of murder.

My brain will not turn off. I finally give up trying to sleep. Staying in bed, snuggled under the covers, I sketch for a while, but flashes of Oli and I in this room overwhelm me. Him pressing me into the dresser, me straddling him on the bed, the feel of his brush strokes on my back as he painted the best picture of me anyone ever has. Even the shower reminds me of him.

After dressing, I practically fling myself out the door, escaping the ghost of Oli that haunts this room. But as I head into the bookstore café across the street, the memories follow me. I get a coffee, but can't sit still, so I go for a walk, telling myself I need fresh air.

Telling myself I'm not sure where I'll wander, all the while with a destination in mind. I end up at the sign where the sticker remains from Oli and my night out. Running around, adrenaline coursing through me, our fingers intertwined, cold sand on bare feet. I take a photo of the sticker, the golden morning sun skimming the ocean waves behind it. Maybe it's the lack of sleep, or maybe it's how much I've thought about Oli since our phone call, but without overthinking it, I text the photo.

Me: Thinking of you.

My fingers are frozen when I finally open the door to Honeybee Bridal. When I heard the name of the shop, I pictured the women working there all with 1950s beehives, but I'm wrong. The owner, an older woman with short red hair, purple-rimmed bifocals, and a massive smile has me try on the dress then flits around me with measuring tape and pins, like a bee on a flower, and suddenly the name makes a lot of sense.

Bridget tries on hers next. It fits like a glove, and Meg claps, doing a little hop of delight. Then it's Meg's turn.

The owner and Meg go behind a curtain with swishes of fabric and hums. Bridget grabs one of the already poured champagne flutes and hands one to me as well.

"Thanks."

"Don't mention it." She leans against the counter, holding her glass up, then she purses her lips to the side. "Meg's really excited you're here."

"I'm happy to be here."

The frown lines on either side of her mouth deepen. "This is Meg's big day. We've been planning it for nearly a year. Just don't leave before the ceremony is over, okay?"

I hold my hand out. "I'm here. Not going anywhere."

She tsks. "Ben thought that once before, too."

"Bridget, that was literally a decade ago. Truly, I didn't mean to hurt Ben. And I know I could've handled it better, but I didn't. There's no way for me to go back and change that now. It wasn't an easy decision to make, and I didn't take it lightly. You act like I left on a lark, but I agonized over it for weeks. I wasn't just breaking up with my boyfriend, I was moving out, saying goodbye to people that had felt like family. Leaving my home. You might not understand this, but even if I was still in love with Ben as more than a friend, at the time, in fact until quite recently, I still would've left before they could leave me."

There's a long pause.

Bridget takes a swig of her champagne, setting her glass down on the counter. "When you were here, it felt like you had everything."

A noise escapes my throat. "Hardly."

"You won the art contest. You had the guy, and all the talent." Bridget bites her lip. "I didn't think about all the things you didn't have. At seventeen, living with your boyfriend sounded like a dream to me. I didn't think about how hard it must've been for you being without your mom."

My throat tightens.

Bridget blows a large breath out and shakes out her limbs like a prize fighter before entering the ring. "Look, I'm trying to say I'm sorry. Okay? I'm sorry I've been such a bitch. Can you forgive me and can we just move on?"

"Yes." I smile, and she pulls me into an unexpected hug then jumps away suddenly with a yelp.

"Pins. Note to self, no hugging when pins are involved."

We both laugh then stop as Meg walks out of the back in a princess-cut white gown, the fabric billowing behind her. Her long hair is in ringlets at her bare shoulder. Bridget lets out a dramatic gasp, and my heart warms. This can't be the first time she's seen Meg in the dress, but her pure joy at seeing her friend is surprising and delightful. We all stand next to each other in the full-length mirror, and tears prick the back of my eyes, because apparently now I'm a crier. But there are worse things to be.

I squeeze Meg's hand. "Thank you."

She turns her megawatt smile on me. "For what?"

"For never giving up on me. For staying my friend no matter how hard I pushed you away."

"We're sisters of the fire. That bond can't be undone." A small tear rolls down Meg's cheek.

The owner steps in. "That's enough of that now. You don't want to get all puffy before the big day."

BACK AT THE INN, I slip into a black dress with a square neckline that comes just to about mid-calf then throw on my faux fur coat and walk to the Vern, which is where the rehearsal dinner is being held. Small snowflakes drift onto the sidewalk as I make the short walk. The door is closed with a sign on it that says *closed for a private event*. I push and am hit with a blast of warmth. There're two long tables with a buffet-style dinner set up, the silver trays still covered. A group of groomsmen are gathered by the dartboard cheering loudly. The tables are full of people with drinks. Meg waves from behind an older woman in a silver dress.

The evening is a blur of faces, some familiar, most not, making toasts to the happy couple. Things between Bridget and I have thawed, so much so that toward the end of the night, she brings me a large whiskey and sits down next to me.

"So, is that tall guy coming to the wedding with you?"

I think about acting like I don't know who she's talking about, but I know and she knows I know. "Nope. Pretty sure I fucked that up."

She nods solemnly. "No fixing it?"

I shake my head.

She waves a hand in front of her face, scoffing, and I wonder how many drinks she's had. She points at the dance floor. "Plenty of men in the sea." She throws back her whiskey then slams it on the table she rises and grabs my hand. "Let's go fishing."

I laugh, and with absolutely no intention of snagging a man, I let her lead me out on the dance floor. The song changes to "Hot to Go," and the crowd goes nuts. Bridget performs some amazing dance moves a little reminiscent of YMCA, and I laugh my way through trying to keep up.

There's more snow on my way back to the Inn, but none of it is sticking. It floats down like stars falling from the sky. I wrap my coat tighter around me and go for a little walk, telling myself I just want to enjoy the snow. Ignoring my cold feet in my heels, I end up back at the sign with our sticker, the moonlit ocean behind it, tiny snowflakes floating. I check my phone, but there's still no response from Oli.

Running my fingers on the cold metal of the sign, I let out a long breath and feel something in my chest unlock. What have I been doing? Trying to ignore my feelings for Oli, from the start. As soon as we got close, I pushed. I called us a fling. I convinced myself we were just about sex, when really, that's not at all the case. And for what? To protect my heart? My pride? Well, both are smashed to shit anyway.

Maybe it's the whiskey, but I dial the phone, my heart racing.

Voicemail.

I'm about to hit the button to end the call, but instead I push my shoulders back and stay on the line.

"This is Oli. Leave me a message."

"Oli. It's Zara. I know you probably don't want to talk to me right now. Which is fair. It was shitty to accuse you of sleeping with Alice. Deep down, I really didn't even think that you were. But it was a good excuse to push you away. And look at that—I did it. It's one of my most honed skills, pushing people away that I love."

I pause, because I didn't mean to tell him I love him on the message. But now I have. And I can't take it back. So I push forward.

"I'm learning…a lot of things, but I'm learning to let people in. I'm learning it's okay to put myself out there. That some people you can trust. And that it's worth it. I know this is a lot to put on your machine. But even if you don't feel the same, I need you to know—"

Click.

The call ends.

"Son of a bitch!"

I pace in front of the stairs. Should I call back?

The ocean waves crash in a hypnotic rhythm and my heartbeat slows. No. I can't call back. It's one thing to let him know how I feel, it's another to leave texts and messages over and over.

I'm a strong independent woman owning my feelings, not a stalker.

On the way back to the Inn, snow falls around me. It's fine. I'm proud of myself, even if he doesn't feel the same.

CHAPTER 35

Another night where I barely slept. I kept checking my phone, seeing if Oli texted or called or anything. In the morning, the light through the hotel room window seems brighter. I run to see and the snow did stick. There is a foot of it coating the streets and speckling the sand beyond.

It's a good thing the church is within walking distance. I check my phone. Shit. Shit. Shit. I slept in.

I call Meg, noticing I have a few missed calls, all from her, I'm sure. She picks up on the first ring.

"Hey, I thought you were going to do your makeup over here. Where are you?"

I think about claiming car trouble, blaming the snow, but I take a deep breath and tell the truth. "Last night, I left Oli a voicemail telling him I love him."

Meg gasps in a very soap opera-esque fashion. "On voicemail?"

"It just came out."

"No!"

"I couldn't sleep. When I finally did fall asleep, I didn't hear my alarm go off. I'm still at the Inn. But I can do my own makeup and meet you at the church."

"Hogwash. Bee's over here doing everyone up. We have plenty of time."

I look at my clock and know that's not true.

"Get your ass over here and we'll fix you up."

There's no arguing with Meg on any day, but especially not her wedding day. I drive over, a bridesmaid dress tucked under my arm. Meg's house is loud even from the porch with the door shut. I knock, and someone yells, "Come in."

The strong aroma of cinnamon rolls and coffee greets me, followed closely by Meg's mom, in a pale-pink dress suit, the lapel beaded, her hair still in curlers.

"Zara!" She wraps me in a warm hug.

"Hey, Mrs. Barner."

"They're in her room."

I head back to find Bridget and Meg in matching satin red robes. Bee from the bridal shop is doing Meg's eyeshadow, and they're all singing along to "That Don't Impress Me Much."

"There you are," Meg says.

We all finish getting ready, them singing along to a country bridal playlist, me smiling, not knowing any of the words or any of the songs besides the Shania Twain ones. I slip into the red satin bridesmaid dress, pulling it over my hips, relishing the smooth fabric on my stomach. Oli would love this dress.

I look over the effect in the full-length mirror, and Bridget comes to stand next to me in a matching dress.

"We're the hottest bridesmaids I've ever seen."

I laugh, and say, "Damn straight."

Mrs. Barner is doing up the ten million buttons on the back of Meg's dress, and Meg's grandma is getting her hair sprayed by Bee, looking at her phone, shaking her head. She mutters, "Terrible. Terrible."

Meg frowns. "What is it, Nana? You don't like your hair?"

Meg's Grandma laughs. "Of course I do." She places a hand on Bee's arm. "The hair is lovely. It's all the crime."

Meg stifles a laugh and rolls her eyes at me. "Nana, what crime? Fortune Falls is pretty sleepy."

"Not according to my Facebook."

Mrs. Barner says, "She's on one of those Facebook groups. I love Fortune Falls, I think it's called."

She nods. "You know the high tide warning sign, near the stairs on the far end of town?"

My heart rate kicks up a notch. Our sign? Is she talking about the sticker Oli and I put up?

"Look at this." She hands the phone to Mrs. Barner. The phone gets passed to Meg, then Bridget, and finally she hands it to me. I look at the small lit screen with trembling fingers, ready to pretend I have no idea how that sticker got there. When I see the photo, I nearly drop the phone. There's a bit of snow on the sign, and on the beach behind, so it must've been taken today. The sticker is still there in the corner, but the rest of the sign is a large painting of a hot dog. The soft amber hues of the bun contrasted against the almost burgundy dog is exquisite. It's painted in a hyper-realistic style. You can practically see the grease glistening on the plump sausage as it lies lazily in the steamed-soft bun. On the dog in scrawling yellow swirls of spray-painted mustard, it spells out, *I miss you*.

I cover my mouth to hide my smile.

"It's terrible," Nana says.

I hand her phone back, my insides buzzing. "Awful."

Excusing myself, I head downstairs and fish my phone out of my pocket. Some of my missed texts weren't from Meg, they're from Louise with a link to a TikTok video.

Louise: Have you seen this?

I click on the video. It's the brick wall near the diner that Oli and I stopped at on our train ride. The little girl with the birds and bones is still there, but it's altered. In her hand that's not reaching out to the birds, she holds a hot dog. Again, the painting of it is stunning, delicate, and careful brushstrokes. The person talking on the video yammers on, "These hot dog additions to OG pieces have cropped up all over the West Coast."

The video zooms in on the dog. Spelled out in mustard, it says, *Still Hopeful*.

My heart is hammering in my chest as I remember our time in the Inn, his mouth on my neck as he whispered about being hopeful in my ear. Are these for me? And if so, then why won't he answer my calls? Well, my one call. There's no time to spiral on those questions.

Meg walks down the stairs, a vision in her cream wedding dress, vintage lace covering her arms. On the way to the venue, I scour the internet for more OG pieces, and find three more, all of them near the Sunshine Express's route. Most of them are additions to existing pieces, but some stand alone. Each hot dog has mustard on it that says something different.

Once we're at the old red barn, I tuck my phone away, and get out, giving Meg a hand. She heads to the back, pointing. "Back entrance. Will you check and make sure everything is all right?"

I nod, following a group of older ladies inside the barn. Meg went all out with the Valentine's Day wedding theme. The barn is strung up within an inch of its life with large Edison bulb string lights. Red roses also fill the space, making it look beautiful and smell heavenly. People are getting situated in mismatched wooden chairs. At the front of the barn is a small stage where Tommy's adjusting his suit and chatting with Ben and his best man, classical music playing over the speakers.

Running around the back, I go find Meg. "It all looks great."

Tears well in the corners of her eyes. "It does?"

I squeeze her hand. "It's perfect."

Bridget grabs her other hand, and we all stand, smiling at each other. Suddenly, I'm overcome with gratitude. For being a part of this day, for Meg always being there for me despite my pushing, for Louise being a part of my life and texting me that TikTok, for Alice always making delicious food and allowing me to be a part of her pregnancy journey, even for Bridget being a spitfire, who I think is now on my side.

Meg's dad finds us holding three bouquets, and the music gets louder, the bridal march ringing through the old wooden rafters. "It's time."

He hands me my bouquet, and I give Meg a wink. Walking out, holding my head up high, I move my feet in time to the music, feeling all eyes on me. Once I'm at the end of the aisle, I scan the crowd. Bridget walks down the aisle next, taking slow, deliberate steps. The music swells as Bridget reaches the end, standing next to me on the stage.

Meg floats down the red runner, her father at her arm, a picture-perfect bride, and an ache settles deep in my heart. I glance at her groom looking at her like the world has stopped. They're so happy. Why have I been running from this?

That hot dog painting on the sign by the beach is so close, it's not lost on me that Oli might be close as well. My fingers itch to text him. After the wedding, as soon as the reception starts, I'll text him.

The officiant clears his throat, and if I'm not mistaken, it's the bartender from the Vern. "Dearly beloved..."

EVERY MAN that shifts in their seat, every man that even moves a muscle, my eyes immediately flick to their face, hoping to see Oli, but none of them are.

The reception is filled with toasts and tears. Cake smashing, excellent roast beef. There's dancing, and Bridget wins limbo.

The music shifts. Melodic piano comes across the speakers. My breath catches in my throat. I know this song.

"Come Away with Me."

I look around. I'm surrounded by people on the dance floor, but I make my way through the bodies with excuse me's and pardon me's. Searching, searching—he has to be here. What are the odds this song, the one we slow danced to in the Inn, the one we kissed and so much more to, would come on now?

But then I look back at the dance floor, Meg and Tommy are holding each other close, swaying with the music, and there is absolutely no sign of Oli.

It must be a coincidence.

I've insisted up and down that life is full of coincidences. That there is no fate. There are no soulmates. Nothing is meant to be, and now it feels like the universe is throwing it back in my face, when all I want is to be proven wrong.

CHAPTER 36

The hauntingly beautiful song plays over the speakers as couples sway on the dance floor, and I can't help flashing back to me and Oli in that small hotel room, on a snowy day a lot like this. My cheeks feel flushed, and I need some air. I keep walking outside, grabbing my coat along the way. The sun dips low in the sky, catching the clouds and lighting them up—golden yellow against the pale-blue sky. Closing my eyes, I inhale deeply the scent of fresh snow and roses.

Opening my eyes, I fish my phone out of my coat and am about to send a text to Oli when a shiny black car pulls up in front of the barn, the tires crunching on the snow.

Meg runs out of the barn, a fur shawl wrapped around her shoulders, followed by Bridget wheeling a suitcase. It must be time for the honeymoon already. But then I get a closer look at the suitcase and do a double take.

That's not Meg's suitcase.

It's mine.

A man in a tuxedo emerges from the car and grabs the bag from Bridget, who is smiling from ear to ear.

"What's going on?" My heart is hammering in my chest, and

my brain is trying to figure out what I did wrong. "Are you kicking me out?"

Meg's smile rivals the setting sun. "It's a surprise."

"I hate surprises."

"Trust me," Meg says as she runs a hand on my arm, "you'll like this one."

The man opens the back door and makes a sweeping gesture for me to get in.

I'm stunned and still trying to figure out what is happening. "Is this a really elegant kidnapping?"

Bridget laughs. "Kind of."

They surround me in a hug, then Meg takes me by the shoulders, points me toward the car, and swats my behind. "Now go, bitch."

The car smells expensive, the leather seats are smooth and toasty under my coat. I sit back and ask the driver, "Where are we going?"

"Can't say."

I watch out the window as the sun sinks below the ocean. We drive through town, stopping right at the train station. The driver fiddles with the trunk, then opens my door, giving me a hand as I step out.

He hands me my suitcase handle and a ticket. "Better hurry."

A booming voice comes over the loudspeaker, "Now boarding Sunshine Express."

I look down at the ticket in my hand: Sunshine Express, Fortune Falls to San Luis Obispo. Sl Cr Rm G.

The voice comes over the loudspeaker again. "Last call: Sunshine Express."

Adrenaline courses through my legs, and I run. My suitcase bumping along behind me, my heels smacking against the tile floor of the station, the sound changing once I get to the concrete. Just as the doors are closing, I make it waving at the attendant. He opens the doors back up.

"Cutting it close there," he says as he tears my ticket and

points me in the right direction, but once I'm on the train, I know where to go. I've been this way before.

Taking slow, deliberate steps, I walk down the hall, my heart in my throat. I realize I don't have a key, but once I get to the room, I find it open.

It's the exact room Oli and I snuck into playing hide and seek. It's set up in the exact same way. There's a bottle of wine and a bag of chips on the table, and two keys lie on the freshly made bed. The gold art deco details shine, catching the waning light cascading through the window. Then I see it.

Lit up from behind, painted on the window by the bed is a hot dog. It's exquisite. The fine brush strokes expertly applied, the mix of color from pinks to browns, the beiges and tan of the bun all go together with the harmony of a Rothko. All offset by the shock of yellow mustard on the top. I set down my suitcase, shrug off my coat and crawl over the bed, sitting right in front of the window to get a closer look.

Spelled out in elegantly painted mustard, it says, *I love you.*

I run my fingers along the paint, cool from the weather outside, and a voice startles me.

"Hot dogs are surprisingly challenging to paint. That guy in the book really must've been the best artist in the world."

Oli walks through the door in a perfectly tailored tuxedo and a red satin bow tie that matches my bridesmaid dress. He adjusts his cuffs, then his lapels, clearly not as comfortable in the suit as in his usual paint-splattered jeans.

I scoot off the bed, walking over to him as his eyes rake over me.

"You look... Wow."

I adjust his bow tie. "You don't look half bad yourself."

A small smirk tugs at his lips. He places his hands on my hips, running his large palm over the smooth satin of my dress. "Zara, I'm sorry. I should've told you about the warehouse piece. I'm so used to keeping that part of my life compartmentalized. Safe and tucked away from the people close to me. It didn't occur to me it would feel like a betrayal, but I see it now. I did leave you out. And I'll never do it again."

I run a hand over his cheek, the light stubble prickling my palm.

He leans into my hand. "I should've never accused you of taking that video either. I was hurt, first that you didn't think what we had was something special. Then you thought I was sleeping with Alice—"

Running my hand down his arms, I gaze up into his color-shifting eyes, the lightest blue right now in the golden light of the train car. "I shouldn't have suggested you were seeing Alice. I wasn't saying you were cheating, just we never really defined what we were... are…"

He nods. "I was worried you thought what we had was just a casual hook up. And my feelings for you..." He pauses, and the look he gives me sends a shiver down my bare spine. "They're not casual. I'm not the best with words. I'm better with spray paint, honestly. But ever since I met you on the train, we talked for hours, and we kissed. You're always on my mind."

He takes my hand and places it firmly around his waist, pulling me closer, his hands at the small of my back. "I'm a one-woman kind of guy. And if you'll have me, I won't keep big parts of my life separate from you."

"And I won't push you away."

The corners of his lips turn up. "So…you and me?"

My whole body tingles, the lightness I feel lifts the corners of lips and makes me feel like I can fly. "We go together like mustard on a hot dog."

I lean in and our lips meet, it feels like putting the first brush stroke on a freshly gessoed canvas. It feels like a beginning.

The train pulls out of the station, lurching forward, sending us staggering toward the bed. We both laugh as Oli motions to the door.

"We should probably shut this, unless we want to wind up all over the internet, again."

As he clicks the door closed, I step out of my heels. He comes back over to me running his hand on my hips again.

"This is some dress."

I smirk. "Isn't it?"

"So silky."

I lean in, bringing my lips to his ear. "You should see what's underneath."

The noise that falls from his lips sends a pulse of want straight between my thighs. We tumble onto the bed, his hands running down the length of my dress then up my leg slowly. The world rushes past us as the train rolls on into the setting sun, into our future together.

CHAPTER 37
EPILOGUE

There's a nip in the air as the wind blows my hair away from my face, and a few yellow leaves whoosh past my feet. Even though the days are still long, fall is in the air, and the smell of impending rain is intoxicating.

I hurry down the sidewalk, running just the tiniest bit late, the drive here taking longer than I expected.

Light streams out of the gallery windows, the sidewalk filled with first Thursday walkers, moving from one venue to the next. Inside, I check my coat and grab a glass of red wine, inhaling deeply, taking a moment to be a fly on the wall. PNWMOA gallery is filled nearly shoulder to shoulder with bodies. Our work is hung on the walls, spotlights shining professionally on each piece. Louise is holding court by her favorite piece, *Season of the Slit*, which sold before the show was even hung, as did most of her work in this show.

Dressed all in black holding her three-week-old baby, Dorothea, also dressed all in black, Alice is talking to an older woman with a bird-like nose. Her exquisite portraits hang behind her, most with red dots on them as well. She's the first one to notice me, and she gives me a little wink as she bounces Dorothea in time to the music playing over the speakers.

A little behind her is Miguel, peering closely at one of Alice's pieces. He's been a more frequent visitor to our neck of the woods and is even talking about moving there to be closer to Dorothea. I'm not sure if romance has bloomed between Alice and him, but I know Alice is all smiles when he visits.

My eyes float to my pieces. A series of paintings of various sizes ranging from Polaroid to a large canvas the size of half a billboard. They're all moments in time, hazy and out of focus. Soft colors mixed with sharp details. Some are reflections, others are of the people I love, the moments I cherish. The fabric that fills my life.

I step away from the bar, but a hand catches my arm. I turn to find Marlene, her hair in the same smooth copper bob, her dress just as low cut as ever.

She drops her hand and clears her throat. "Congratulations, Ashford. This show is a real coup."

I swallow back my surprise. We haven't spoken since she fired me, and I can only assume Louise or Alice invited her, or possibly the gallery. But I am glad she's here. "Thank you."

"Your work is exquisite. Were you painting like this the whole time you worked for me?"

I gaze over at my paintings, each a little piece of me, each one hours of work, each stroke coming from a new found place of self-love and confidence that when I worked for Marlene, I absolutely did not possess. Shaking my head, I say, "No. No, I wasn't."

Over at my wall of art, a man stands in front of a close-up of Alice's hand running over her very pregnant belly, and sparklers ignite in my breastbone.

"Thank you for coming, Marlene. If you'll excuse me."

Turning from her, I stride across the room and tap him on the shoulder, my heart in my throat as he turns around. Despite living together since he moved a few miles from Louise's in June, I still get excited every time I see him.

Oli turns, a smile on his face. "There you are."

"Here I am."

He wraps me in a hug and whispers in my ear, "You did it."

Pulling back slightly, I look around the packed gallery. "It's not a solo show."

Oli looks at me, his eyes soft and his voice low. "Would you want it to be?"

Looking around at all the faces, some familiar, some not, watching Louise animatedly chat up the critics and Alice bounce little Dorothea in front of her stunning photographs, I shake my head. "I really wouldn't."

Oli laces his fingers through mine, and we weave our way through people, looking at the show. I squeeze his hand. "Do you think our gallery will ever be this full?"

Oli shrugs. "We have a stellar lineup of shows. It's in a much smaller town, but maybe. How'd it go with the contractor?"

"Good. The work should be complete in a few weeks. We should be able to open by the next first Thursday. We just have to come up with a name."

Oli wraps his arm around my waist. After Oli and I reconnected on the train, we dated long distance for a month or so, but we missed each other too much. I loved my job working for Louise, still do, and I wanted to be there to support Alice and the baby. Oli had nothing tying him to where he was living outside LA, so he moved and we got a place together.

One night we were walking downtown after a big spaghetti dinner at the Italian place in town, when we saw the old fabric warehouse was going out of business.

I pointed to it. "That would be the perfect place for a gallery."

Oli raised an eyebrow. "You think?"

"Yeah, have you been in there? It's huge, with massive old wooden rafters and a concrete floor. The front windows let in a ton of light, plus there's some skylights but not enough to damage the work. It'd be perfect."

He took my hand in his. "Let's do it."

I laughed. "What?"

"Let's open a gallery."

I thought it was the wine talking and laughed it off. But we both just kept bringing it up over the next few weeks. How fun it would be. What shows we would have. How we could host classes, too.

We talked ourselves right down over to the rental office to sign a lease, Oli's substantial OG bank account making the process smoother than I expected. The very next day, Oli and I put up a mural on the side, at night, so no one would find him out. It's a massive hot dog with mustard scrawled on the top spelling out *hopeful*.

We move through the crowd, stopping in front of one of Louise's paintings, and Oli says, "The Hopeful Hotdog?"

I shake my head.

"Imagination Station."

"No."

"But all our train history." Oli's fingers find my hip.

I laugh. "Yeah, I get it. It sounds like a Sesame Street song."

We keep walking through the space, and I whisper in Oli's ear, "What about Roadside?"

He nods, his smile lighting the room more than the hot gallery lights. "What about Roadside Reflections?"

"It's perfect. I love it."

He nuzzles into my side. "I love you."

Louise holds up her phone. The loud sound of a siren erupts, sending a shock wave through the crowd. The chatter stops, and everyone turns to look. Louise tucks her phone back into her sequined purple coat and clears her throat. "That's better. I just wanted to say a few words. I know that's not done, but it's one-third my show and I'm old. So humor me."

There are a few giggles through the crowd. I try to breathe normally, which is hard not knowing at all what Louise is about to say.

"Thank you all for coming. Thank you, PNWMOA Gallery, for

having us. This past year has been one of the most creative periods of my life." Tears well in the corners of her eyes, and I can feel some prickling the back of mine as well. "At my age, I thought that part of my life might be done. It had been so long since I had new, fresh ideas. I had truly lost hope. I was trying to make peace with the fact that my creative life was behind me. But I couldn't. Something in me wouldn't let go. Then I went to Marlene's artist retreat. Where is she?"

Marlene raises her glass from the back of the room.

Louise continues. "Her retreat, well, to say it changed my life would be putting it lightly. Thank you for inviting me. And a huge thank you for firing Zara."

A few gasps and titters of laughter ripple through the crowd, while Marlene's face turns from beaming to like she sucked on something sour.

"Zara is the best assistant I've ever had. And one hell of an artist. Zara, Alice, come up here."

I smooth my hair, and Oli gives me a tiny pinch on the rear. Alice comes over from the other side, Dorothea snoozing on her shoulder.

"There you are. These girls, well, not only is this the most dynamic, lively group show I have been a part of since the seventies, but...they..." Louise wipes a tear, and I pull her close to my side. Alice comes in, and we share a group hug. When we part, Louise says, "They're family. Thank you all for indulging me in my ramblings. Drink up and buy lots of art."

Louise raises her glass. The crowd does as well.

"Louise..." I start, but she waves me away.

"No more sappy shit," she says as she wipes a tear off her cheek. "Go sell your art."

At the end of the night, Oli and I are the last to shuffle out of the gallery, besides the owner. Alice had to leave once Dorothea woke up and was not pleased about the gallery lights. Louise left around nine, saying it was past her bedtime.

Oli intertwines his fingers in mine, and we walk down the

road to the hotel we booked for the night, a chill having washed over the city.

"You've been working so hard on that show. Was it everything you wanted it to be?" Oli asks.

I inhale deeply, the smell of fresh leaves and his spicy leather and mist scent filling my lungs. "It was."

We pass an alley that has a large electric box with a few tags on it. Oli stops, looks around, and pulls a sticker out of his pocket. It's one of the girls surrounded by diamonds. He peels it quickly and sticks it on, then grabs my hand and we run down the street, all the way to the pier, our shoes smacking on the wood planks of the boardwalk, the lights of the Ferris wheel shining on the water. We slow to a walk, breathless, passing street artists with paintings lit by battery-powered lanterns.

Strolling along, we buy coffees from a cart and take them closer to the water, leaning on the railing, looking out at the inky surface, the lights reflecting on it in streaks reminiscent of an impressionist painting.

Oli takes a large sip then turns so he's leaning against the railing, facing me. "Zara Bytheway..."

A smile tickles the corner of my mouth. "Yes, Oliver Really?"

"Do you think you'd ever want to get married...to me?"

The smile on my face grows. "Are you proposing?"

He shakes his head. "No. When I propose, you'll know. There will be a ring, and music, and probably a large art installation of some kind. Maybe I could get a Weiner mobile?"

I laugh.

"I wonder how much it would be to book the entire train?" Oli's eyes are wild scanning through the possibilities.

I snuggle into him, and he stills, wrapping his free arm around me.

"One day, I would like to marry you, Oliver Grant. But for now, let's just enjoy this night. Then tomorrow we can go back home and work on opening Roadside Reflections. One major life-altering thing at a time."

"I love you." He sets his coffee down on the ledge, taking a finger under my chin and tilting my face toward him. He places his soft lips on mine, and we melt together, the light reflecting all around us.

The End

ACKNOWLEDGMENTS

Thank you so much for diving into the art world with Oli and Zara. As a former art student this one was super fun for me to write. If you loved it please consider leaving a review.

This year has been a whirlwind and I could not have done it without my romance writer girlies Robin Blackburn and Stephanie Paul. Thank you for always be willing to chat about my ideas, read my stuff and comment thoughtfully (at astonishing speed) and for our monthly chats. Love you both!

Thank you to Haley Catherine for your feedback and support. It means the world to me.

Thank you to my parents for always being willing to help out with childcare when I need to get some sh*t done.

Thank you to my daughter and my husband for always supporting me and making me want to be a better me.

And a huge thank you to all the readers. Of this book and The Now in Forever. Thank you for spending your time with me and the characters so dear to my heart. I hope you'll consider doing it again.

A PEEK AT CHAPTER ONE THE ROAD NOT TAKEN

As my best friend in the whole world sits barefoot on my floor, neon green margarita in hand, eyes swollen nearly shut with tears, I wonder when I became such a heartless bitch.

She arrived at my house two hours ago, sobbing because, on her way to pick up chips for our regular Margs and Meg third Tuesday of the month (where we drink too much tequila and watch Meg Ryan movies), she passed her boyfriend in his car in the back of the parking lot, his chair leaned back, his eyes closed. She walked up to knock on the window playfully, flirty, and then she saw *her*. She saw all of it. His hot co-worker, who he insisted nothing was going on with, was giving him head, right there in the parking lot.

And as she told me all of this over the course of two margaritas, I thought, of course. Of course, he's a cheating, lying piece of shit. Despite the fact that I've always had a weird feeling about her now ex, even if this hadn't happened, something would have. He would've gotten bored, or she would've. They would fight over future children that they don't have. Or which streaming service they should drop to save money. Someone would've gotten sick. Something always happens to make a relationship end, which is why I don't do relationships.

But I am not a complete asshole, so I'm keeping those thoughts to myself. I pull my mass of blonde curls up into a messy bun on top of my head. The last notes of "A Thousand Years" play on Heather's phone. She taps the screen, and it starts over for the fifth time. *Fifth*. It's time to intervene.

"Honey, maybe we should—"

Heather hums over me.

I snatch the phone off the black and white tiled floor. My hair escapes its bun and gets in my face as I do. I toss it back over my shoulder and move to the other side of the kitchen island. After a few clicks, "I Forgot That You Existed" blasts out of the tiny phone speaker. Enough wallowing. It's time to get mad.

"Ruby McVeigh! Give me my phone back."

"Only if you agree we're moving on to the empowering women playlist. No more sad songs."

"I'm not ready to move on. I don't want to move on." Heather slumps back onto the floor. We've been friends since kindergarten. This is not the first breakup we've waded through together, but I've never seen her this dejected. Guilt prickles my chest. I shouldn't be dictating how this goes. I sit next to her, the cold December air making the kitchen tile freezing even through my jeans.

I put a hand on her knee. "You'll find someone else, someone better."

Heather looks up at me, silent tears running down her face. "I don't want someone else. I don't want someone better. I just want him." She shakes her head, bringing what's left of her margarita to her mouth, and says so quietly I almost don't hear her, "You wouldn't understand."

Her words pack an unexpected sting. I *do* understand. Kind of. I know heartbreak, just not really of the romantic variety. Which is on purpose. I am careful. I have rules. I protect myself—and others, really—from it.

A fire sparks in my belly, partly tequila, but mostly bloodlust. I want to pummel her ex. Saying that won't help right now. Instead,

I pat her knee. "I get it. Really, I do, but he's such a prick. You're better off."

"I'm not." Heather stumbles to her feet again, shaking her head so hard, I worry she might be doing some damage. "You can't possibly understand. You're always doing the dumping."

She's drunk, drunker than I realized, and now she's lashing out. I'm a thirty-two-year-old woman. Of course, I've been dumped. Haven't I? And anyway, it's not like I dumped them exactly. We both agreed to just have fun, and that's exactly what we did. No labels. No hard feelings.

"No one was dumped. If you don't take it all so seriously, then no one gets hurt. And if no one gets hurt, then everyone has fun."

Heather shakes her head. "Some of your beaus didn't get the memo. You may think it all didn't mean anything, but they were left heartbroken."

Her voice catches on the last word, and she doubles over, clutching her stomach, her shoulders shaking with sobs.

I really don't think that's true. But there's no time to argue about this right now. I hop up off the floor and wrap her in a big hug. "Let's order a pizza and watch Meg."

We were going to watch *The Women*, but since Meg catches her husband cheating, that's out. *Innerspace* it is.

Heather lays her head on my shoulder. "And open some wine?"

Not a good idea, but the girl's been through trauma. "Sure. This will all feel better in the morning."

———

The light is too bright as it streams in through the single-paned living room windows. The air is practically Siberian. This house used to be my grandmother's, and before that it was *her* grandmother's. There have been some updates, but some is still original. Like the hardwood floors, the tile in the bathroom and, unfortunately, the windows.

I sit up and stretch my neck, each vertebra popping as I do. Not sure if Heather is going to feel better when she wakes up, but I really don't. Red wine and tequila do not mix. When will I learn?

Heather is on the other side of my oversized couch, snuggled in the blanket nest we made last night. I get up and make my way to the kitchen, the massive bay window making the light even brighter in here. The tile is so cold under my bare feet that I wince as I put some grounds into the filter and fill the machine with water.

Small whirs and gurgles of the coffee percolating warms my heart. A shame it can't warm my feet. I sit at the yellow kitchen table, watching the snow fall lightly outside the window and running my hand along the smooth Formica. This table also used to be my grandmother's and has sat in this corner by the window for as long as I can remember. When she passed, my mother suggested I spruce up the place. Get some new furniture. But I couldn't bring myself to get rid of Grandma's stuff. She loved this house, this table. Even her clothes are still hanging in the closet of her untouched bedroom.

The snow is picking up speed as I go to pour myself a mug of coffee. Hopefully, it doesn't snow too much, or walking to my shift at the bar later will take a lot longer than usual. I take my coffee back to the blanket nest, turning on an episode of *The Great British Bake Off*. I try to zone out on the intricacies of puff pastry, but Heather's words from last night keep nagging at me.

After the second episode, I can't sit still anymore. I shove my feet into my fuzzy suede slippers and go back to the kitchen. Putting a saucepan on the stove, I pour in milk and heat butter. I've made this recipe so many times, I know it by heart. Once the butter is fully incorporated, I pour the mixture into a bowl, testing the heat with my pinky. Feels right to me. I scoop out some yeast and set the timer on my phone for ten minutes. The snow is still falling steadily.

Heather is wrong. All the men I've dated felt the same way I did. We were having fun until we weren't. Then we parted ways, no hard feelings. Except maybe a few. Mentally, I start tallying up my relationships but am barely past tenth grade when my timer dings.

Adding the flour half a cup at a time, I stir until my spatula gets stuck. Then I start to knead. The dough is firm and squishy in my hands. My muscles in my biceps turn on. It's all so familiar and soothing. But my mind is still swirling in agitated circles, like a shark with blood in the water.

After covering the dough, I take my coffee back to the couch and start the next episode of *TGBBO*. One and a half episodes later, Heather finally opens her eyes. I'm so worked up, I blurt out, "You really think I left them heartbroken?"

Heather immediately shuts her eyes and throws the blanket over her head. Through the muffled layers, she yells, "Coffee."

I get up, taking my now empty cup and feeling like a bitch once again. My poor, actually heartbroken, hungover friend just woke up, and I immediately pounce on her with my own shit. Filling a cup for Heather, I place it on the coffee table, setting it down carefully in case she's fallen asleep under the blanket. Back in the kitchen, I make the cinnamon and sugar filling, roll out the dough, and pop the whole thing into the oven.

Refilling my own cup, I snuggle on the couch in the blankets. The room is extra cozy with the colorful lights from the Christmas tree in the corner. Heather is holding her mug of coffee with both hands, her eyes puffy and focused on the screen, which she has changed to *You've Got Mail*, our favorite of all the Meg movies.

"How are you feeling?" I ask gently.

"Terrible."

I nod. "Will cinnamon rolls help?"

Heather sighs. "No, but I will eat them."

"Do you have school today?" I ask as I set my coffee down.

Heather teaches ninth grade at the high school down the street.

She shakes her head slightly, wincing as she does. "Canceled for the snow. Then, lucky me, after this weekend, it's winter break."

I bring us both a plate to the couch. We spend the morning eating, sipping coffee, and watching movies. But the accusation from before that I dumped all my past boyfriends lies heavy on my heart. It nags at me so much that eventually, I make my way back to my bedroom.

Opening my thick red curtain, I let the light in, the snow still falling. Looks like the walk to work will take a bit longer today. I kneel and reach under the bed, slipping the vintage suitcase out and placing it on top of my comforter.

My breakup suitcase. Ever since I was fourteen, I've taken all the mementos I'm not ready to get rid of and have shoved them into this vintage faux crocodile skin luggage. I usually don't pull it out unless there is a new batch of things to put in.

Heather comes through the door, coffee in hand. "The breakup case? I should get one of those."

I snag a Polaroid out of the side pocket as Heather sits and starts riffling through movie tickets, teddy bears, and love notes. In the picture, I'm sitting between Josh's legs, tilting my face back, and we are locked in a passionate embrace. My blonde hair looks darker in the old photo. My already fair skin is even paler, but there's a rosiness to my cheeks. I look great. Ah, the built-in filter of youth and Polaroid film.

Josh and I dated all through eleventh grade, up until the prom, when he decided to take someone else. I'm still not sure what happened there. We weren't ever exclusive, but it was a shock all the same. I definitely didn't dump *him*. Before its disastrous end, Josh and I were like peas and carrots. I show it to Heather. "Exhibit A. If anything, Josh broke up with me."

Heather takes the Polaroid and shakes her head. "That boy was head over heels for you, and you always had one foot out the door. You pushed him away."

She digs through the side pocket, bringing out more Polaroids. She flips one to me. It's another one of Josh and me. We're at a party. He's sitting close, looking at me intently, and I'm leaning away. She points. "This! Josh always wanted to hold your hand or be so close to you, and unless you were making out, you were always pulling away."

Is that true? I look through the stack of photos of Josh and me. In every one of them, if we're not kissing, my body is turned away from him. But we were kids. And I'm not really the most casually affectionate person.

"Hmm." I'm still examining the evidence when Heather gasps so loud, I jump back. "What? Is it a spider?"

I fucking hate spiders. Adrenaline shoots to my heart, and I scan the room for something I can use to kill it. I land on a baking magazine, quickly snatch it off my bedside table, and roll it up. I really don't want to get bug guts on it—inside, there's a recipe for a pear tart I'd really like to try—but desperate times…

I hold it up and rush to Heather's side, but there's no spider. No creepy crawly critters at all, in fact. Heather is holding a small blue velvet box. She snaps it open. Inside is a gold ring with a solitary square diamond. It's simple and elegant. On the top of the box is a little note that says in cursive, *Marry me.*

"Ruby!" Heather says. "What the fuck is this? You were engaged? Why didn't you tell me? Who gave this to you? Was it from Nick?"

I shake my head and realize I'm still holding the magazine like I'm going to whack the ring. The gorgeous ring that I have never, not once, seen in my entire life.

"I have no idea," I say, throwing the magazine on the bed. "Where did you find it?"

Heather hands the ring to me. "It was just at the bottom, under some of the books."

My first thought is Grandma. Somehow, someway, this ring is her doing. Handing the ring back, I run out to the hall closet with Heather calling after me.

"Where are you going?"

I'm back a moment later with a thick, leather-bound photo

album. I start flipping through the plastic pages, yellowing now with age. There's my grandmother and her sister as little girls, drawing on the wall with crayons in this very house. There's Grandma in her graduation gown. Heather points to a picture of a man on a motorcycle with a cap on instead of a helmet. He's leaned over with a cigarette hanging out of his mouth.

"Who's that?"

"No idea." I look closely. The black-and-white photo is slightly out of focus and very grainy. It could be my grandpa. I don't think he ever smoked, though. I keep flipping because it's not what I'm looking for. A couple more pages, and I find it. A picture of my grandma and grandpa with her hand over her heart. Her engagement ring is the focal point of the picture, with an oval-shaped diamond. I know we buried her with it on her finger five years ago.

I take the ring again, holding it up to the picture. "It wasn't my grandma's. This one is square."

"Princess cut," Heather says.

I look at her. "How do you know that?"

"How do you not?"

If this ring isn't just left over from the suitcase, then how did it get in there? Was one of my exes really going to propose? Who? Maybe one of them did have deeper feelings than I thought.

The clock on the nightstand switches over and, in bright-red, announces it's already noon. With all this snow, I'm going to be late.

"Shit. I have to get ready for my shift at the bar." I hand the ring back to Heather like we're playing a game of hot potato and practically run to the shower. I scrub like I can wash away the millions of questions swirling through my head—the main one being, where the hell did that ring come from? I throw on jeans and a black sweater. The snow hasn't stopped, so I put on my thickest socks and dig out my snow boots from the back of the closet.

As I put on my cropped puffer coat, wishing I'd gone for the full-length one when I bought this last year on a trip to Seattle. Heather's back on the couch, ring box clutched in her hand, eyes fixed blankly on the screen.

"Honey, I have to go to work, but you're welcome to stay."

"Okay," she says without looking away from Harry meeting Sally.

I head over and wrap her in a big hug. "I love you."

"I love you too." We part, and she looks up at me. "Which one of the boys you dumped was ready to propose, do you think?" She hands me the ring box.

"Heather. I didn't dump…" I don't know what to say. If one of my exes was going to propose, then clearly their feelings ran deeper than I realized at the time. Maybe she's right. Maybe I really did dump them all. Guilt coats my stomach as I shove the box into my coat pocket and give her a kiss on top of her head. "Come by the bar later if you want."

Coming November 1st!!!!!!

ABOUT THE AUTHOR

I received a BFA in mixed media studio art. With a degree in the arts and no solid plan, I've had the opportunity to hold many different jobs; video store manager, barista, photographer's assistant, toy store clerk, and yoga instructor at a retreat in Puerto Rico are just a few. Hands on research for her books.

Currently, when I'm not writing, you can find me working at a title one elementary school library, crafting with her little girl, or hosting the podcast, *So I Wrote a Book...Now What*, where I interview fellow authors about their revision process.

Want to join my newsletter?

ALSO BY NC BARTON

The Now in Forever: A Small Town Second Chance Romance

Coming soon! The Road Not Taken: A Friends to Lovers Christmas
Roadtrip Romance